FIC Lynch

Lynch, Daniel, 1946-

Yellow : a novel /

1992.

YELLOW

YELLOW
A Novel

DANIEL LYNCH

WALKER AND COMPANY
NEW YORK

To Kevin, to make him proud

First published in the United States of America in 1992 by Walker Publishing
Company, Inc.

Published simultaneously in Canada by Thomas Allen & Son
Canada, Limited, Markham, Ontario.

Library of Congress Cataloging-in-Publication Data
Lynch, Daniel, 1946–
Yellow : a novel / by Daniel Lynch.
p.   cm.
ISBN 0-8027-1226-6
I. Title.
PS3562.Y417Y4   1992
813'.54—dc20   92-17332
CIP

Printed in the United States of America

2   4   6   8   10   9   7   5   3   1

AMBROSE BIERCE
MEXICO, 1914

I have always been one, in a perilous emergency, who thinks with his legs. This character trait has preserved me these seventy-two years. Now, however, I confront an enemy from whom I cannot run. I burst with fever. My aged heart pounds with the fury of the microbes' attack. I fear I soon may be done with this business of breathing, the mad race run. I find this a sobering thought—the very worst kind.

My fever swept over me after the consumption of copious quantities of God's next-best gift to man. I was celebrating a victory with the *compañeros* of the Mexican Insurrecto. We downed a liquid that has the capacity to induce lunacy in abstainers. In me, however, it has always instilled a warmth and wit I might otherwise lack. I staggered off to bed gloriously drunk; I awakened afire.

I lie abed now on a whore's mattress of cornhusks. I fear I have finally had the misfortune to overtake the pleasure I have always so earnestly pursued. The scene of my travail is a bug-infested adobe hut, deserted by the Insurrecto forces whose activities my master, Hearst, sent me to Mexico to chronicle.

"Bierce," The Chief instructed me, "send me dispatches from the war—colorful dispatches in your own distinctive style."

"And if I find no war?" I asked him, setting myself up for the response I knew he longed to make.

"You furnish the dispatches," he said, chuckling. "I'll furnish the war."

It was our joke, more his than mine. It stemmed from the cables The Chief was supposed to have exchanged with Frederic Remington when The Chief sent him to Cuba. Remington, the story goes, found little action, so he sent a cable to New York, saying, "There is no war here. I wish to return." And The Chief is supposed to have responded, "Please remain. You furnish the pictures, and I'll furnish the war."

The story is a canard. Its source was one James Peatam, a Pulitzer man whose animosity toward The Chief was monumental—proof positive that hatred is nothing more than a sentiment appropriate to the occasion of another's superiority. Remington found action in Cuba, almost more than he could bear. I know this because Remington told me so shortly before the Christmas of 1909. His story touched my heart, the same organ that now labors so mightily.

The pounding is immense. It thuds in my ears, a rapidly faltering cannonade. What is a heart, after all, but a pump, subject to the ravages of age more than any other organ? I have never believed the heart to be the seat of emotions and sentiments. It is now known beyond all doubt that the sentiments and emotions reside in the stomach, being evolved from food by chemical action of the gastric fluid. The precise process by which a beefsteak—or an enchilada, for that matter—becomes a feeling has been patiently ascertained and convincingly expounded upon by M. Pasteur. The good doctor left little question that hard-boiled eggs can be converted into religious contrition, that a caviar sandwich can be transmuted to a quaint fancy, and that love is nothing more than a product of alimentary maceration.

Perhaps, then, it is because I have never been much of an eater that lasting love has always eluded me. Unless, of course, one counts Small Maria, the whore whose bed now threatens to be the scene of my last thought. She approaches me, her luminous eyes aglow with an abundant affection. She bathes my wrinkled brow with a soft, moist cloth. She lays soft hands upon my burning, shrunken flesh. Small Maria is comely and tidy, but she makes no secret of what she is. Like all women living in the vicinity of man, she has only a rudimentary susceptibility to domestication. The female species is the most widely distributed of all beasts of prey, infesting all habitable parts of the globe. It is lithe and graceful in its movements, omniverous, and cannot be taught to remain quiet. Small Maria is living proof of this.

"Señor Bierce," she says to me, adoration in her youthful eyes, "how do you feel?"

"Cold," I respond as I shiver. "Cold and lonely, bereft of friends in my final hours."

"You are not alone," she tells me. "Small Maria is at your side."

"Count my breaths," I instruct her, struggling for air. "When they cease, be sure to let me know. The number will be of considerable interest to me."

"No," Small Maria says, clutching my hand. "There will be too many breaths for me to count. They will go on forever."

I chuckle—no small task, all factors considered. Then I say, "Count, Maria. Count my breaths while I count my friends who still share breath. Their numbers have dwindled in recent years. That is the price of attaining that period of life in which we atone for the vices we still cherish by reviling those we no longer have the enterprise to commit."

Small Maria stares at me, mystified. She is a sweet creature, but mystifying her is no great chore. I seem able to manage it even on my deathbed.

"Who are your friends?" she asks me.

"They are those with no favors to bestow," I tell her. "They are destitute of fortune, addicted to truth and common sense."

"Your finest friend," Small Maria asks, working to keep me talking and breathing. "Tell me of your greatest friendship."

I am touched by her efforts, although appreciative of their futility. Humor the child, I tell myself. Where's the harm?

"He was an artist," I tell her, "a fellow Hearstling—the only man with whom I ever felt true communion of the soul."

Small Maria, the childish whore who is distinguished by her name from another whore called Big Maria, stares at me in utter bafflement. "Communion?"

"Forgive me," I say apologetically, "These are only the sickbed ramblings of a battered relic who misses his friends and their tall tales of adventure."

"Tell me of the adventures," she instructs me with urgency. "As long as you speak, Señor Bierce, your breath will flow."

I ponder her words. *As long as you speak . . .* A powerful argument for conversation, although the likelihood that she knows whereof she speaks is remote. I rest for a long moment, gathering my precious and fading breath. Which of Remington's fabulous stories should I relate to her? Perhaps one of the encounters with wild Indians on the Great Plains as he burned into his brain the images he would later re-create in oil and bronze? Redskins, they are called—and incorrectly. Their skin is not red. At least, not on the outside.

"A Remington adventure," I muse. "Perhaps you would like to hear of the Insurrecto."

"I know of the Insurrecto," she tells me.

"Do not be a bore, Maria. That is a person who speaks when you would prefer her to listen. I speak of another Insurrecto—a glorious little Insurrecto, splendid in its pointlessness and brought about by rulers mostly knaves, and soldiers mostly fools. And, most conspicuously, by scribblers. We scribblers brought war by dark of night. Our profession enjoys eternal amity with the midnight hour."

Her smooth brow furrows with profound confusion. I feel a surge of guilt at toying with this guileless child, but not so much that I shall cease. She is too fine a target, and I am too cruelly skilled a marksman.

"This is a story told to me in 1909 in Connecticut by Remington.

[3]

He probably lied considerably, as was his habit. It was one of the reasons I was so fond of him."

"Tell me, Señor," Small Maria begs, "and breathe deeply as you speak."

I take this advice for what it is worth, which is nothing. I will soon be a dead sinner, consoled only by contemplation of the continuing discomforts of the living.

"The story begins," I tell her, "at a party where I had the good fortune to be in attendance, as a servant of my master. More than a decade later, when Remington told me the tale in its entirety, he began with that evening, which he knew I would recall. He reminded me of a fine town house on the east side of Manhattan—New York City. It was one of many fine homes owned by a man of unspeakable wealth. Remington was chatting with the great T.R., of whom even you have surely heard."

"T-R?" Maria asks, baffled once again.

"Theodore Roosevelt," I explain, recalling with sudden and startling clarity the version of events as recounted, just before Christmas Day five years ago, by Remington as he sat in a chair in the pleasant library of his new home in Ridgefield . . .

ONE

Frederic Remington
Ridgefield, Connecticut, 1909

No one can blather quite like T.R. As blatherers go, Bierce, T.R. has even you beat—no mean accomplishment, to be sure. Not that the world seems to mind. Eight years now in the White House, and the torrent of blather continues to captivate the great unwashed, as you so delight in calling them.

Some years before that night at Carnegie's town house in Manhattan, I'd illustrated a series of articles that T.R. had written for *Century*. The articles had been published later in book form. T.R. had called it *Ranch Life and the Hunting Trail*. I have a copy of it around here somewhere. It wasn't my best work, so I don't keep meticulous track of it.

T.R. and I'd struck something of a friendship with that collaboration. Or, at least, as much of a friendship as a reasonable man such as I can strike up with a lunatic—despite his virtues. T.R. had taken a real fancy to my work. He bought me a wonderful steak dinner at Delmonico's after I was awarded a silver medal at the Paris Exposition in eighty-nine. The following year, he asked me to sign a copy of *Hiawatha* for his daughter, Alice. I'm certain someone must have bought it for him. T.R. never pays for anything if he can get it for free.

You do recall, Bierce, that I did several paintings and drawings to accompany Longfellow's poem? It was a wonderful break for me when the bloody thing became so popular, although I personally was never terribly fond of it. Oh, it had its charm, but historically the thing was wildly inaccurate. Hiawatha was an Iroquois. Longfellow, for reasons obscure, made him an Ojibway. That's like turning a German into an Italian—or a Spaniard into a Cuban. I had specific occasion later to take note of how towering a perversion that would be.

Since Longfellow felt no compulsion for historically accurate prose, I felt none in my artwork. I gave the Ojibways feathered bonnets like the Sioux. The thing sold wildly, regardless. People, Americans in particular, always prefer a romantic lie to the prosaic truth. As a journalist, I'm sure you can vouch for that.

[5]

On that night at Carnegie's town house, T.R. hadn't seen me for a while, and he battened onto me like a vampire. He was bending my ear endlessly about some hapless moose he'd dispatched up in Quebec. It was a profound relief for me when McKinley finally arrived, accompanied by his military aide—a fellow named Curry. This Curry chap was a lieutenant colonel and not yet forty, all decked out in his braid and ribbons like a bloody European field marshal. T.R. was greatly impressed by the uniform. He was less impressed by the President, as always.

It was quite a pleasant evening. Stag, of course. Carnegie buried us under an avalanche of food and drink, and the surroundings were appropriately palatial. You recall the splendor of the place, I'm sure. It's what God would have done if he'd had the money.

Carnegie made a great fuss over McKinley. I'd never before met the man, and I was young enough to still be impressed by politicians. I was—let's see now—I would have been thirty-six that evening, three years younger than T.R. Or, another way of putting it, T.R. was five years younger than I am now when he became president. A humbling thought, that. On the other hand, by the time he was my age Alexander had conquered the world and been peacefully dead for fifteen years.

It was a gathering of notables. Carnegie was always taking his private railroad car from Pittsburgh to New York to hobnob with the social and cultural betters who were his economic inferiors. Sam Clemens and I were there as representatives of the artistic community. I'd come down from my place in New Rochelle, he from Hartford. Sam was off in a corner with Carnegie and some others, spinning wonderful tales about nothing in particular. I would have preferred to have been over there, listening to Sam's marvelous lies, but T.R. had me firmly in his grasp, and I was stuck with him and his luckless moose. I figured it was probably worth the price. I'd begun to do bronzes only a few years earlier, and it was good business to cultivate those with the resources to pay the outrageous prices I was charging—even someone as notoriously tightfisted as T.R.

T.R. was New York City police commissioner that year. Why he would ever have wanted that job I could never imagine. The coppers were all Irish, a good number of them immigrants. T.R. was in perpetual conflict with them. He always enjoyed a good battle, so I imagine that was the attraction, although he was bucking for something more even then. There were no unfortunate moose to mow down on the streets of New York.

I'd seen McKinley only in sketches in the press. When he came sweeping into the room, I was surprised to realize that he looked disturbingly like his reproduced image in the yellow sheets. As an artist, I view the world through atypical eyes, but I found nothing whatever remarkable about this man. He was a bit on the heavy side, and his tailcoat was slightly frayed at the cuffs. It was hardly the imposing image I'd expected a president to project. He looked like what he was, an Ohio lawyer grown large beyond the wildest surges of his imagination.

We hadn't yet sat down for drinks when you and The Chief made a late entrance. You were your usual self, Ambrose; you were well warmed with brandy even at that early hour. How is it that you've described brandy—one part thunder and lightning, one part remorse, two parts bloody murder, one part hell and the grave, and four parts clarified Satan? I believe I have it right. You looked as though you'd consumed a barrel of the stuff.

The Chief, however, was unexpectedly restrained. I hadn't had occasion to meet him before that gathering. I was startled to realize that he was a few years younger than I was—by far the youngest man at the conclave. You recall what he looked like in those days, Bierce, before he began to put on weight. He was tall and rangy and just a trifle overdressed. The classic rich man's son, so full of quiet confidence and utterly unconcerned with the trivialities of life, like paying bills. The Chief once told me, you know, that he has no idea how much money he has. He looks upon money the way some men look upon silverware. He has enough even for emergencies, and he concerns himself with the topic no further than that.

That evening, The Chief's sandy hair was combed to the side, and he was sprouting that pitiful mustache he'd been trying to make bloom since college. I'm glad he finally shaved the damned thing off. I was startled, too, by his voice, so high and thin and reedy. It wasn't at all the voice I'd expected of a press baron.

We were all in white tie and tails, if you'll recall. Except for Clemens, that is, whose white suit was his uniform except in the very pit of winter. Carnegie enjoyed the trappings of the upper classes, although he still had brass spittoons in every corner of every room of that enormous house. I visited his estate outside Pittsburgh once, much later, and the spittoons were missing. I only hope that whoever told him they were no longer fashionable did so gently. Andrew possessed such tender sensibilities.

Carnegie's idea of a sprightly party was to gather together men of steel and flint and watch them strike sparks off one another. I can't imagine why the President subjected himself to such indignities. Well, I can, actually. Carnegie gave obscene amounts of cash to the Republican party. As a major contributor, his posterior demanded osculation, even from a president. Especially from a president, now that I think about it.

Anyway, we were seated in Carnegie's elegant sitting room when you and The Chief arrived. Clemens was holding the group captive to some story about a jumping frog. You headed immediately for the brandy while The Chief made the rounds. When he got to me and T.R., we struck up a lively conversation. The Chief was something of a collector even then, and he informed me that he owned a few of my oils.

"My congratulations on your taste, sir," I said to him.

"My congratulations on your talent, Mr. Remington," he responded. "Your fame is well earned, but it's a shame your work isn't even better known among the masses—and not just your painting and sculpture. I read *Pony Tracks* and found it most impressive. A man equally at home with both pen and brush is a decided rarity. Perhaps we might find a way to make your work more visible to a mass audience. Would that appeal to you?"

"Any mechanism for enhancing my capacity for communication appeals to me, Mr. Hearst."

"Good," said The Chief. "You might stop by my office at the *Journal* tomorrow—say about ten? Perhaps we can talk a little business."

Since he was untroubled by the necessity to earn a living, this conversation had bored T.R. mightily. He'd wandered off in search of someone else on whom to inflict his tale of the moose. But the sight of McKinley, standing by the fireplace and blustering on about tariffs and the like, was apparently more than T.R. could bear. Before anyone knew it, T.R. was storming up to the President and demanding with characteristic bluffness: "About this Cuba business, sir. How long is the United States of America going to permit the Spanish queen to impose her imperial tyranny so close to our coastline? Surely we Americans can no longer tolerate a Spanish military presence only ninety miles from our shores. Isn't it time to kick the bastards out of Cuba and send them packing back to Madrid to slaughter their bulls in their own hemisphere?"

He didn't let it show, but McKinley was taken aback by this performance. Outwardly the very picture of aplomb, the President turned to Carnegie.

"Andrew," he said. "Do all your guests behave so impetuously? Is every president who visits your house compelled to defend his policies on such short notice—and to so vociferous an attacker?"

It was McKinley's attempt to defuse the situation with a quip, but the President wasn't much of a quipster. And such a maneuver would have been lost on T.R. at any rate. He has always been so weighed down with the troubles of the world. He merely plowed ahead, as is his habit.

"Sir," T.R. lectured the President, "my query merits a response of a certain gravity, as I'm certain that Mr. Hearst here will agree. Do you not, Mr. Hearst?"

The Chief smiled like a crocodile, all teeth and glittering eyes and without humor whatsoever. This was one of his favorite topics, and T.R. had opened it with all the delicacy of a child falling upon a Christmas present.

"Most assuredly," The Chief replied. "There are those of us, Mr. Preident, who consider the matter of Cuba to be the most crucial issue facing our nation. As long as Spain controls the southern seas, there'll be no canal through the Panama isthmus. And, of course, there's also the small matter of the Cuban people bleeding beneath the heel of the Spanish tyrants. That also is worth considering."

McKinley harrumphed grandly. He was mightily disturbed by this sudden assault, and his face turned the color of young port. I'm struggling here, Bierce, to contrive an analogy you might appreciate. The President turned back to T.R. and said, "And your solution to this problem, sir, would be to wage war against the Spanish? How free you seem to be with the blood of others. Perhaps you would care to volunteer for such a campaign?"

This was precisely the wrong thing to say to T.R. If McKinley thought he was dealing with some drunken, drawing room blusterer, he'd badly misjudged the opposition.

"In a heartbeat, sir," our hero responded, his eyes blinking furiously through his glasses. "Our nation is perched upon the precipice of greatness. I would consider it a singular honor to risk my life to consolidate American power in this hemisphere. So would any man in this room."

Since T.R., The Chief, that Curry fellow, and I were the only men in the room remotely young enough to take part personally in such a conflict, the rest were more than delighted to back T.R.'s boasts.

"Hear, hear," said someone, and the cry was immediately taken around the room—ringing from the dry throats of old men positively enthralled with the prospect of sending young men off to die for the financial betterment of their elders. McKinley was conspicuously annoyed. He fixed T.R. with what was designed to be a withering glare and said, "I am not accustomed to discussing the intricacies of foreign policy in such settings. These are vastly complicated matters, and they merit better attention than thoughtless huzzahs over brandy."

Then T.R. ripped it, as he so often does. The man is a model of indiscretion, and he enjoys moments when he would not stand out, intellectually, in a flock of sheep. He said simply, "Such vastly complicated matters, Mr. President, deserve the attention of a chief executive whose backbone bears less of a resemblance to a chocolate éclair."

Whatever good humor there had been to the exchange—and there had been precious little from McKinley's standpoint—evaporated immediately. He abruptly turned his back on T.R., struggling to maintain some modicum of dignity. After that, the gathering very rapidly drew down. I, for one, had no interest in lingering at a session at which the President of the United States of America had been so rudely insulted.

I told T.R. before I left, "That was a bit much, old man."

"He's a fool and a weakling," T.R. said. "He should never have been elected. We live in historic times, Frederic. Nothing less than the destiny of the nation is at stake."

"Which means," I said, "that you're not in the least chagrined by your conduct?"

"Not a whit." T.R. grinned his toothy grin.

As I headed for the door, shaking my head over T.R.'s bullheadedness, The Chief intercepted me.

"At ten tomorrow, sir?" he reminded me.

"I've not forgotten, Mr. Hearst."

And, to be sure, I hadn't. I suspected there might be money at stake. I could smell it in the air, Ambrose. The odor of money has always been The Chief's perfume.

TWO
New York City, 1897

I have no idea where you were that day, Bierce. You might have been en route back to your home roost in San Francisco, after spreading gloom and desolation around New York for a few weeks. In any event, you were nowhere to be found the following morning when I wandered into the *Journal* newsroom looking for The Chief. That illustrates how little I knew at the time about big-time newspapering—that I thought the editor and publisher actually operated out of the newsroom, as had my father.

The first fellow I encountered was a clerk of some sort. He seemed none too sober even at midmorning. Clearly, this was a man after your own heart, Ambrose. When I asked to see the boss, he directed me not to The Chief but to the city desk. I'm aware of your antipathy toward editors in general, but you always demonstrated reasonably high regard for Sam Chamberlain. I'd never before met him, and I hadn't expected the elegant, continental figure I encountered. He was such a dapper, trim man with his monocle and his meticulously trimmed goatee. Chamberlain was magnificently tailored and looked more like a Wall Street banker than the managing editor of a yellow sheet.

I found him busily engaged in preparations for that day's late edition, so I stood by waiting to attract his attention and witnessed my first bit of newspapering in a big city. In general, the city room of a decade ago was quieter than today's version. Typewriters were still new, and there weren't many around that room. For the most part, the only sound created by the act of writing was the slow, stifled scratching of pen upon paper, precisely as it had been at the small-town newspaper of my youth.

I was startled that even on a large newspaper, amid all the time pressure created by multiple editions, reporters still took pains with their penmanship. It wasn't until later that I came to realize and appreciate their mortal fear of the *New York Journal*'s copy desk. As you well know, it has never paid in newspapering to scribble sloppily. God alone knows what horrors an overactive copy desk might inflict even upon a story legibly inscribed. At the *Journal*, a story marred by awkward penmanship was fair game for any copy editor with a lust for altering a colleague's work. I suppose all copy editors suffer from that malady.

Nonetheless, that close to deadline the city room was a frantic place. People ran hither and yon, shouting frantically. Chamberlain, however, remained impassive. In a business where time is money and crisis normality, he was a study in serenity. When I reached his side, he was chatting with a young reporter. Chamberlain was asking how a particular murder story was going.

"Just fine, sir," the young chap replied. "I'll have it finished in plenty of time to make the final. Johnstone just made a photo of the victim at the morgue."

Chamberlain frowned at that. It wasn't until I'd grown to know him better that I realized the depth of his discomfort with photographs. Until the process of transferring photographs to printing plates had been perfected, Chamberlain had relied on drawings. An editor could always make a drawing look the way he wanted. Photographs reflected only reality, and trading in such a mundane commodity would have made the *Journal* a far less popular publication.

Had he not been confronted with the inhibiting reality of the photograph, Chamberlain would have had the reporter describe the victim, and one of the *Journal*'s illustrators would have created a likeness. Or, if time were short, the illustrator would have pulled a file drawing of someone famous and altered it to look like the victim as the reporter described him. I was somewhat surprised when I learned that this was the pattern at the *Journal*, but it did explain why so many yellow-sheet portrayals of slaying victims bore a startling resemblance to Jenny Lind and so many ax murderers looked remarkably like Benjamin Harrison.

As an artist, I had great sympathy for the aesthetic aspects of Chamberlain's point of view. As a journalist trained in gentler circumstances, however, I must confess that it troubled me.

I stood by, more or less ignored, as Chamberlain pondered the problem of the photograph. Finally he said, "Well, a photograph taken of a dead man in the morgue just won't do. We can't print a photograph of a corpse. Women and children read the *Journal*, young man—or look at the illustrations, at any rate."

"Yes, sir," the young chap said, "I realize that. That's why I instructed Johnstone to have one of the illustrators paint in eyes and a collar and tie as well. The victim will, I assure you, look precisely as he did the very moment before his wife severed his head, sir."

Chamberlain merely grunted. It was his signal for agreement—or, in this case, surrender. The victim might appear a bit glassy-eyed in the *Journal*, but the illustrator's tampering would provide the managing editor with at least some small measure of control over the terrible tyranny of fact.

That matter resolved, Chamberlain turned and inquired as to my business in his city room. I told him I was on the premises at the invitation of Mr. Hearst.

"Of course, Mr. Remington," he said, expansively shaking my hand and grasping my shoulder. "The Chief is expecting you. Permit me to escort you to his lair."

He led me from the city room, up two flights of stairs, and into a suite of offices whose style of decoration can best be described as something from *Gulliver's Travels,* a not inappropriate comparison, all things considered. The decor of each room was enormous. Seated behind a desk outside a pair of towering, mahogany doors was a lean, neat man of about my age.

"George," Chamberlain said, "Mr. Remington is here."

The secretary—for that's what he was—stood and extended a thin hand. "George Pancoast," he said.

And thus it was, Bierce, that I met two men who were to become my finest friends in the Hearst Empire. And the luster of my affection for them has been dimmed only slightly by their obviously high and misguided regard for you. Just as Chamberlain—with his polished, Parisian background—was not what one would expect in a ranking editor of a yellow sheet, neither was Pancoast a likely secretary for a press baron. As you know, he was a former printer who'd gotten his job only because he'd played some stunning practical joke on a friend of The Chief's. I don't recall precisely what the joke was, but it was outrageous enough to attract The Chief's attention and persuade him that a trickster of such perverse creativity deserved a higher station in life.

"The Chief awaits you," Pancoast told me. "I take it you've met him before."

"Only briefly," I replied.

"Well, then," Pancoast said, "you should be prepared. The Chief is quite busy, and you'll likely have only a moment with him. After all, Mr. Hearst is running both the *New York Journal* and the *San Francisco Examiner.* That's number one. Two, The Chief is . . ." And here Pancoast hesitated, groping for words. "Well, let's say he's a unique personality. You'll soon see what I mean."

He then turned and threw open the two looming doors. With Chamberlain at my side, I entered a gigantic room with soaring ceilings. The floors were covered with thick Kirman carpets, the walls paneled in rich, gleaming walnut. Thick velvet draperies hung from floor-to-ceiling windows. Directly before us were a Chippendale sofa and two delicate wing chairs. Over the mantelpiece, a mile or two away, was Cabanel's *The Birth of Venus*. I was simply aghast at the thing. It's over seven feet long, you know, and more than four feet in height. It's a wonderful work, and I had a fair idea of its value, which was unspeakable.

But as surprising as I found the richness of the furnishings and that remarkable painting, most surprising of all was The Chief himself. He was at the far end of the room, standing atop a gleaming desk, waving an enormous sword. He was slashing ferociously at a totally imaginary opponent. As the tall figure of the publisher launched a vicious thrust at his ghostly challenger, I noted the presence of another in the room—a strikingly handsome fellow in his early thirties who was laughing uproariously at The Chief's performance. I paid him no mind and, thus, didn't recognize him at first, so taken was I at the spectacle of The Chief on his desk.

"Visitors, sir," Pancoast announced.

The Chief glanced over at us and smiled broadly. He bounded from the desk top with enviable agility and crossed the broad expanse of carpet, his free hand outstretched.

"Remington," he said grandly. "How good of you to be on time. I see that you've already met Mr. Chamberlain. And I believe you know Richard Harding Davis, the finest reporter on the face of God's green earth."

And so I did. Davis had been the editor of *Harper's Weekly* during one of my assignments for that esteemed publication. We'd enjoyed only a nodding acquaintance, since I always dealt directly with Henry Harper. But I recalled Davis, and he, of course, knew me.

"Good to see you again, Remington," Davis said.

We shook hands while The Chief dismissed Pancoast with a quiet nod. The contrast in wardrobes could not have been more vivid. Pancoast—a former song-and-dance man, he once told me—was soberly attired in a good suit of dark gray. The Chief, scion of the San Francisco Nob Hill Hearsts, was decked out in the outlandish style he favored at that time. He was, if you'll recall, caught up in his Broadway swell period for several awkward years. His suit was broadly striped, and the jacket hung open to reveal, in all its questionable splendor, a gaily patterned vest of watered silk with bright gold buttons.

I'd seen that sort of waistcoast on many young men on the make who dressed and talked with a brashness uniquely New York in character. It wasn't at all what I'd expected. It was to be only the first of many surprises in dealing with The Chief over the years.

He said to me, "Like Davis here, I'm a great admirer of your work, as I believe I mentioned last evening. I must confess, however, to an appalling ignorance of you aside from your work. Do tell me a bit about yourself, Remington. Where are you from, for instance?"

I must say, Bierce, that I was somewhat taken aback. I'd not gone there to recite my life's story, and I sought to make it terse and get down to business.

"Well," I said, "I was born in Canton. That's a little village in the Adirondacks near the St. Lawrence. My father published a small newspaper, although I never was too involved in it. As soon as I was able, I left to see the larger world. I return to Canton only occasionally, to escape the rigors of a crueler universe."

"College?" Hearst demanded.

"Yale," I replied. "I studied fine arts. I was the only man in a class of twenty-three women. So, to demonstrate the stiffness of my wrist, I played a little football."

"For the finest football team in the country," Davis broke in with what was, after all, only the truth. "And you played more than a little, as I recall."

I nodded in a failed attempt at modesty. Then Davis added, "I seem to recall that you were also, for a brief time, Yale College heavyweight boxing champion."

"Mmmmm," The Chief said. "You strike me as a bit small for a heavyweight boxer."

I said, "I'm only five-foot-nine, sir, but my current weight is two hundred and forty pounds—only fifteen or so over my fighting weight. I found that size sufficient for the task."

"I wouldn't have guessed you to be so heavy," The Chief said, appraising me from a height several inches above my own. "You must be a powerful fellow, Remington, under that fine suit. How did you happen to head west, if you don't mind my asking?"

"At nineteen, I lost interest in the academic life. The West beckoned to me, and I heeded her call."

"And we're all grateful you did," The Chief said in his incongruously high-pitched voice. "I had the opportunity to see one of your bronzes last week—the *Bronco Buster*, I believe it's called. A marvelous work. Quite different from your paintings. My favorite painting, by the way, is *Roping Horses in the Corral*. The action is nothing less than remarkable. No camera could have captured the moment with such faithfulness."

I bowed slightly, not at all embarrassed by the praise. I'd worked too long and hard to inspire such words from the lips of the mighty.

"I'm a Harvard man myself," The Chief announced. "Would have been class of eighty-six, but they threw me out. Harvard takes itself entirely too seriously. Never take yourself too seriously, Remington. That's the surest pathway to buffoonery."

I asked, "For what reason did they eject you, if I might inquire?"

"You might indeed," The Chief replied, grinning. "There were several reasons, but it started with Charlie."

"Charlie?"

"Yes. Champagne Charlie, I called him. Great fun at a party, Charlie was. He was an alligator."

"I beg your pardon," I responded, smiling involuntarily.

"An alligator," Hearst replied. He was clearly amused at my amusement and returned to his duel with his imaginary antagonist. "Long, green tail, big teeth. You know the type, Remington. Terrible drinker, though. His liver finally gave out, and we buried him in the yard. Harvard didn't care for that. Seems they felt that Harvard Yard wasn't a proper cemetery for an alligator."

"And that's when they threw you out?"

The Chief shook his head. "No, they were merely unpleasant about that. They threw me out over the chamber pots."

"Chamber pots?" I said, slightly nonplussed. The Chief was alight with that mischievous energy he sometimes gets. He was bouncing about the office, whishing the sword through the air. The trait still disconcerts me somewhat. I'm sure it does you as well, Bierce, although you're not likely to exhibit the character to admit to such a human frailty.

"Take that, Joe Pulitzer," The Chief said, thrusting the weapon at the empty air once again. Then he turned back to me and said, "Yes, the chamber pots. I bought a supply of them and sent one to each of my professors. Each pot had the professor's name ornamentally lettered on the bottom—on the inside. That's what did it. 'Out,' they said, without even the charity of a smirk."

The explanation provoked a muffled chuckle from Chamberlain, a somewhat more spirited laugh from me, and a positive guffaw from Davis. The Chief immediately drew his sword down to his side and fixed Mr. Davis with a ferocious glare.

"So," he said grimly, "you think it's amusing that I was summarily ejected from Harvard, do you?"

Davis—not the type to be easily intimidated, as I later learned—replied, "Under the circumstances, sir, I find it hilarious."

There followed a brief, awkward moment of silence. The air was pregnant with disaster—for Davis if for no one else. But this was only another of The Chief's many games. Hearst's grim visage gave way slowly to a bemused grin, and he chuckled. "So did I. As I said, Harvard takes itself entirely too seriously."

Hearst then turned back to me. He leaned upon the hilt of his sword and said, "I would like very much, Remington, to persuade you to work for me. Do I seem the sort of fellow you might enjoy working for?"

I said, "I admire much of what you've accomplished."

"For example?" The Chief asked, already pleased with my response.

"Well," I told him, "I'm enamored of your accomplishments with the *San Francisco Examiner*—how you fought the trusts and the railroads, how you stood up for the people of California against the robber barons. When you bought this moribund newspaper in New York, I expected work of a similarly lofty character."

"And . . ." he pressed.

I thought about it and decided that candor was the best policy.

"I've seen some of that," I said finally, "but I've also seen a great deal of much lighter material of a lower tone."

Clearly, The Chief was not entirely pleased with this response, although he didn't dispute it. He began to pace the room, his sword over his shoulder.

He said, "A newspaper must reflect the interests of the readers it serves. We serve a different audience here in New York, Remington. Moreover, you can accomplish wonders with a newspaper in good financial health. The *Examiner* is healthy. We have many more readers now than we had in the beginning, but the *Journal* is still struggling. It's my hope that we'll soon prosper, however—and my father's hope as well. As of now, the *Journal* is costing my father and me a fortune every month."

"I'm sorry to hear that," I said honestly.

"Well," The Chief said, smiling, "I have a fortune to spend. My father, you should know, has this remarkable knack for knowing precisely where to dig for gold and silver. It's really quite an uncanny skill, and he's not uncritical of me for my comparable knack for spending it. I've gone through nearly eight million dollars of his money in the past three years keeping this newspaper alive. As you may have heard, Remington, the key to success in the newspaper business is circulation."

"So I've been told."

"Which newspaper in New York would you imagine has the most circulation?" he demanded.

"Offhand," I replied, "I would say the *World*."

The Chief flashed a grin, obviously pleased with my response.

"And you'd be right, sir—absolutely right. Joseph Pulitzer's *World* is the circulation leader."

He leaned close to me, his voice taking on a conspiratorial tone. "Right now," he said, stabbing the air with his sword.

"Pulitzer has more circulation than do I, and he consequently enjoys more advertising dollars. But, my dear Remington, we at the *Journal* will soon outstrip the *World* in circulation. And can you imagine how?"

I shook my head. The Chief immediately snapped to attention before me and raised his sword in smart salute.

"*Cuba Libre!*" he shouted.

The man stood like a guard at Buckingham Palace, the point of his sword pointed toward the ceiling way above us.

"I beg your pardon," I said.

Hearst looked at me as though I were a cretin. "The revolution going on down there, Remington, is not at all unlike our own treasured American Revolution a mere century or so ago. The Spanish are terrorizing the poor but honest Cuban people, who are fighting valiantly for their liberty and for democracy. And when the colonists of this great nation were fighting the imperial British for independence, who came to our aid?"

I admit it, Bierce. He had me baffled. I'd gone there expecting a generous commission, perhaps a bronze bust of the great man himself, and now I was undergoing a history lesson at sword point. I could see little choice but to play along.

"The French?" I replied.

"The French!" Hearst bellowed in triumph. "That's absolutely correct, Remington. Apparently, you learned some history at Yale, second-rate school though it may be. France, at the time, was the dominant military power on Earth, and she came to the aid of the gallant American rebels and helped us secure victory against the British."

It was a marvelous show, Ambrose.

"It's my opinion," The Chief continued, "that the United States today has an obligation to play for the Cubans the same role the French played in our behalf so many years ago. Unfortunately, as you saw last evening, President McKinley is improperly appreciative of the situation's destiny. And that's why the *Journal* is about to embark on its greatest ever crusade."

He leaned over to me, his voice low, his words intense. "We, Remington, are going to free Cuba."

I gazed at the man in undisguised amazement. The Chief broke into a merry grin and added, "And, if the *Journal* were to pick up a little circulation in this glorious cause, it would hardly be a disappointment to either my father or myself."

That's when Hearst handed me the sword he'd been swirling about all through the meeting. I recognized it as a saber. It was well made and richly decorated. Its gold handle glittered with diamonds. I shuddered to think of its cost.

"It's quite lovely," I said.

The Chief instructed, "Read the inscription."

With difficulty, I tore my eyes away from the ornate hilt, which was worth more than any of my paintings or bronzes—at that point, at least. On the gleaming steel blade I found these words:

To Maximo Gomez, Commander-in-Chief of the Army of the Cuban Republic. Viva Cuba Libre.

I glanced back at The Chief. He was still grinning.

"I've been trying," he said casually, "to find someone fool enough to carry this elegant sword to Gomez. I'll be perfectly frank with you, Remington. These inscriptions would be devilishly hard to explain to the Spanish army if that somebody happened to be caught, wouldn't they?"

"Indeed, they would," I agreed.

"Strangely enough," The Chief went on, "the intrepid Mr. Davis here has agreed to deliver my sword to the commander. I swear I don't know what else to do with the damned thing. If I keep it around here, I'll end up slicing my hand off. If you're nabbed with it at sea, Davis, I suppose you can chuck it overboard."

Davis responded cheerfully, "And if I get surrounded on land, perhaps I can swallow it. But I'll take my chances. I'm quite definitely the fool you've been looking for, Mr. Hearst."

"And where," I asked, "might I enter into this grand plan of yours?"

That's when Chamberlain piped in. "We see the delivery of this elegant weapon as a story of some magnitude, Mr. Remington. Davis will write up an account of his adventures, and the *Journal* will also need sketches to illustrate them—sketches of the finest quality by the finest American artist of the age."

"You want me to go with him, then?" I asked.

"It'll be a great adventure," The Chief assured me. "I'll ship you both down there on my private yacht for a landing somewhere where you won't have to explain this sword to the Spanish authorities. What do you say, Remington? Are you up for a bit of sport?"

I must confess, Bierce, that the project—as wild as it was—held considerable allure for me. As you know, my father was a hero of the Civil War, a man of immense courage, and I'd never seen war. Unless, of course, you count Indian wars. They were hazardous enough to qualify, I suppose, but I'd never seen war in its classic sense. Moreover, I'd been in New York for several years. As I approached middle age I found myself longing for the freedom and excitement I'd known in the West. Like all young men, I had been too callow to fully appreciate the grandeur of the enterprise I had undertaken.

As I weighed the relative merits and drawbacks of the offer, Pancoast came in through the towering double doors behind us and said, "Excuse me, Mr. Hearst, but the Willson sisters are here for your luncheon date."

· As Pancoast spoke, two young women—expensively dressed and extraordinarily lovely—burst upon us. Hearst beamed at their arrival, as did we all.

"Gentlemen," The Chief announced, "may I present the sisters Willson—Millicent and Anita. Ladies, these are Mr. Chamberlain, Mr. Davis, and the illustrious Frederic Remington, the celebrated painter and sculptor."

I handed the sword to Davis and bowed to the young ladies who had all of New York buzzing. The Chief's youth, his undeniable flair, his money, and his sheer cheek were enough to establish his reputation as a dashing New York rake. But his association with the Willson sisters, each a startling beauty with family connections in the theater, had confirmed our master's reputation about town as a playboy of some note. He was seen everywhere with them, and no one could say which was the lovelier.

"Charmed, gentlemen," they said, almost in chorus, and favored us with graceful curtsies.

"Well, Remington," The Chief demanded as he took a Willson sister on each arm, "what do you say to my proposal?"

I was interested. I was, however, reluctant to agree until I'd cleared it with my wife, Missie, and there was an equally practical concern to be addressed.

I replied, "It has a certain undeniable appeal, Mr. Hearst. There is, however, the matter of what I might be paid to embark upon an adventure of such a perilous nature."

Heast merely threw back his head and laughed. "How much do you want?"

I quickly named an outrageous sum. "Three thousand a month would have to be my minimum, sir."

The Chief never blinked. "So be it. Chamberlain here will make the necessary arrangements. Good day to you, gentlemen, and the very best of luck."

"That's what I'm getting, too," Davis whispered to me as The Chief swept out the door flanked by his duo of lovelies.

"Really," I said, hoping my annoyance didn't show. I was furious at myself for asking for too little. It was a mistake I seldom made.

"The Chief's private yacht can be ready to sail from Key West by the end of the week," Chamberlain told us. "I'll make train arrangements for both of you to meet up with it. I do trust, gentlemen, that neither of you is subject to seasickness."

"It has never bothered me," I said truthfully.

"Nor I," Davis assured us both, uttering one of the more innocuous distortions, if not outright lies, that already swirled so merrily about the Cuban rebellion.

THREE

There's no place quite like Key West, Bierce. It's drenched in sunshine, caressed by gentle sea breezes, and blessed with a seemingly bottomless well of white rum. You'd like it there. Just your sort of place.

Davis and I'd gotten there under a cloak of secrecy the military would have envied. At The Chief's orders, we met late one night at the *Journal* office and were taken by closed hack to the train station. I'd brought my usual outfit for outdoor living—my Duke of Marlborough field garb and British Empire pith helmet. I thought I looked rather dashing, but Davis had outdone me. He was dressed in some sort of pseudo-military uniform with all the white-hunter trimmings. You'd have thought the fellow was going to stalk elephants for trophies instead of stories for a newspaper.

We took separate trains out of New York and met up several days later at Key West's Duval House. The Chief's yacht, however, wasn't quite ready. It was being painted a pale gray so it could blend in more effectively with the fog. With nothing better to occupy us, Davis and I fraternized with Navy personnel in watering spots along the shore. One afternoon, after a few drinks, I talked one officer into letting us aboard the U.S.S. *Raleigh* so I could play with the guns. I practiced with a five-incher until I could cut the flagstaff off a target with just one shot. It gave me a certain appreciation for why we were hanging around Key West until the yacht was made less visible to Spanish patrol boats.

I also took the opportunity to write several times to Missie. She'd grown used to my absences. Traveling was part of what I did to earn my living then. But this was my first lengthy trip since we'd moved out of Brooklyn. There, she'd enjoyed a neighborhood surrounded by friends. In New Rochelle, we'd bought a big old house in a neighborhood where she knew virtually no one. Still, my Missie was a good sport. The three thousand dollars a month was a powerful balm to ease the pain of my extended absence.

The Chief's yacht was something special, indeed. He called it the *Vamoose* because it could run at enormous speed. The vessel was a mackerel-shaped speedboat of sheet iron and shallow draft. She ran 138 feet, a trim little sliver in the sea. She was powered by three triple-expansion steam engines. In her hull, she carried enough coal and water for a journey of seven days. When the paint was dry, we boarded her at night. Davis began throwing up almost immediately.

By midday, we were well out at sea, steaming south by southeast. Davis had turned a fetching shade of gray-green. He fought his sickness by the simple expedient of not eating. His theory was that if he consumed no food, then no food could come up. It was a sound enough plan, rooted firmly in science, but it failed to take into account a phenomenon well known to sailors, expectant mothers, and drinkers of herculean proportions like yourself—the dry heaves. So, except for brief trips to his stateroom, Davis spent most of the journey hung over the rail of The Chief's yacht, wracked with spasms and wishing fervently that death—if it was coming—would hurry along.

Our second day out, he was hanging over the rail beneath a heavily overcast sky—the very best sort, from our perspective. The captain, whose name I can't recall, was a huge, blond-bearded fellow with a voice like a lion. He made no secret of his concern about the patrol boats. He also made no secret of his disdain for Davis and me, who were placing him and his boat in such peril. I was enjoying the air and casually sketching Davis in his unwilling pose. Then he shifted position, and I groaned.

"Davis," I complained. "You went and moved on me."

"What do you mean, 'I moved'?" he moaned. "I haven't moved from this rail since we left Key West. How long have you been spying on my misery, Remington?"

I handed him my sketchbook. "Long enough to do this."

It was only a rough bit of work, a figure study in soft pencil, but it intrigued Davis. I did manage to capture the flat lighting and the general limpness of Davis's frame. I even managed to hint at his pallor.

"Lovely," he muttered. "This is why The Chief sends an artist along with me, to draw me throwing up my guts into the Atlantic?"

He turned unsteadily and started lurching along the pitching deck. I flipped my sketchbook shut, deposited my pencil in my jacket pocket, and followed. We had to reach out every few steps to grab at a piece of railing or bulkhead to keep from being thrown to the deck as the *Vamoose* cut its rocky way through the waves.

"I have to get used to drawing you," I explained. "It's essential that I be able to provide a good likeness when I do the drawing of you presenting the sword to General Gomez."

"I'll never live to make it to Cuba," Davis told me. "None of us may survive this trip."

"You worry too much," I said. "How heavy can the Spanish sea patrols be? The rebels don't have a navy, after all. They're strictly land troops."

Davis sank into a deck chair. "They're not really troops at all, Remington. They're farmers and peasants. And they're a reasonably brutal bunch, too."

"I thought the Spanish were the brutal ones," I replied. "They're the ones slaughtering civilians, after all."

It was almost painful for him in his current condition, but Davis laughed when I said that. He told me, "It doesn't pay to attach too much veracity to what's printed in The Chief's paper or, especially, Pulitzer's. When it comes to Cuba, Remington, the yellow sheets are good mainly for the artful prose of immensely talented writers like myself. That doesn't mean, though, that the prose is to be taken literally, however lyrical it might be."

That stopped me for a moment, Bierce. I was not, after all, totally unfamiliar with newspaper journalism, and I'd certainly done enough coverage of my own for magazines and national weeklies like *Harper's* and *Collier's*.

"Explain yourself, Davis," I said. "You talk like an expert on this war. I suppose you're right. When all's said and done, I know only what I've been reading on the topic."

He leaned back in his chair and stared out over the rolling sea. He thought for a moment, then he said, "Well, Remington, it's more or less like this: When the rebels catch a Spanish soldier, they cut off his head. When the Spanish soldiers catch a rebel, they sometimes cut off his head, too. But more often they just throw him into prison, where he can't cut the heads off any more Spanish soldiers. And they wouldn't have thrown him into prison in the first place if he'd been working in the cane fields like he was supposed to be doing instead of running around decapitating Spanish soldiers."

I had to admit there was a certain logic in that perspective. I said, "I guess that's one way to look at it. Listen, what about this Spanish general? What's his name—Weyler? What sort of chap is he?"

Davis fought back a ferocious belch and said, "Valeriano Weyler. I saw him once. It was in Madrid, before they sent him out to replace Captain-General Martinez Campos as military governor in Cuba. Actually, the rebellion in Cuba had been fairly quiet when Campos was in charge, but Weyler gave the yellow sheets a glorious new target. He wasn't in Cuba a week before one of the yellows—either The Chief's or Pulitzer's, I can't remember which—started calling him 'Butcher Weyler.' He was 'Weyler the brute, the devastator of *haciendas*, the destroyer of families, and the outrager of women.' It was a catchy phrase, so I committed it to memory. He was also described as 'pitiless, cold, and an exterminator of men.' I wish I'd written that, Remington. Nice rhythm there."

I must confess to some puzzlement at what Davis was telling me. I said to him, "All of which means what?"

He sighed deeply. "It means Weyler's not really all that bad a fellow, Remington. He's a stern man in a trying circumstance. The rebellion was already well under way when Maria Christina, the queen regent of Spain, sent Weyler in to restore order in the cane fields. You should know that this is, in fact, only the latest in a long series of rebellions. They've been going on for years. They love to rebel, these Cubans. Personally, I think it's all that coffee they drink. A few sips of Cuban coffee will stop your heart, if you're not used to it. They down a couple of quarts of the stuff a day. No wonder they're always running around looking for yokes to throw off."

I took the chair next to Davis. He was still sadly sallow. "That's your theory on the war?" I asked him. "That it's all the fault of Cuban coffee?"

"Laugh if you like," Davis said. "The fact is that Maria Christina didn't send in Weyler until the rebels elected a president and proclaimed Cuban a separate nation."

"But what about all the atrocities Weyler has committed?" I demanded.

Davis leaned toward me. "Do you know about the Junta? That's a group of Cuban sympathizers who occupy offices in Florida and New York and Washington. They have one purpose, and one purpose only— to inflame the American public through planted newspaper stories. Surely, Remington, you've heard of the Peanut Club."

I had, in fact, heard of the Peanut Club. It was a group of reporters who met regularly at the offices of the rebel sympathizers to glean all the latest news of the war.

I said, "The people I've met who know the rebel representatives consider them quite reliable sources of information."

"I'm sure they do," Davis snorted. "They're all people, like yourself, who've never seen Cuba. They depend for their stories on representatives of the Insurrecto whose primary purpose in New York is to raise money for the cause. These reporters get their information from men like Jorge Gonzales, who's in the stateroom next to mine."

I was stunned. "We're not the only passengers? Who's this Gonzales fellow? I haven't seen him."

Davis only smiled slyly. "I've seen him. I bumped into him on one of my trips below deck, and I asked one of the crewmen about him."

I was almost sputtering with the surprise of it all. "Well, who is he?"

"He's one of the Florida operatives of the Insurrecto. He's being ferried along with us back to Cuba."

I shook my head wearily. "Wonderful. If a patrol boat intercepts us, we can always throw that silly sword overboard and pretend that we've merely wandered off course. But with a Cuban revolutionary on board the vessel . . ."

Davis smiled ruefully. "Gonzales will be the least of our problems if we're intercepted, Remington. You should worry considerably more about the guns in the hold."

I swear, Bierce, that I felt my heart miss a beat when Davis uttered those words. "We have guns on board? What in God's name are you talking about, man?"

"The rifles and ammunition are being sent to the rebel army by representatives of the Insurrecto who're working in Florida. That's why they're there, after all."

I was almost beside myself. "This is serious. Do you really know what you're talking about?"

Davis merely fixed me with a bemused glare. "A few months ago," he said slowly, "a large fund-raising affair was held at Madison Square Garden. That's where it was decided to have the sword in my cabin delivered to General Gomez. It was also where money was raised for the guns and ammunition. That's the main reason we're being dropped off on the coast of the Santa Clara Province, Remington, instead of simply steaming into Havana Harbor like civilized journalists. Gonzales will deliver the guns to the rebels. Then, if we're lucky, we'll be taken to Gomez where I'll give him his fine sword and where you'll draw a fine picture of the historic event. Then we'll scurry back to the coast to meet up with the *Vamoose* and sail back to Key West to avoid a Cuban prison cell—if we're lucky."

I muttered a curse—and not a mild one, either. "Marvelous. Just marvelous," I added.

"Well," Davis said philosophically, "what did you expect for three thousand a month—a picnic? When you work for The Chief, you earn your money, Remington. I just hope your drawings are up to his standards."

"Our smallest worry," I told Davis, whom I was beginning to dislike rather intensely, "will be the quality of my drawings."

Then I excused myself and wandered off along the deck. I was fretting—just a bit, anyway. From the bow, I cast a glance back at Davis. He'd returned to his spot at the rail, his digestive system again in full revolt.

Which, given the circumstances, struck me as no more than just.

FOUR

Let me tell you about Gonzales.

He was a dark man of medium height with a trim waist and a deeply furrowed brow. He was perhaps the age I am now—mid-forties, or thereabouts. One might call that middle-aged, if one felt an entitlement to live to ninety. His hair was the color of india ink, although it had receded to the middle of his skull, leaving him with a high, domed forehead. His was a most arresting face, and his dark eyes gleamed luminously beneath bushy black brows. It was as though a blast furnace were smoldering deep within his brain.

In fact, I suppose, one was. Jorge Gonzales was a man utterly without humor, without a shred of frivolity, and without even the meanest appreciation for the absurdity of the comedy in which we're all such baffled players. He smoked constantly, but seldom drank. He was a totally asexual creature, as near as I could determine. Women weren't even a convenience to him. He shunned most male comradeship as well. I later realized that was because comrades had a disturbing tendency to step in front of Spanish bullets, as he'd learned to his sorrow early on in the fight.

Gonzales was the ultimate pessimist. He seemed convinced that the worst is inevitable and keenly aware that a man's final act is the one he struggles all his life to avoid. I'm not sure he thought about it in precisely these terms, but I suspect he believed in predestination. He seemed vaguely bitter that although his fate was preordained, he had no idea what it might be. He spent much of his time fighting impulse, and his impulses were invariably violent.

He was very much a killer, and he felt no remorse whatsoever at killing because it's the job of a soldier—his very reason for living. And Gonzales was, above all, a soldier—a creature of discipline and self-denial, of regimentation and acceptance, of obligation and obedience. He was that most dangerous of creatures, Bierce—a totally committed man. One glance at him would make much of what I've described evident to even the densest bumpkin. You could sense the tension in the way he moved—always coiled to strike, like a desert rattler.

So it was that when he came up on deck, I realized immediately that he was seeking not relaxation or companionship but information. You could read it in his face. He was asking himself, What sort of chaps are these who have been sent with me and my guns? How can I deliver my cargo without burdening myself with these soft gringos from Nueva York?

After our conversation, Davis had gone below to suffer in privacy. I didn't care for the vessel belowdecks. A fellow my size felt decidedly cramped down there. So I was reposing in splendid isolation on a deck chair near the bow when I saw Gonzales stalking the long deck directly toward me. He was a sinuous figure in a broad-brimmed hat, a somber business suit, and a flowing canvas coat to protect his fancy garb from the spray. A long, thin cigar was clenched in his teeth. He shifted his balance nimbly as the ship pitched. As he came on, the sun suddenly emerged from its den and shone brightly on the waves, producing the sort of shimmering highlights that can be captured properly only in oil. It was a dazzling display of God's skill in stage lighting. Gonzales, I'm sure, noticed none of it.

"You must be the artist, Remington," he said.

I told him, "I am. Davis is below, napping."

He permitted the smallest of smiles to play about his lips beneath the thin line of charcoal mustache. "Some stomachs, they are not built for travel over water. My name is Gonzales. May I sit?"

"Please do," I told him, and not without a measure of caution. Jorge Gonzales exuded menace.

He gazed for a moment at the sea, as if noticing it for the first time. Then, to my surprise, he flashed me a brief smile, white teeth gleaming against his olive skin. I kept my eye on the man, Bierce. I felt as though I were sitting next to a cobra.

"What might I do for you, Mr. Gonzales?" I asked. "And I'm curious as to how you might have gotten aboard this boat. My understanding had been that Mr. Davis and I would be the only passengers."

He said, "Is that what my good friend Señor Hearst told you? Or is it something you merely assumed? I boarded slightly before you and your friend of the restless stomach. Señor Hearst is a fine friend of the Free Army of Cuba, and he was kind enough to offer us the use of this fine yacht for the transport of supplies."

I said merely, "So, you're the man in charge of delivering a hold full of guns and placing Davis and me in danger of being captured."

He shrugged casually. "I am told that you have something to deliver as well."

I was taken aback by the depth of the man's information. I told him, "We're delivering an object of ceremonial value to General Gomez, compliments of Mr. Hearst."

"I have seen this sword," Gonzales said evenly. "It is a thing of great beauty. I wish I had known earlier that it was going to Cuba on this voyage. You see, while Señor Hearst did not tell you about me, he also did not tell me about you. I can save you a dangerous journey, Señor Remington, by delivering the sword myself to General Gomez. The journey inland to the free Army is both difficult and hazardous."

"So," I said, "General Gomez won't be picking up his guns in person, then."

Gonzales shook his head. "No, señor, he will not. He is busily engaged inland, killing Spanish soldiers."

"Well," I said dryly, "I appreciate the offer, but Mr. Hearst asked us to deliver the sword in person. I plan to sketch the presentation so the *Journal* can run an appropriate illustration with my colleague's story. I'm afraid, Mr. Gonzales, that we'll just have to travel inland with you."

Gonzales shook his head, as though speaking to a somewhat slow child. "There is much danger inland. Surely, your talent will permit you to produce such a picture from the fertility of your imagination."

"I have no idea what Gomez looks like," I protested.

"He is a heroic figure," Gonzales snapped, his small supply of patience wearing thin. "A drawing of a heroic figure in a fine uniform will suffice."

I said to the man, "You know little of journalism, sir. We must spend time with the rebel army, reporting on its activities and its spirit. This sort of thing is news, you know, and the readers of the *New York Journal* have exhibited an intense interest in this war."

Gonzales made a careless motion with his cigar, as if warding off my arguments. "There will be vastly more news for you to report in Havana, señor, where our agents will keep you well informed of our activities inland. You will have your news delivered to you daily as you sit sipping fine Cuban rum in the lobby of the Hotel Inglaterra. Is this not a much more agreeable arrangement?"

"Not for us," I told him. "Davis and I will report only what we see and hear with our own eyes and ears." I then delivered what I thought would be a harmless, rhetorical thrust. I said, "I wasn't aware that there was a Peanut Club in Havana."

Gonzales's eyes clouded over instantly. I'd been more or less lounging in my deck chair, but I found myself possessed of the distinct impression that—for a moment, at least—my life was in serious danger. I still can't explain precisely how or why, but I suddenly realized that Jorge Gonzales was capable, had he considered the task of sufficient profit, of calmly squeezing the life out of me. And then of casting my corpse over the rail without even a hint of remorse.

I was, of course, considerably larger than he, and in the prime of my vital years. Strangling me would have posed something of a chore. Still, the realization that he would have tried it without a second thought was chilling. I sat immediately upright, bracing myself. But by then the fire in the man's eyes had burned down a bit, and I heard him speak in a voice hoarse with restraint.

"You do not understand, Señor Remington," Gonzales told me. "Some of what happens in war can be misunderstood—especially by civilian *periodistas* with the power to mislead, quite unintentionally, the readers of the *New York Journal*. Go to Havana. Enjoy the warmth of the Cuban sun. Enjoy the Cuban women. We will see that you have news to print."

He then stared at me, clearly expecting a response. I cleared my throat and said, "The message I get from all this, Mr. Gonzales, is that your people will feed us lies while we sit and grow fat in Havana. That won't do, I'm afraid. We're here looking for stories, and we'll find them ourselves."

There was a moment's silence between us. Gonzales's gaze was steely. For a moment, I had the impression that I might have once more gone too far—that this dark and threatening man next to me was again considering how best to throttle me. I realized also that I was only about fifty percent confident of my ability to stave him off, despite the difference in our respective bulks. I must confess that I briefly weighed the prospect of jumping up and running, but the realization of how ridiculous that would be—and that outrunning him would be unlikely—kept me glued to my chair. Well, I thought, if you're going to do it, I'm ready for you.

We suffered through a long and awkward silence, our eyes locked on each other's. Then Gonzales said at last, "You are a most difficult man."

"When necessary."

The Cuban rose, glared down at me, and stalked off. I kept a careful eye on him as he moved back along the deck and disappeared belowdecks. Then I slumped back in my chair and heaved a great sigh of relief. I found myself utterly drenched in sweat.

And so it was upon the occasion of my first meeting with Jorge Gonzales, Bierce. And I couldn't help but wonder:

If this was what our allies were like, then what in God's name could we expect from the Spanish?

FIVE

I was choking. I felt strong fingers closing on my throat, and I realized that looming up over me like the Angel of Death was the Cuban. I struggled. I pounded fiercely on the man's face. But I still couldn't breathe, and I could hear this terrible booming in my ears. It was awful—as though the whole world were ending, not just my own.

Then I sat bolt upright in my bunk.

A slanted funnel of morning sunlight streamed in the porthole and across the deck of the little stateroom I occupied on the *Vamoose*. Slowly, I realized that I was completely alone—that I'd been alone all along. I've never been much of a dreamer, Bierce, either before or since the Cuban adventure. I sleep like the dead. But this dream had been startlingly real, right down to the dull explosions that had so assailed my ears.

Then I heard another. It was almost painfully loud, like a crack of thunder booming from only yards away. Through the porthole, I heard an enormous splash. The *Vamoose* shivered from its impact, and I felt the great steam engines take hold deep within the narrow hull. Then came another blast. And another splash.

I leapt to my feet, ran to the porthole, and stuck my head through to peer out on the gleaming swells. Only a few hundred yards to the stern, a white, wooden boat was cutting through the waves directly toward us. It was smaller than our vessel, and nowhere near as fast. But it was moving at full speed, and we weren't. I could see men scurrying about its deck. And I could see that the vessel was armed.

I'd stripped to the skin when I'd retired the previous evening, and now I was pulling my head back inside the vessel and struggling into my pants in those infernal close quarters. I was sweating and swearing and smashing my elbows against the bulkhead as the *Vamoose* built speed against the force of the sea. The pants were enough, I decided, and I tore up to the deck, barefoot and barechested. The sunlight was ferociously bright. I merely stood for a moment next to the hatch, blinking in its glare.

Then I heard a voice call out, "Mr. Remington, get down! Down with you!"

I blinked again as my eyes sought the source of the voice. It turned out to be a member of the crew, flattened on the deck.

"It's a Spanish gunboat, Mr. Remington," he called out. The man was clearly terrified. "They're firing on us. Please get down, sir!"

As the crewman spoke, I heard another booming explosion off our stern. I turned and spotted a rise of smoke puffing off the bow gun of the Spanish vessel. Then, a scant ten yards from the port bow of the *Vamoose*, a plume of water shot up two dozen feet above the deck. I immediately dived for cover.

I then spied Davis's head popping out of the hatch. I couldn't determine if the sallowness of his skin was a byproduct of seasickness or fear.

"What's happening, Remington?" he shouted.

I raised myself up just slightly and motioned toward the stern. "Spanish gunboat. Keep your head down, man."

But no, not Davis. It was my first experience with him in such circumstances, and his conduct at that moment demonstrated to me that he was utterly incapable of any rational assessment of risk. He pulled himself on deck and stared at the gunboat. He didn't even bother to duck.

I lifted my head with considerably more care than Davis had chosen to exhibit. I saw the Spanish boat making better time against the waves than I would have expected, given the rotundity of its hull. The boat was perhaps fifty feet long with a high cabin and a raised prow that shed water like a turtle's shell. It was close enough that I could clearly see the cannon and the two soldiers manning it. They wore the beige tropical uniforms of the Spanish military and floppy, wide-brimmed hats to guard against the sun's cruelty. Their actions were directed by an officer, similarly dressed but waving a saber.

This vessel had obviously begun life as a fishing boat. It was awkward and bulky, designed for shallower coastal waters instead of the deep, blue sea. Billows of smoke belched from its single stack as the pilot pressed his throttle. He must have tied down the safety valve on his boiler because the boat was making better time than it had any right to make.

That, in fact, had apparently been the salvation of the *Vamoose*. The patrol boat's bow was rising and falling as it plowed so vigorously through the waves, and accurately directing the fire of the bow cannon was an impossibility. The Spanish knew that, and they were flogging the boat forward, firing as they came, in a desperate attempt to narrow the range before the *Vamoose* built up speed and outran them.

I could see the officer's sword arm fall. As it did, another shot boomed out of the bow cannon. Davis merely stood erect, gazing at the sight without perceptible anxiety. I concluded that he'd lost his mind entirely and dragged him down beside me. The shell from the gunboat struck ridiculously close to our hull. It created a towering spire of water that crashed down on deck, drenching both of us.

"They must have spotted us as the sun rose," Davis told me in the most casual of tones, as though he were merely a detached observer. "They must have signaled us to stop for inspection. And when we didn't—"

"Where's that sword?" I demanded. "The damnable thing is going straight to the bottom."

Davis merely laughed. "A gesture of questionable utility, Remington. You forget the guns in the hold. But we might be able to outrun them before they land a lucky shot. Let's hope so."

We were, however, enjoying limited success in that regard. The *Vamoose* operated on a twin boiler system, and one boiler had apparently been permitted to cool to an unacceptable level during the night. We had only half our power available, and many of the crewmen were huddled on deck so they could swim for it if a shell happened to penetrate the hull. They were crewmen on a rich man's yacht, not fighting men, and they weren't inclined to go down with the ship. I could hear the captain bellowing at them with his bull-like voice, but they were paralyzed with fear.

The gunboat was rapidly narrowing the distance between us, coming perilously close. I could almost make out the faces of the gun crew. The Spanish flag fluttered arrogantly over the cabin. As I watched, the officer's sword arm dropped once more. Another blast issued from the bow cannon. I went flat on the deck, and I heard the whistling of the shell as it flew no more than a dozen feet over my head, miraculously missing us. I must confess to a certain amount of alarm at that moment, Bierce. I was certain that they must have had the range by now.

All of us aboard the *Vamoose*—with the exception of Davis, who possessed no sense at all—were busy ducking or praying, so none of us actually saw Gonzales come topside. But, suddenly, there he was amongst us, in trousers and boots, his white dress shirt open to the waist and his sleeves rolled up past his elbows. He was stalking across the deck, the wind whipping through his thinning hair, and he was squinting against the sun at the gunboat. Like Davis, who had escaped my protective grasp, Gonzales stood fully upright. He strode purposefully. I had my cheek pressed firmly against the *Vamoose*'s wooden deck as the polished boots passed my face. I reached up and grabbed at the Cuban's shirttail.

"Mr. Gonzales," I cried out. "Get down!"

He merely gazed down at me, his features contorted by the most naked of sneers. He pulled away and marched across the deck to the steel railing that encircled it. It was then that I saw the rifle he carried.

The weapon was fresh from its crate. While I was certain that Gonzales, the soldier, had taken time to clean its firing mechanism and barrel, the Cuban had not bothered to wipe the grease from the rifle's skin. It was a bolt-action carbine, a military weapon. It was designed for one purpose only—the killing of men. Gonzales handled the thing with affectionate familiarity. As he stood at the rail, vulnerable to enemy fire, he slowly produced a handkerchief and wiped away the excess grease. Then he jammed a clip into place. He turned back to me. His eyes were no more than slits revealing bits of black fire between the hooded lids.

"Cowards hide," he said crisply. "Patriots fight."

As he spoke, still another shell struck the water only yards beyond where he stood. Gonzales ignored it. He calmly and meticulously wiped down the greasy rifle with his handkerchief. Even Davis was impressed. We stared at one another in amazement.

Gonzales concluded his task and tossed the handkerchief overboard. He then dropped to one knee and rested the barrel of his weapon against the railing of our pitching vessel. I glanced back at the Spaniard. I could see the officer raising a pair of binoculars. I was studying that image when Gonzales's rifle barked. I spun my head about to see the barrel jump up a few inches off the railing from the recoil. I immediately turned back to the Spaniard to see the officer flying off his deck and into the churning sea.

I tell you, Bierce, I witnessed some impressive marksmanship during the Indian wars. I saw Apaches who could shoot a coin out of your hand from a galloping horse at fifty yards, and I saw troopers who could best them. But I would not have thought possible such a shot as Jorge Gonzales made that day off the Cuban coast.

I was gaping at the magnitude of his feat as he lowered the rifle, made a minute adjustment to the sights, then worked the bolt to jam another cartridge into the firing chamber. Once again, he raised his rifle and rested it on the railing of the jumping, heaving ship. He sighted for less than a second and fired twice in rapid succession. I spun my head about to watch the two-man gun crew on the bow of the Spaniard crumple to the deck.

Instantly, the gunboat slowed, then turned sharply to port at the hands of its prudent pilot. I rose to study the two fallen soldiers on the bow—I remain certain that each was dead—and the officer floating motionless in the trough of a wave to the vessel's stern. There was no doubt whatever that he had been dispatched to his maker, saber and all.

The Spaniard continued its port turn until it showed us its ungainly stern. Then the water churned about its rear as the pilot opened his throttle. The Spanish were running, and I couldn't blame them—not with three crew members dead in a matter of seconds. The survivors must have been astonished to have been converted so quickly from hunter to prey.

A rousing cheer erupted from the crew of the *Vamoose*. Gonzales put his smoking rifle under one arm, produced a long, thin cigar, and casually lit it with a wooden match cupped in his hand against the wind. He took a puff or two and tossed the match overboard. Then, his expression utterly noncommittal, he turned and walked back across the deck to the hatch. He stopped and stared down at me with obsidian eyes. I felt a chill run through me. Then he was gone belowdecks.

I clambered to my feet and found Davis, grinning, at my side.

Davis said, "This Gonzales chap's not terribly friendly, but he does seem to have his good points."

SIX

After the encounter with the gunboat, just south of the Tropic of Cancer, both the *Vamoose*'s boilers were kept hot. We moved at full cruising speed to get as far as possible as quickly as possible from the site of the conflict.

"Where there's one gunboat there's others," the captain grunted to Davis in his flat, Maine accent.

By late afternoon, with the burning orange ball of the sun hovering on the western horizon, a dim and sprawling shadow appeared over the waves to the south.

"Cuba," Davis told me.

By nightfall, the *Vamoose* was moving eastward a few miles off the Cuban coastline. On the captain's orders, only small lanterns necessary for the reading of maps and charts were permitted. Davis and I stayed on deck watching the inky sky to the south blend with the stygian mass of land. At one point, a small, winged creature flapped across the deck, narrowly missing my head. I ducked and swatted at it.

"Even the sea gulls here are aggressive," I complained to Davis.

He merely grinned at me in the shadows. "That was a bat, Remington—a big, Cuban jungle bat. We've moved into some sort of sheltered anchorage. We seem to be quite close to shore, actually."

I was dozing in my favorite deck chair when I heard the anchor splash. When Davis and I made our way to the bridge to find out what was happening, we came upon the captain and Gonzales studying charts spread across the navigation desk. A tiny lantern lent their faces a Halloweenish cast.

Painters can't help but notice lighting. There are, I suppose, portions of our brains that take special note of color and light and their incredibly subtle and infinite variations. We see the world as others do not. I would imagine that musicians hear it differently as well.

The Cuban was dressed in tropical tans. He wore a broad-brimmed Panama hat. I noted, too, that around his waist he boasted a belt and holster that was home to a large, evil-looking revolver. Gonzales gazed at the chart for a brief moment, then turned his glare toward the darkened shoreline.

"You are certain that this is the spot?" he demanded of the captain. "Why then do I spy no signal?"

The captain stiffened at the Cuban's tone. He was by far the larger of the two men, and he was making a special effort to communicate to Gonzales that he would not be intimidated.

"I've checked the charts over and over," he said. "This is the right spot—La Bahia de Paz. If there's no signal, then that's somebody else's fault."

Gonzales didn't even bother to look at him. He simply stalked off the bridge. And, as he did, he snapped, "We wait."

Davis and I watched him go. Then Davis said to the captain, "Are we just going to sit here? We must have every patrol boat on the northern coast looking for us after what happened this morning?"

"We'll sit," the captain said grimly. "Until the sun starts to come up, anyway. I don't want to be trapped against this shoreline, gentlemen, but I also want to be rid of those damned guns in our hold. Small boats are supposed to meet us here and take that cargo off our hands."

The captain motioned with a huge hand to the deck below. Through the glass of the bridge, I could see crew members struggling up from the hold, bent under the weight of the gun crates. Davis and I went down to the deck to inspect the process. We found Gonzales, smoking another of his thin cigars, supervising the crew. He betrayed his nervousness only by a slight tapping of his foot.

"How long do we wait?" Davis demanded.

"As long as is necessary," Gonzales replied.

"And what if your small boats have run afoul of a Spanish patrol, Gonzales?" I asked. "What then?"

Gonzales favored us with a small, cold smile. "Then, truly, God is not smiling on us."

Davis frowned deeply. "Your sense of humor leaves a bit to be desired."

I can assure you, Bierce, that was one of the longest nights I've ever spent. We stayed on deck trying to remain alert to every sound, but the wild cries of the bats and the birds from the shoreline almost drowned out our feeble attempts at conversation. There was, thankfully, no sign of Spanish patrol boats, but neither was there sign of the party for which Gonzales was waiting. Finally, I went to my deck chair and dozed fitfully. At some point in the night, Davis settled into the chair next to me, and I noticed that he had with him the Gomez sword. He spent the remaining hours of darkness fondling its jeweled hilt—

thinking, I'm sure, of how much the thing had cost. And brooding over the peril in which we now found ourselves.

As the first, faint glow of dawn embraced us, the captain became embroiled in a ferocious argument with Gonzales. The Cuban wanted to stay and await his comrades. The captain insisted on fleeing for deep water so he had at least a chance of preventing his lovely yacht from being shot out from under him. Davis and I awakened from our fitful rest and enthusiastically joined in, taking the captain's side. But, as we began to rail at one another, Gonzales pointed toward land. A band of men clad in white peasants' garb had emerged in the dim light from the lush vegetation that surrounded La Bahia de Paz. They bore small rowboats on their shoulders. As the boats were pushed into the surf, one of the band flashed a lantern—once, twice, three times.

"There they are," the captain bellowed joyously.

"Indeed," said Gonzales, his tone a mixture of satisfaction and relief. He turned to Davis and me. "Soon the guns will be unloaded, and this fine yacht will be taking you to Havana, gentlemen. I assure you, you will find Havana enchanting."

"Wrong, Mr. Gonzales," Davis said flatly. "We get off here. We go with the guns to General Gomez."

Gonzales merely shot the reporter a withering glare and stalked off to supervise the unloading of the weapons. Davis was fuming.

I said to him, "This Gonzales fellow is almost enough to make you root for the Spanish."

It took the dozen or so little boats the better part of an hour to fight through the surf and make their way out to us. The sun was well off the horizon as they came alongside.

The rebels certainly weren't the polished, efficient, and dashing military figures the New York papers had made them out to be. They wore tattered versions of either the white cotton pajamas and wide-brimmed straw hats of peons, or cast-off garments of varied hues and shades. Some were even attired in stolen Spanish military garb.

There was not a fat man among the forty or so rebels in the boats. Each was so thin as to seem cadaverous, but they exuded the same leather-tough quality that Gonzales exhibited. Their expressions were hauntingly strange, Bierce—a mixture of sadness and . . . something else. Resignation, I suppose. It took me a few moments of study before I came to the conclusion that each of these men was marking time until violent death arrived, as it inevitably would, and each was fully prepared for it. Each of these skinny, humorless men already considered himself dead, and he therefore would fight like a demon when called upon to do so.

I studied their faces as they clambered up the rope ladder hung over the side. The faces were different and yet all the same—flat, somber expressions, burning eyes remarkably like those of Gonzales, who stood at the top of the ladder greeting each man. He would have a handshake for one, a pat on the back for another, an informal salute for still another.

All of these rebels were quite young, some barely more than boys with wispy beards. Then, up the rope came a much older man, his hair and beard almost white. He moved with economy—strong, wiry hands on the ropes. As the older fellow reached the deck, Gonzales reached out a hand. For the first time, I actually saw his face light up.

He burst out, "Cosio, *mi amigo*. You're not dead?"

The two men embraced. My Spanish was only fair at that point— what little I had retained of that language from my time painting Apaches and troopers in the Southwest—and I couldn't catch much of what they were saying. At first their manner was joyful, the reunion of old friends. Then the old man mumbled gravely about something involving his daughter, and Gonzales's uncharacteristically sunny expression reverted to its usual smoldering glare. I was watching from a few feet away when I realized that Davis was standing near me.

"Did you hear that?" he asked me.

"Not much of it, I'm afraid."

"It's a sad story," Davis said. "The old man's name is Cosio. He was a prisoner on La Isla de Piñons, the Isle of Pines. That's a prison off the southern coast. His daughter went to the prison. But when she tried to help him escape, she was captured and presumably raped by the commandant of the prison. Now she's in Recojidas Prison in Havana awaiting trial for sedition."

"Davis," I said, "I'm merely a scrawler of pictures, but it does seem to me that the old man's troubles might make a fairly interesting story."

He cast me a surprised glance. Then his eyes brightened. "You're right, Remington—absolutely. It would make a terrific story."

Davis immediately walked up to the two men. He ignored Gonzales and stuck out his hand to Cosio.

"Do you speak English?" he asked.

The old man nodded.

"Sir, I'm Richard Harding Davis of the *New York Journal*. This is my colleague, the famous artist Frederic Remington. We couldn't help but overhear what you were saying to our good friend Mr. Gonzales."

Gonzales flushed visibly at that characterization, but Davis pretended not to notice the menace that appeared in the man's eyes.

"I'd like to interview you," Davis said, plowing merrily ahead. "I'd like to put your story in the newspaper. A story like this, sir—as sad as it is—might be helpful to the revolution."

The old man shrugged. "It pains me to discuss this situation, señor. But if it could help my Evangelina . . ."

"It'll help, believe me," Davis assured him. "A young woman abused, imprisoned, and ravished merely because she defended her father? It's what we in journalism refer to as a natural, sir. Tell me, do you have a picture of your daughter?"

Cosio reached around his neck and removed a small, gold locket. "Only this."

I stepped in to view the image. It was a photograph of a stunning young woman. She was utterly breathtaking, Bierce—enormous dark eyes, cascades of luxurious black hair framing an oval face, a full, sensuous mouth. Davis, I could tell, was even more startled than I at the woman's beauty. For a moment, he merely stared at the image, unable to speak. He took the locket from the old man's hand, and—finally tearing his eyes away from her face—dropped it in my outstretched hand.

"Remington," Davis said, "surely you can make a sketch from this and return it to . . . Mr. Cosio, is it?"

The old man nodded. Davis immediately slipped an arm around his shoulder and steered him away from Gonzales and down the deck.

"Now, sir," Davis said, "let's start at the very beginning . . ."

I went below to get my sketch pad and Davis's notebook and pencil. When I came back topside, Davis and Juan Cosio were in deep conversation. I sketched his daughter's face as Davis interviewed the old man and scribbled notes. Even in English, Cosio was an articulate man. For nearly an hour, as the sun rose steadily off the horizon and blazed down on us, the old man spun his tale. He was a widower, a college professor, and Evangelina was his only child. She was eighteen and enchanting—a willful, clever girl who was utterly devoted to him. When he'd been arrested, she'd gone to his island prison in an effort to make life as comfortable for him as possible. He recounted calmly a horrific tale of imprisonment—the rats, the brutal treatment, a dramatic escape attempt with his daughter in a small fishing boat. Only the Spanish had fired on them as they put out to sea, and the boat went down.

"And after the boat sank?" Davis asked. "What happened then?"

Cosio's expression grew even more somber. "I saw the guards drag my beloved Evangelina from the sea and disappear into the island. I felt myself being pulled by strong currents out to sea. Knowing that I could not help her, I let myself go, expecting to drown."

"How long were you in the water?"

"Perhaps four hours, señor. It is difficult to say. Then a fishing boat rescued me from the sharks, which were beginning to gather. I was taken back to the mainland. From there I made my way over a period of weeks to the Insurrecto forces inland, with the help of many patriotic *compañeros.*"

Davis slapped his notebook shut. "That's a very dramatic story, Mr. Cosio," he said gravely. "Once this story is printed, you'll have the sympathy of every newspaper reader in America—and especially every parent."

Davis turned to me. "How are you doing on the drawings, Remington?"

Given the limitations of newspaper reproduction, I was working in pen and ink, and conditions weren't the best. But I thought I'd done rather well, considering. Portraiture has never been my strongest suit, but I'd produced an acceptable likeness of the girl from her locket photograph. Davis gazed longingly at that sketch. I swore the man had gone lovesick. Then he set that sketch aside and flipped through the others. I'd captured Cosio, head down, the very image of dejection. I had another of him talking, his expressive hands moving as he told his tale. They were reasonably detailed, and Davis was impressed, as he should have been. He'd worked with other artists, and he knew quality when he saw it.

"Fine work," he told me as Gonzales approached us. Davis said to him, "I have to write this now. I see that the guns are almost loaded, but you'll have to wait until the story is ready so we can leave with you."

"You are not leaving with us, señor," Gonzales said sharply. "I am leaving with my guns and my *compañeros,* and you are staying on this fine boat until it puts into port in Havana Harbor."

Davis began to sputter, but I'd had enough of this. We had, not twenty-four hours earlier, been fired on by Spaniards. It wasn't my first such experience, but stray bullets from a few Sioux or Apache warriors really don't produce the terror created by artillery shells sailing your way in shark-infested waters. Gonzales was a killer, true, but I was prepared to defend myself, Bierce, and I wondered how this Gonzales chap might stand up to a few stiff jabs followed by a solid right cross, were it to come to that.

"I've listened to all I'm going to take from you, Gonzales," I bellowed at him. "What makes you think you've got the authority to order us around?"

"I am a colonel in the Free Army of Cuba," he replied evenly.

"We're not in your damned army," Davis finally got out. "Our employer financed this trip. I don't know if he actually financed those guns, but he financed this sword, and he's given us orders to deliver it personally to General Gomez. We intend to do just that, Gonzales, whether you like it or not."

Gonzales seemed slightly amused by this outburst.

"So," he told Davis with a malevolent smile, "the rooster crows."

I'd begun to lose my initial surge of indignation, but Davis was fuming. "You'll find that this particular rooster can do you and your cause real good or real harm. If I have to take this boat to Havana, then I'll simply take it back to the United States instead. And if I have to do that, I'm going to do everything I can to convince Mr. Hearst that he's backing the wrong side in this little war of yours. Maybe I can succeed at that, and maybe I can't. But for you, Gonzales, that's a pretty big *if*."

Gonzales glared at the reporter, his face dark.

"On the other hand," Davis said more quietly, "if I write this story about Mr. Cosio and his daughter and send it with Remington's sketches back to the States with the captain of this boat, you can bet it'll mean a good deal of sympathy for your cause and probably a lot more money to buy guns."

Then I got back into it. I said, "But the price for this story and the sketches, Gonzales, is a trip inland to visit General Gomez and his army. Take it or leave it. Frankly, sir, I hope you turn it down. I don't much care for being on the same side as you."

The man's gaze flicked back and forth between us. You could almost see the wheels turning inside his head. Davis, I'm sure, had no confidence whatever that he could back up his threat. I certainly had none. Neither of us had any real access to The Chief in those days, and I couldn't conceive that we could convince him that the rebel cause was anything other than a parallel to that of the United States 120 years earlier. The Chief viewed the Cuban rebellion as one of those crucial moments in history, and he wasn't likely to back off that position just because of the personal prejudices of two hired hands. Gonzales was no fool, and he surely understood much of that.

Yet, I did hope that the risk of barring us from the journey inland would be too great for him to take. The Chief was, in no uncertain terms, the linchpin of the Cuban rebellion. Without his support, money would dry up, and all but the most fanatical of the revolutionary fighters would go back to work in the cane fields rather than face Spanish troops unarmed.

"Very well," Gonzales said finally. "Write your story in haste, señor. We have much ground to cover, and we must be on our way."

While I returned to my deck chair, Davis retired to his cabin and produced a finished piece in less than an hour, scribbling in longhand. He was always fast, but that was an accomplishment even for him. If it contained an error or two, it was on the side of the rebels, and Mr. Cosio was unlikely to complain to the editors about being misquoted. Davis was just emerging from the hatch when the captain shouted down from the bridge.

"I see something out there in the open water, you fellows," he bellowed. "Sweet God, don't let it be another gunboat."

SEVEN

I immediately climbed the ladder to the bridge to see what I could see. The vessel was well out at sea, but from the towering height of its steam plume there was little question that it was making for us at full power.

Our captain shouted down the voice tube to the engine room, "Get ready to get the hell out of here."

I took the opportunity to pick up his glass and aim it at the speck steaming toward us. It took me a long moment to find it, and when I did I felt a surge of true alarm. This was a larger boat than the first, a legitimate naval vessel perhaps a hundred feet long and fully capable of open-sea travel. Like the first one we'd encountered, it was painted a showy snow white, and the Spanish flag was clearly visible through the glass even at that distance. More disturbing, however, was its weaponry. It boasted a bow cannon and one amidships. I could also see what looked like a Gatling gun mounted on the cabin roof.

I put down the glass and took a deep breath. The captain had already stormed off the bridge and was down on the deck. I followed after to find him glaring wrathfully at Gonzales, Davis, and those few of the rebels still on deck.

"We've hung around here too damned long," the captain snapped. It was an accusation. "Get off my boat—now!"

Then the captain turned his back on them and began bellowing instructions to the crew. "Weigh anchor. The Spanish are on our asses good this time."

Gonzales was motioning the last of his people over the side and into their heavily laden rowboats. Davis rushed to the captain's side and pushed his story and my sketches into the man's big hand.

"These have to be delivered to Mr. Hearst's office in New York as soon as you drop anchor back in the States."

The captain's face was the color of sherry beneath his blond beard. He shoved the papers into his pocket and said, "I've got to get through the mouth of this bay before that gunboat can cut me off. If you're getting off my vessel, Mr. Davis, I suggest you do it immediately."

We felt the huge engines kick into life below deck, and then Davis and I were sprinting toward the rope ladder. Only one rowboat still bobbed beside the *Vamoose*. In it, waiting not at all patiently, were Gonzales, Cosio, several of the white-clad rebels, and two rough-hewn cases of guns and cartridges, all broken open. Gonzales sat at the stern with a rifle across his legs. The others were similarly armed, although I couldn't imagine what use such puny weapons might be against a deck cannon and a Gatling gun.

As we settled into the boat, Gonzales said to us, "You *norteamericanos* move at a leisurely pace."

We pulled away from the *Vamoose* as the pilot applied the big boat's throttle. The twin props churned up bubbles and white foam. As she began to move, we could see the crew scampering frantically around the deck. Several of them had arms of their own, and they were taking up defensive positions.

I turned my head toward the mouth of the bay and felt my stomach drop to my knees. The patrol boat was perilously near now. If the *Vamoose* could make the mouth before the gunboat, then it had a chance to break free into open water. If not, however, she would find herself trapped along with us, and the yacht couldn't fade into the jungle, as could we.

All around us, the rowers of the small boats were pulling furiously toward shore. The land was a half to three-quarters of a mile away across open water. We not only had to make the beach, we also needed time to get the rifles in their heavy crates into the trees, an action that would expose us further to fire.

We rowed madly while I kept my eyes on the *Vamoose* steaming toward the open sea. It was soon obvious that, with her narrow hull and greater power, she would indeed beat the gunboat to the mouth of the bay and have her chance to run in open water, although the Spaniard was beginning to lob shells in her direction. Gonzales was also studying the situation.

He said, "The patrol boat's captain will be forced to make a choice as soon as the *Vamoose* breaks through the bay's mouth. He will have to decide whether to chase the yacht or try to catch us before we make shore and unload."

"What do you think he'll do?" I asked anxiously.

Gonzales lit another of his small cigars. "If I were him, I would come after us. He has seen the yacht's speed now. We are slower, and we are clearly loaded down with contraband."

Even as Gonazales spoke, we could see the patrol boat turning to bear down directly upon us. I turned back to Gonzales. The Cuban was gazing across the water at our pursuer, and the hint of a smile played about his lips. I recall thinking, my God, this lunatic actually enjoys this.

"You should have been a Spanish officer," I told him.

"I was," Gonzales replied coolly.

He rose slightly in his seat and shouted in Spanish to the other boats. Immediately, some of the rowers in each boat released their oars and began breaking into the crates of rifles and ammunition, as had already been done in our boat.

I turned to Davis. "What did he tell them?"

"He said for some to row and for some to get ready to shoot," Davis told me. His voice was no more than a croak. His throat was bone-dry.

Once through the mouth of the bay, the patrol boat found itself on smooth water. That meant it could move with greater speed and fire with accuracy. The bow gun began to speak directly to us, as did its brother amidships. They fired almost simultaneously. One shell fell thankfully short, but the other landed squarely on a small boat sixty or so yards off our port bow.

It was astounding to see, Bierce. The shell had some explosive capacity, which is common to naval ordinance. The boat erupted into an oily ball of orange flame. It was rendered instantly into kindling. I caught the briefest glimpse of a man—his white, pajama-like garment afire—flying two dozen feet into the air, arms flapping bonelessly like those of a rag doll. He landed with a dull splash. As the smoke cleared in the offshore wind, pieces of wood floated where the boat had been. Then the bodies began bobbing to the surface, floating motionlessly in the water amid the splinters. There were perhaps a half-dozen of them.

The suddenness of the violence was blood-chilling. The riflemen in the surrounding boats immediately returned fire, a gesture of utter futility. The patrol boat was still some distance away, but it was coming on like a locomotive. I stole a glance at Davis, whose face was ashen. Cosio crossed himself with a quick gesture, but the old man's well-seamed visage showed no sign of undue alarm. He simply raised his rifle and fired in the general direction of the oncoming engine of destruction that bore down on us so relentlessly. The report of his rifle so close to my ear left my head ringing.

Gonzales was on his feet now, waving his arms and shouting furiously in Spanish. He looked like a high-wire walker, balancing as he was in our bobbing little boat.

I asked Davis, "What's he saying?"

Davis merely motioned toward our starboard bow. There, still some way off, I could see that the bay had changed color. The water was lighter in hue, as though the broiling sun had bleached away its true blueness. For a stretch of several hundred yards along the length of the shoreline, and perhaps twenty yards in width, the bay was a pale turquoise.

"He's telling them to row toward the shallower water," Davis told me, "toward that reef. He's apparently hoping that the patrol boat will draw too much water to follow us over it. You know, you really must brush up on your Spanish, Remington."

I must confess to being absolutely stupefied at such a remark delivered under such circumstances. I replied, "I was just thinking—at this very moment, Davis—about signing up for a language course or two."

I glanced down at the reef as we went over it, and even in such a life-threatening circumstance I was struck by the wonder of the thing. I've read a great deal about reefs in the years since that day, but then I could only guess at how such an edifice could come to be. In the beginning, it had been no more than a low ridge along the floor of the bay. On that fateful day, however, the reef had grown to a depth of nearly two fathoms—the skeletal remains of millions of mindless creatures dead for millenia serving as home to still millions of other unthinking life-forms.

It was a teeming hive of activity beneath the bay's surface. Along its sharp edges lived restless sharks and an endless array of brightly colored fish. Deep within its caves lived moray eels with teeth sufficient to sever a man's arm with a single snap.

There were only two classifications of life in and around that reef—hunters and prey. And that day, up on the surface, we had become the prey of the Spanish. Our little boats cleared the jagged top of the reef by mere inches in some spots. As we passed into paler water, I peered over the side. The reef was clearly visible almost to its foundations in glass-clear tropical water. I saw black fish with yellow stripes, blue ones and yellow ones and red ones with vivid yellow and blue markings, all scattering by the hundreds as the boat passed overhead.

Davis, the writer, saw none of the immense physical beauty that so struck me, the painter. He merely noted aloud, "It's shallow as hell here."

Gonzales was squeezing off a few shots at the patrol boat fast closing on us. "Not so shallow that we cannot get over it," he said. "Let us pray that they cannot follow."

Other shells came our way, but none as accurate as that first salvo. I grabbed an oar and lent my back to the effort. I pulled maniacally, and then—in a moment or so—we were past the reef, and the water was again a rich blue-green. When I looked up, my heart nearly stopped. The gunboat was so close now that on the cabin roof I could see the beige-clad Spanish soldiers in broad-brimmed hats preparing to employ their Gatling gun. They were startlingly near. The cannon crewmen on the bow were bending over to pick up rifles. This was, I recall thinking ruefully, what was meant by shooting fish in a barrel.

The gunfire from each side produced a fearsome roar. All the individual shots seemed to blend into a single, enormous explosion that assaulted the ears. I could actually *feel* the physical force of the blasts, particularly when the Gatling gun erupted. The collective immensity of the sound was so profound, in fact, that no one—not even the Spaniards, I'm sure—actually heard the awful cracking, crushing sound the patrol boat's wooden hull must have made as it smashed into the reef.

Several things happened then.

First, the patrol boat continued on for another yard or two, albeit at a considerably reduced speed. And, as its powerful engine drove it straight and true, the vessel's hull was rent by a gaping hole longer than most men. The wound was inflicted just at the waterline, behind the port bow. Within only seconds, the engine must have been awash in seawater, its boilers quenched forever. The engineers belowdecks, I'm sure, must have been knocked off their feet by a crushing wall of bay water, and I would imagine that they were drowned in an instant.

The Spaniard slid to its sudden and unexpected halt and listed lazily to one side as water rushed into its guts. On deck, the list caused the cannoneers at the bow to slide off the slippery planking into the water. Other crewmen—I didn't see more than a dozen—were jumping off the stern into deeper water or sliding over the side onto the reef, where they were chopped to bloody bits by the razor-sharp coral. Still others slid more carefully off the deck into the knee-deep water atop the reef and landed on their feet, their rifles still in their hands and expressions of sheer horror on their swarthy faces.

Standing in only a few feet of water, they became perfect targets. Our riflemen in the rowboats made short work of them. The bloody unfortunates who staggered up from where they'd fallen on the reef were next. Then came the hapless Spaniards splashing about in deeper water at the stern of the mortally wounded patrol boat.

One man remained visible on the boat. He was a large fellow with a bristling black beard. He lurched out of the cabin, an incredible gash on his head, obviously a souvenir of the crash. He motioned blindly toward our rowboats.

I heard him shout, "*Socorro por Dios.*"

My Spanish was good enough to decipher that he was crying out, "Help me, for the love of God."

The man staggered to the bow and collapsed against the barrel of the cannon. Gonzales raised his rifle and shot him squarely in the forehead. The sailor flew off the deck and landed with a splash. In only a few more seconds, the patrol boat was sliding off the reef, pulled down by the weight of water overwhelming its stern. Amid a frenzy of bubbles, it slipped beneath the waves to become, eventually, a part of the reef that had taken its life. The corpses of Spanish soldiers floated in the water. Then, on the far side of the reef, one disappeared beneath the surface. After that, another was pulled down.

Sharks, I realized.

I must confess that I turned my face away from the carnage. So did Davis, I noted, only to come face-to-face with the grim countenance of Jorge Gonzales.

"This is war," the Cuban told Davis, with surprising gentleness. "This is what you wanted to write about."

Then Gonzales leaned back in our boat and lit yet another of his small cigars. He fixed me with a coldly amused stare.

"Welcome to Cuba, Señor Artista."

My voice falters as I recount Remington's tale, I find the effort of inhaling and expelling air enormously taxing. Small Maria shakes me with all the furious energy her tiny form can generate.

"Señor Bierce," she cries out in alarm, "you must keep speaking."

I nod weakly, acknowledging the imperative but begging for time to comply. She is a truly lovely young thing, small of mind but large of heart. And as I teeter at the precipice of the eternal pit, her kindness consoles me.

It has been said of me that I view the world with such a jaundiced eye that I celebrate its warts and belittle its roses. Is that to be my legacy? It is not, surely, how I am viewed by this gentle rose of a whore who crouches at my bedside. Of course, she cannot read, which means she does not truly know me. I am real only in my writings and will be recalled for them only. The rest of my life need not have been lived.

"Speak," Small Maria begs. "Continue the story. Breathe, Señor Bierce."

She wants this so much. I cannot deny her. And so I continue.

I say, "I knew the captain of The Chief's yacht. I had been The Chief's guest aboard the *Vamoose* on several occasions. After Remington told me his story, the captain confirmed that portion of the tale and embellished it with his own recollections."

"Yes," she says, almost gleefully. "You must tell me."

Her pleasure renews me. I say, "How can I tell it all to you? Without the politics of it, the history, surely you cannot understand."

"Tell me," my whore implores. "Tell me all of it."

And who am I to deny her?

I say, "The *Vamoose* slowed immediately when the Spanish patrol boat veered off after the smaller vessels. Whatever might befall the men in the small boats, the captain knew, he and the *Vamoose* were safe, but he wanted to observe so he could report the event to The Chief.

"He monitored the chase through his glass. When the patrol boat shuddered to a sudden halt in the bay and began to list so dangerously, the captain guessed immediately what had happened. He had studied the charts of these waters, and he knew that reefs were everywhere.

"He heard the gunfire, clear and crisp over the water. Through his glass, he saw the Spaniards die, saw the patrol boat slip beneath the waves in a fury of bubbles, saw the rowboats make the beach. Then he lowered his glass and made for his anchorage in Key West. From there, he took a train to New York. That, Small Maria, is a sight you should behold some day. See New York, and see the apex of civilization in all its degradation.

"The great city before the new century was a choked sea of brownstone and painted wood, of church towers and odd, contorted creations of stone rising from the landscape like obscene statuary. It was a metropolis of mansions, tenements, and outhouses, its streets littered with horse droppings and tattered derelicts.

"Our captain arrived in the late afternoon several days after the journalists and the guns and the ever-precious sword were set ashore in Cuba. He was bound for the *Journal* building to deliver the papers that Davis had entrusted to him. He went by horse-drawn trolley, the most common form of mass conveyance, though cable cars have since grown in popularity. Bicycles, too, have become such a rage that they present grave traffic problems.

"Our captain, Small Maria, shared the car with a polyglot pool of immigrants chattering in a dozen languages—further proof that you would not be unduly conspicuous in New York if you were to depart this terrible place and go there after I draw my last breath. The city demands strong backs. Those backs come from Europe in steerage in seemingly endless waves, more than a million a year crowding into filthy tenements and firetrap shanties, their noses filled with the stench of one another's sweat and body wastes.

"They take the hardest, dirtiest, and lowest-paying jobs. The Poles and Italians and Slavs and Russian Jews who come to New York arrive to find that the prize positions are solidly in the hands of other immigrants who had come to America with a special advantage.

"Our Dutch-founded New York remains very much a city dominated by the Irish. They began coming during the famine, and they arrived at the gates of New York with an edge no other immigrating ethnic group possessed before or since; they had taken the language forced on them by the British centuries before and mastered it as no other people has ever managed. They could make it sing in poetry or bray in political slogans. Their command of the tongue of their new land was vastly better than that of its natives.

"While other immigrating groups tend to be forced into the most menial jobs for a generation or two, the Irish moved immediately into the political process. They organized, pooled their votes, spoke their minds with spirit, and generally scared the hell out of New York's political bosses, who promptly bought them off with tax-supported jobs.

"That period before the war in Cuba broke out in earnest was a time of almost total ethical bankruptcy throughout the power corridors of America—even worse than today. It was a time when millions were made or stolen in business, when industrial and financial geniuses like Jay Gould and my friend Andrew Carnegie were elevated to the status of demigods. It was a time when it was widely accepted that at least one president, Rutherford B. Hayes, had taken the helm of the nation through nothing less than sheer fraud. William Vanderbilt could proclaim openly, 'The public be damned,' and get away with it.

"And damned they were—to a level of poverty and squalor the equal of any found on the globe. The city outside the trolley car in which our captain rode was a surging mass of struggling life, human and animal. Horses labored under their loads; humans buckled under theirs. As the horses were whipped, so too were the laborers. Behind grime-encrusted windows, children slaved twelve hours a day, six and seven days a week in sweatshops. For them, the sun was no more than a rumor. Thus, it was no surprise that the feverish brew of Marxism bubbled in the tenements and shanties. The workers' chains were tight in those days in New York, Small Maria.

"Saloons lined every street, whores and hoboes in their doorways. Three-card monte operators and shell-game specialists plied their trade on the sidewalk. No city on earth was ever dirtier, ever more vividly a festering wound of sin and sadness and decay.

"It was in this city that my Chief produced his newspaper. In this huge, churning caldron of a city where a half-dozen newspapers battled for readers among the literate and politically sensitive Irish who made up the bulk of their audience. Here the journalistic battles were waged by Pulitzer's mighty *World*, by the stodgy *New York Post* Alexander Hamilton had founded, by the lofty *Tribune*, by the scrappy *Herald*, by the dull and insignificant *New York Times*.

"It was a city, Small Maria, that had already produced legendary editors. Among them was Horace Greeley, whose alleged admonition, 'Go west, young man, go west,' had helped push back the frontier. And we must not forget James Gordon Bennett, who had sent a reporter named Henry Stanley to darkest Africa to find a mysterious geographer and explorer named David Livingstone. And, in so doing, had emblazoned forever in history the words the exhausted Stanley had uttered upon cornering his quarry: 'Doctor Livingstone, I presume.'

[53]

"What a fool, that Stanley. He had stumbled across the only other white man for a thousand miles. Who else might it have been?

"The newspaper was a vital and living organism to New Yorkers. Their world was turbulent and dramatic, in a constant state of technological, political, and social flux. Popular music, now becoming the opiate of the masses with the growing popularity of the Victrola, was available only to the relatively well-off who had the time and money to enjoy the performers live. Spectator sports were not a popular diversion, although the New York Giants had a loyal following. Books were expensive, but newspapers were cheap and useful. They were exciting and available in abundance. Newspapers were the common denominator in New York, and both The Chief and Pulitzer had aimed their products at the commonest of that denominator. They sold crime, sex, and excitement at two cents a copy. New Yorkers saw it as a bargain and could not get enough.

"So what if there were breadlines? There were plenty of customers in New York for Budweiser beer, for Sweet Caporal cigarettes, and for Ivory soap. And those products were prominently advertised in the pages of the city's newspapers. Where else could they be advertised? The newspapers had the audience, and the audience craved excitement they could obtain nowhere else.

"When The Chief moved his center of operations from San Francisco to New York, he knew he was moving into the most competitive newspaper market on earth. Its population was ten times that of San Francisco, and its readers would not tolerate being bored. The Chief responded by bringing in the best of the stable he'd built up at the *San Francisco Examiner*—myself and Annie Laurie among the group. And he brought along Sam Chamberlain to conduct the orchestra. I later returned to San Francisco. Sam and Annie stayed. New York got into their blood as it never got into mine, although I dropped by from time to time.

"The *Journal*'s shabby plant was located directly across the street from the *New York Sun* and only a block south of Pulitzer's *World*. The Chief immediately made over his new acquisition as a carbon copy of the *World* and dropped his newsstand price to but a penny. He advertised his new product in trolley cars and elevated trains. He recruited highly paid staffers from around the nation. By the end of his first year, he had pushed the *Journal* above one hundred thousand in circulation, most of it at Pulitzer's expense. Then he began raiding his competitor's staff. By the end of 1896, when I went back home, he had topped one hundred fifty thousand in circulation, and the war with Pulitzer was on in earnest.

"By the time coverage of Cuba began to dominate the front pages of both papers, the war in New York was the talk of the town. It was fought with ink and not bullets, but it was no less vicious than the clash in Cuba. In both cases, the underdog was committed to winning at any cost.

"When our intrepid captain finally found his way to the *Journal* building, he was ushered up directly to see Pancoast. They chatted a bit, and then Pancoast opened the packet. He was much impressed with what he saw, and he and the captain immediately hurried off to the Herald Square Theater, since it was now nearing evening and Pancoast knew precisely where he would find The Chief. Our leader was watching the opening of Clara Lipman in *The Girl from Paris*.

"The buxom Miss Lipman was well into her second solo of the first act when Pancoast and the captain slipped into The Chief's private box at the theater. Pancoast rubbed his eyes to accustom them to the dim light, and then he made out The Chief, in his white tie and tails, an elegantly decked-out Willson sister on either side.

" 'Excuse me, sir,' Pancoast whispered. 'The first dispatch from Cuba has arrived. I have it with me.'

"The Chief's face lit up. He said, 'Let's go outside. Excuse me, ladies, if you will.'

"The three of them slipped into the hallway. Pancoast opened the packet and handed The Chief its contents. The Chief leaned back against the wall and began reading. His reading style was always unique. He tends to read aloud, but in a stream-of-consciousness style that often leaves his listeners puzzled.

" 'Father taken prisoner,' The Chief mumbled. . . . 'Hmmm . . . escape attempt . . . yes . . .'

"Then he moved on to the next page of Davis's dispatch, and his eyebrows shot up. 'Ravished by Spanish soldiers? My word.'

"The Chief then raced through the balance of Davis's story, lips moving as he read, occasionally mumbling to himself and shaking his head. Then he mulled over Remington's sketches and looked up abruptly.

" 'George,' he pronounced, handing back the packet, 'this is marvelous stuff. Have it put on page one of tomorrow's editions. Let's have the headline read . . .' And here he thought for a moment, rubbing his chin and gazing up at the ornate ceiling of the theater.

"He snapped his fingers as inspiration struck him. 'How about: The Joan of Arc of Cuba? How does that strike you, George?'

"Pancoast nodded his head quickly. 'Very fine,' he said. Indeed, it was a brilliant headline.

The Chief continued. 'Big type, George—all across the front page. Red ink for the head, of course.'

"Then The Chief smiled broadly—that charming, winning smile of his that exudes perfect confidence. I've seen it often. It never fails to inspire my fellow Hearstlings, though I've always found filthy lucre a more effective motivator.

" 'I think we have a story here,' " The Chief observed.

"Pancoast merely nodded. If The Chief said it was a story, then it damned well was a story—and not just because The Chief had pronounced it so. For all The Chief's youth and showiness, Pancoast knew what all of us knew, from Sam Chamberlain on down. The Chief has a natural sense for what might appeal to the rabble. Had he not been subjected to the misfortune of being born a millionaire, he might even have succeeded as a reporter. As it is, he is one of those truly inspired newspaper proprietors who approach the news as a salesman. He knows what will sell. In fact, he always knows. Even when his editors doubt the intrinsic value of a story, The Chief never fails to gauge accurately the depth of its interest to the unwashed hordes.

"Pancoast and the captain, who had uttered not a word throughout these proceedings, were shoving the papers back in the packet in preparation for their departure when The Chief grabbed one of Remington's sketches. It was the one Frederic had done from the locket photograph. The Chief studied it carefully before handing it back.

"He said, 'Lovely, isn't she?' Then he rubbed his palms together with undisguised glee and chuckled, 'Let's see how old Joe Pulitzer likes this one.' "

I pause, my capacity for speech temporarily exhausted. My heart pounds threateningly again. Small Maria gazes down at me and places a cool hand on my brow. I turn my eyes to her, silently beseeching. She understands what I want to know, and she answers silently, with a shake of her head.

The poor child has not the faintest clue to what I am talking about.

EIGHT

Frederic Remington
Cuba, 1897

It happened, I was told by one of the rebels, several hundred years before the *Vamoose* appeared off the sun-washed Cuban shore. A Spanish missionary was engaged in a search for Taino Indians to convert to Catholicism. One summer night as he journeyed along the shoreline the skies suddenly opened up in one of those fierce tropical downpours for which Cuba is so famed. The priest sought shelter beneath some palm trees.

Tons of water poured from the night sky into the lush greenery and the hungry sea. In the morning, the rain swept on, and the priest continued his journey along the coast. Only a few hundred feet from where he'd rested during the storm, he rounded a bluff and came upon a huge lagoon—a vast field of sunlit blueness where the water was mostly calm and the beach protected by a reef that occasionally popped through the surface at low tide.

It was a spot of such unsurpassed loveliness that the priest, an aging Franciscan friar, stopped for several days to doze in the sun, to frolic in the smooth water, and to give thanks to God for his bounty. The friar named the place La Bahia de Paz, the Bay of Peace, although—strictly speaking—it wasn't a true bay at all, merely a large cove protected by the great reef.

Several days later, as he traversed the beach some miles to the east, the friar encountered the Indians to whom he'd sought to bring the true faith. He was thanked for his efforts by the forcible separation of his head from his body. His journal, which he'd kept faithfully since his arrival in Cuba, was confiscated by an Indian warrior, who kept it as a good luck charm until the day other, less benevolent Spaniards attacked his village in a quest for slaves. The warrior was killed and his stolen book was found amid the rubble of his hut.

The conquistadores read of the beautiful spot along the shore, marked it on their maps as La Bahia de Paz, and promptly forgot about it. Over the years, the designation the long-dead priest gave the lagoon has appeared on many maps and charts of the thirty-five-hundred-mile

Cuban coastline. But, because of the enormous reef, the area has been only sparsely settled. No vessels of any size could put in there.

This was not, however, a problem for our tiny rowboats as we pulled up on the shore of La Bahia de Paz—a spot that had been anything but peaceful on that bloody day. Despite it all, though, I was awed by the placid and gentle atmosphere of the spot. The Spanish gunboat rested on the lagoon's bottom, and if the corpses of its crew still floated in the waves, we couldn't see them.

"A beautiful spot," I said to Gonzales.

He merely grunted. "Beauty is of no value when your stomach is empty. And in Cuba, very few stomachs are full, Señor Artista."

It took only an hour or so to unload the weapons and load them on the backs of burros that had been hobbled in the trees. The boats were left on the beach for recovery by the fishermen who'd donated them. Gonzales issued each man a rifle and a ration of cartridges. Many of the rebels also reclaimed weapons they'd left hidden with the burros before boarding the little boats for the trip to the *Vamoose*. Some of our companions carried Spanish army–issue firearms. They seemed to have a special fondness for pistols. All of them sported ugly knives with blades two feet long.

"The machetes are used to cut the cane," Gonzales explained when he saw me eyeing the ugly things. "They are in the hands of Cuban peasants almost from birth. We have found that they will also draw Spanish blood. In fact, our crack raiding parties—made up of our very best men—they are called 'the Machetes' after the weapons they wield with such skill."

"Interesting," I said in response.

As we began the journey inland, I was struck by the wet blanket of heat that enveloped us once we left the breezes of the sea. The dry, desert heat of the American Southwest is one thing, Bierce, but the moist furnace of the tropics can be unbearable.

We found ourselves in a vast rain forest mixed with swampland— a hostile world of molten sun reflections from shallow, stagnant water, razor-sharp weeds, and saw grass. The soil beneath our boots was soft, the debris of rotting vegetation a million years old. Towering trunks of ebony and mahogany loomed, their majestic boughs stretching high into the heavens, blotting out the sun. They had been old even during the Renaissance. Mixed in among them were soaring palms the height of a dozen men. I was struck by the abundance of fruit trees and bulging banana plants crawling with spiders as large as a man's hand. Davis spotted mangroves and a strange-looking growth that Cosio told us was a rare cork palm tree.

And the birds, Bierce; they were everywhere, screeching and singing, screaming and howling—sweet-throated nightingales, parrots, an occasional royal thrush. I was most struck by the startling abundance of hummingbirds, their tiny wings buzzing with the quickness of thought, hovering above the avocado and papaya plants that filled the tiny spaces between the towering trees.

My painter's eyes were almost overwhelmed by the wild colorations of the orchids that grew on everything. They were vivid, almost obscenely hued flowers strung like Christmas ornaments among the festival of wild growth. It was a vast, seething, primitive incubator of a world in which we found ourselves, filled with such a startling abundance of life and death and growing things that my mind swam with the fertile frenzy of it all.

Once, as our party staggered through knee-deep water, I stepped on a partially submerged log. I was startled when it began twisting beneath my feet. I lurched to one side, and one of the rebels quickly pumped two quick shots into the log. He then slashed at it with his machete until it rolled over and ceased its thrashing. I was aghast.

"An alligator?" I managed to get out.

"A crocodile," Gonzales said matter-of-factly. "Cuba has two distinct species of crocodile."

I was fully out of the water now, counting my legs for reassurance. "What's the difference?" I demanded, still somewhat shocked by the closeness of that call.

"It's in their jaws. The crocodile bites differently. Also, our Cuban crocodile is somewhat nastier than your American alligator."

"For some reason," Davis broke in, "I don't find that surprising."

Several miles further inland, we stumbled into a flock of lordly flamingos—huge, pink birds that rose from the muck of the swamp by the thousands. Their flight erased the sky. I was surrounded by countless great, flapping wings and gleaming black eyes and by innumerable sticklike legs drawn up against feathered torsos. They then were gone, leaving us to calm the startled burros.

By the end of the day, which we spent chopping a rude path for the bawling burros through the vast orgy of growth, we'd encountered several more crocodiles. They'd been considerate enough to merely slide into the fetid waters of the swamp. We'd also come across huge frogs, bigger than anything in North America, and an endless variety of snakes, many of which surely were poisonous. As night fell and we settled down to an exhausted rest, great jungle bats shook free of their daytime roosts in the huge trees and flapped upward into the night sky, splitting it with their shrieks.

Gonzales permitted us a fire. Over it, the rebels heated an enormous vat of a thick, black soup that I found surprisingly good—

especially with onions chopped up into it. The warm food was welcome, but the fire was a mixed blessing. We appreciated the illumination in such a frightful setting, but it only added to the terrible heat. I could feel tiny seas of sweat on every square inch of my flesh. My Duke of Marlborough togs clung to me everywhere, wet and exceedingly ripe.

Most annoying of all, however, were the insects.

They were everywhere, Bierce—great, shifting clouds of them, forever alighting on my face as we tried to sleep, stabbing into our flesh with needlelike mouths. After several hours of swatting at them, I was simply too weary to continue the combat. I surrendered to their ministrations and drifted off in a daze.

I don't know how long I might have been asleep when the rains came. It was as if someone had thrown a bucket of water in my face. I awakened to find the jungle a solid wall of rain, like a waterfall. Davis had collapsed next to me, and I shook him awake.

"Who can sleep in something like this?" I grumbled.

He said, "I could, Remington, if you'd be kind enough to permit it. This is the end of Cuba's rainy season. In the past few months, the island has gotten more than fifty inches of rain."

I told him, "Fifty inches of rain fell during the past minute and a half. This is like trying to sleep at the bottom of a lake."

There was nothing to be done about it. I pulled my helmet down over my face and, to my surprise, actually managed to go back to sleep. I awakened to the sun peeking through the roof of savage greenery and accepted a cup of the fierce Cuban coffee the rebels were brewing over a renewed fire. I felt as though I'd been trampled by a herd of buffalo.

Gonzales came around. "Did you sleep well?" he asked smugly.

"Like a baby," I assured him.

He said, "Good. I am glad you are properly rested, Señor Artista. Today the travel should be somewhat more difficult."

He wasn't lying.

The first day's journey had taken us deep into the heart of the rain forest that bordered the northern coast east of Havana. That second day we emerged from the rot of the jungle to a great plain of cane fields. It was here, Gonzales told us—where the great plantations occupied mile after rolling mile—that we would face our greatest peril.

"First," he said, "we shall enjoy little cover. We shall cross broad fields, hiding in stands of cane where they exist. And it is here that the Spanish patrols will be the thickest."

"Why here?" Davis inquired.

"Because this is where Cuba's wealth is stored. Ninety percent of our exports are sugar. In a good year, these fields will produce nearly two million tons of sugar, most of it bound for *los Estados Unidos*. Of course, we have not enjoyed a good year in some time."

"Because of the revolution?" I asked.

Gonzales nodded grimly. "Last year, we burned enough sugar and sugar mills to keep production to less than two hundred thousand tons. This year, we may be able to drive production even lower."

"Doesn't that mean that your own people starve?" Davis asked.

Gonzales said, "Death is the logical and inevitable result of war, my rooster. There used to be two million people living in Cuba. Today, we are but a million five. Besides, the people do not own these fields. They are the property of the great landowners, who have driven small farmers off the land from Havana to Port Principe."

Then Gonzales merely fixed Davis with a disdainful glare. "How could they have sent us a man who knows so little of our history?"

My first instinct, had I been Davis, would have been to respond harshly to such a criticism, but he seemed to recognize some justice in it. Or his calm was part of his reportorial technique. He said only, "Just tell me about it, Gonzales, then I'll know—your side of it, at any rate."

Gonzales emitted a grunt of annoyance. "The Cuban sugar industry is the most mechanized on earth. The *ingenios*—the mechanized sugar mills—dominate the landscape. The land has been raped, my rooster. The landowners have chopped and burned back the lovely forest and planted cane everywhere. And this great industry which provides more than one-third of the world's sugar has no work for the farmers except as slave labor—except as peons working their own land for small coins which do not buy enough food to fill the stomachs of their small children."

Gonzales waved his arm at the line of solemn, dark-faced men who marched with us. "Why do you think my *compadres* are here, carrying guns through the cane fields instead of working their own farms? Their land has been stolen from them by Spanish landowners and rich Cubans who care more for profits than for justice. Our people are starving."

Davis had produced his notebook and was scribbling. He said, "If things are truly so bad here, then why do you think the United States has failed to step in and help?"

"A very good question," Gonzales snapped. "Were it not for the efforts of your gracious employer and others—too few others—our Insurrecto would stand no chance. We can succeed ultimately only if we have *los Estados Unidos* on our side. And only now that we have done serious damage to Cuba's economy is this a realistic possibility. *Los Estados Unidos* has fifty million dollars invested here, and in good times Cuba and your country do more than one hundred million dollars every year in trade. Now that American dollars are at stake perhaps we will receive the help we need to achieve our independence. That is, if you Americans have not lost your stomach for fighting even when honor demands it."

Davis merely took notes, but the comment prompted me to flare. I said, "Don't worry about the American stomach for a fight, sir. We may not go looking for them, but when they arise we can certainly handle them."

A flicker of cold amusement flashed through Gonzales's dark eyes. "We shall see, Señor Artista. We shall see."

Little did I know, Bierce, that later in the day I would find myself provided with an unwitting opportunity to demonstrate my point. In our party was a rebel named Ernesto. He'd given me coffee that morning and told me the story of La Bahia de Paz as we chatted. He seemed a pleasant, diffident sort of chap. As we moved through the cane and the dirt roads that snaked through the fields, Ernesto's job was to range ahead of the party as an advance scout. He was a short, slight, very dark man of no more than twenty-five. By midafternoon, he'd grown slightly careless. So it was that he was astounded when, upon moving out of a stand of cane onto one of the dirt roads, he came face-to-face with a Spanish soldier—like Ernesto, an advance scout for a routine patrol.

Ernesto was dressed as all Cuban peasants dress, in white cotton pajamas, and barefoot. The machete at his hip was not an uncommon sight in the cane fields. The soldier therefore took a brief moment to inspect this man before him—to decide if this was a rebel or just a cane worker—and that was his undoing. Ernesto took that opportunity to draw his machete and neatly cleft the fellow's skull from crown to chin.

Ernesto dragged the unfortunate Spaniard into the cane and waited to see how large a party he was scouting for. In a few moments, a troop of Spanish soldiers marched along the dirt road. They were led by a strutting young officer with a saber at his hip. When the soldiers had passed, Ernesto remained in his hiding place for a count of one hundred, then slipped back through the cane to find us.

He came bursting out of the waving stalks. Several of our party, startled, reflexively drew machetes. But Ernesto snapped out, "If you want blood, fools, the Spaniards up ahead will be delighted to oblige."

Gonzales was all ears when he heard that. "Where?" he demanded.

Ernesto told him that a Spanish patrol was following the dirt road around the vast field of waving cane through which we were traveling. Their route would bring them disturbingly near us, and there was no way a party like ours—laden with burros and heavy crates of weapons—could count with absolute certainty on escaping detection.

"What are you going to do?" Davis asked him.

"We will fight," Gonzales told him quietly. "This is what soldiers do."

Davis and I were for trying to hide in the cane field. We pointed out that we were noncombatants on a mission to deliver the sword—which I had the misfortune to be carrying at the moment.

We tried to dissuade him, but Gonzales was determined to carry out his ambush. Davis and I had only two choices. We could remain with the two men detailed to watch the burros or follow Gonzales and the bulk of the party to the edge of the cane field to engage the enemy. We elected to travel with the larger, better-armed group. Neither option was particularly safe, but we felt more secure with the strength of numbers. And, if our party were to lose, we'd surely be captured in any event.

We crawled with Gonzales and his men to the edge of the field. Our movements and even our breathing were shrouded by the rustle of the wind through the cane. Once at the edge of the road, we simply lay down among the stalks and waited.

In only a few moments, I heard muffled footsteps as Spanish boots fell on the soft earth of the road. I heard faint laughter and good-humored banter in the lispy Spanish of the Continent. I tried to remain motionless, but could sense rather than hear the intake of breath from the men around me. I knew their fingers were on the triggers of their rifles or the hilts of their beloved machetes. I hoped that no one could hear the thumping of my heart or the rush of blood that sounded so loudly in my ears.

The sounds drew nearer until a Spanish boot suddenly came down less than a yard from my nose. Davis, lying next to me, literally jumped, and I thought we all were undone. But, by then, Gonzales was ordering the attack. I could hear his voice, thick with that controlled rage that was so much a part of his temperament, sound out, *"Cuba Libre!"*

His comrades fired in a sudden, ragged explosion that deafened me. Then, amidst the smoke and din, I was aware of men leaping up and out of the cane, their machetes flashing, echoing the cry that had begun the engagement.

"Cuba Libre! Cuba Libre!"

The two forces collided in the narrow road in a flurry of curses, cries of surprise and pain, gunshots, and clanking metal. Davis and I would have liked nothing better than to have stayed precisely where we were, lying in the dirt several feet off the road and obscured from the combatants by a half-dozen thick, lovely stalks of green cane. Unfortunately, within the first few seconds of the clash, the warm corpse of a Spanish soldier came crashing through our blind and right on top of Davis. He howled in alarm and immediately pushed it off him and onto me, which I also found somewhat unnerving.

I scrambled from beneath the poor fellow and leapt to my feet. I took several steps away from the fallen man and cast a glance into the road. There I saw Ernesto, our scout—his eyes narrowed to burning slits—moving toward the young Spanish officer. In Ernesto's hand was his bloody machete. I saw their eyes meet and silent communication flashed between them. Then, inexplicably, a grin split the young officer's face, and he slashed viciously at Ernesto with his saber. Ernesto neatly sidestepped the blow and responded with one of his own, which the Spaniard parried rather gracefully.

I was mesmerized, Bierce. I staggered to the edge of the cane, unable to pull my eyes away from this terrible dance. I'd done some fencing at Yale, and I'd seen plenty of matches. But never a duel conducted with deadly intent—never a match to rival this one.

Ernesto was a cobra, and the Spaniard was a graceful cat. They circled one another in the soft dirt, several yards from the main body of the fighting. Each carried a razor-sharp blade, and their eyes were fused in a death stare. Ernesto was a lithe man. He danced in nimbly on his bare feet, slashed once more, and once again was bested by the Spaniard's effortless parry.

Then the Spaniard dropped into a classic fencing stance, and I saw instantly that the man was a master. He was trained in this, and his saber was no more than an extension of his will. Ernesto saw it, too, and he blanched beneath the darkness of his skin.

What happened next took place more quickly than I can describe it. The Spaniard was thrusting, moving forward with exquisite grace and economy of movement. Ernesto managed to stave off one thrust, then another, then a third. But the fourth caught him squarely in the middle, just below the breastbone. The saber sank in a good eight inches before it struck the bone of his spine and stopped. Ernesto immediately slumped against the saber blade, head up and his eyes filled with hatred.

The Spaniard gave his weapon a powerful twist to break its point free of Ernesto's vertebra. My comrade—for that's indeed how I thought of him—shuddered once and collapsed in the dirt. The Spaniard stood over him, placed a boot on his chest, and pulled his weapon free. Then he turned, his eyes searching for another victim and—

—focused directly on me.

I couldn't believe it, Bierce. I glanced over my shoulder, hoping there was someone—anyone—behind me who was the true target of this swordsman's stare. There was only cane, waving high over my head. I turned my eyes back to the Spaniard. He merely smiled, as he'd smiled at poor Ernesto.

"*Su espada,*" he said softly, and motioned with his blade.

I followed the point of his weapon, and my eyes came to rest on the ornate hilt of the sword I wore about my waist—the Gomez sword. I began jabbering, trying to explain that the sword wasn't mine, that I was here only as an observer. But by then the man was coming on. He sliced almost carelessly at me, and I leapt back, not yet convinced this was truly happening. His second blow in my direction was more purposeful, missing only by a hair's breadth and severing several stalks of cane. I could feel the breeze of it. And then it was clear I had no choice in the matter.

I lurched into the road to provide myself with more room, and I drew the Gomez sword. As I said, I'd done some fencing at Yale, but I wasn't in this man's class—never had been. I managed to parry his next slice, but the vibration numbed my arm, and the sound and feel of metal edge against metal edge sent a profound shiver through me. Moreover, his saber bounced off the blade of the Gomez sword and into my face. I turned my eyes away in time to save them, but I was left with a neat groove along my left cheek. If you look closely, you can still see the mark, all these years later.

I put my fingers to the wound. They came away bloody. I glared at my antagonist. There was no way out of this, and there was only one course of action left open to me.

I simply threw myself at the Spaniard, hacking away with a fierce intensity born of anger and sheer terror. I was by far the larger and stronger man, and that gave me a momentary advantage. He was driven back by the vigor and surprise of my attack. He parried each blow and thrust with almost careless skill, if not ease, and finally feinted to his right and stepped to his left. Like a bull in a ring, I went tearing right by him.

By the time I managed to regain my balance, the fellow was on the offensive again. Frantically, I swung the Gomez sword about to block the Spaniard's blows. He was not only more skilled than I but also considerably faster, and I found myself driven back. I don't mind confessing, Bierce, that the anger I'd felt the moment before had given way to cold fear. The young officer grinned again. It was a hard, cruel smile—the smile of an efficient killer. I'd seen that same smile on the face of Gonzales, and I'd grown perceptive enough to recognize it for what it was.

And then I stumbled.

To this day, I can't tell you what I fell over. It didn't matter. What did matter was that I was suddenly flat on my back in the dirt, staring up into the Spaniard's face with its mocking smile. The Spaniard laughed once—a sharp, triumphant sound. Then he raised his blade, and . . .

. . . his eyes bulged almost out of his head.

The fellow just stood there, transfixed. His eyes were enormous with shock, and his mouth began to work soundlessly. Then I saw a tiny stream of blood trickle out the corner of his mouth before he crashed down directly atop me.

I shoved him away as though he'd died of the plague. Strong hands reached down for me, and I found myself pulled to my feet in the ironlike grasp of Jorge Gonzales. Gonzales wiped his machete blade on the uniform of the dead officer, whose back he'd rent with a sharp, twisting thrust. Then he simply glanced at me and tapped the sword still clutched in my right hand with the blade of his machete.

He said, "We cannot have the sword of General Gomez stained with blood just yet, can we, Señor Artista?"

He stalked off to gather his men. The battle had lasted only a few moments. The fusillade of shots from the cane had wiped out nearly a third of the Spanish troop, and another third had been overwhelmed by the rush of machete-swinging rebels before they'd known what was transpiring. The final third, led by the Spanish officer, had battled fiercely for only a few moments before they, too, had been overcome. Gonzales quickly calculated his losses. Four dead—including the invaluable Ernesto—and none of the others so seriously wounded that he would be forced to shoot them.

"Come," Gonzales announced to his sweating colleagues, whose breasts were heaving with their exertions, "we must depart this place."

The rebels faded back into the cane for the spot where we'd left the burros. I found Davis standing beside me. We exchanged wordless glances. Yes, I indicated, I'm fine. He merely grinned and slapped me good-naturedly on the back. He pointed over to Gonzales.

"Our friend there definitely has his good points."

AMBROSE BIERCE
Mexico, 1914

I awaken to the pallid rays of a new dawn in the squalid hut of Small Maria. My voice and wind spent, I drifted off at sundown yesterday expecting to awaken in my tomb—in the House of Indifference.

Tombs are by common consent invested with a certain sanctity, but when they have been long tenanted it is considered no sin to break them open and rifle them. Archaeologists are the greatest proponents of this point of view—and hyenas.

"Protect my bones from seekers of knowledge," I urge Small Maria, who continues to kneel at my bedside in a display of loyalty monumental in its simplemindedness. She seems delighted that my weary heart continues obstinately to perform its duties, but I feel it waning, and my instructions will not wait.

"Tell no one but your priest where I lie," I order her. "Bury me deep and take the secret of my grave to your own resting place. I will not have my grave become a waiting room for the arrival of some industrious medical student."

"Señor Bierce," she says gleefully. "You sound so much stronger today."

"It is but illusion," I assure her. "I soon will reside in a carniverous hole in the ground with the peculiar property of devouring its contents. Your priest will perform over this pit a semireligious ceremony fixed by law, precept, and custom, with the essential oil of sincerity carefully squeezed out of it. Reveal to no one, Small Maria, the location of the pockmark in the earth that contains me. Promise me this."

She nods. It is almost a surrender on her part, this silent admission of my mortality. In my weakened state, I am moved to console her in her obvious grief over the inevitable.

"For now, however," I tell her, "let us endure the present—that part of eternity dividing the domain of disappointment from the realm of hope. I will continue my story, if you like."

She nods. "Speak to me, Señor Bierce. Keep talking, *por favor*."

I respond, "I perform few tasks with more practiced skill. Shall I tell you of the story recounted to me years later by my friend, Gardener? He told me this tale after he had fled the Pulitzer empire for the more benevolent fold of my own master. Gardener's portion of the tale becomes more or less pertinent at this point, and some of it might even be true."

"Talk," she urges.

And, so I do.

"There were fourteen stairs," I tell her. "Joseph Pulitzer knew this because he had counted them. He had done so long ago, when his eyesight had commenced to dim. It had occurred to him that if he was to continue functioning as the proprietor of the *New York World*, he would have to do so largely by memory. He would have to recall from that vast storehouse of facts that resided in his skull the precise number of steps between floors in his newspaper building, the number of paces between his desk and the doorway, the layout of the newsroom, the precise location of the washroom.

"As he hit the fourteenth and last step, Pulitzer turned around and stared down sightlessly on my friend Gardener, who he knew would be only a step behind, waiting to catch the great publisher if, for some reason, the old man's memory should fail him and he came crashing down the stairs. Gardener had better be there if that were to happen.

" 'Hurry up, Gardener,' Pulitzer ordered curtly.

"Gardener sighed. 'Yes, sir,' he said softly.

"Pulitzer fixed his editor with a piercing, utterly blind gaze. Then he strode purposefully down the hall to his office, precisely forty-eight steps from the top of the stairs. Gardener pulled out a handkerchief and mopped his brow. He dreaded his master's monthly visits to the offices of the *New York World*. He dreaded the publisher's probing questions, uttered in Pulitzer's thick, middle-European accent. Gardener dreaded the unending criticisms of him and his subordinate editors. He dreaded the violent outbursts from Pulitzer at the slightest sound.

"Most of all, however, Gardener dreaded the necessity of explaining to Joseph Pulitzer that Hearst's *New York Journal* had badly beaten the *World* on an important story. He dreaded that as he dreaded death itself. For the thousandth time he asked himself why he endured this agonizing existence. For the thousandth time, he provided himself with the answer—money.

"Gardener followed Pulitzer down the hallway. As he arrived in the great man's outer office, he heard the publisher's secretary already reading his boss the lead story in the *Journal*. Gardener toyed briefly with the idea of going back down the stairs, gathering up his hat and walking stick, and walking out the front door once and for all—as he eventually did one afternoon. On this particular day, however, he rejected that plan. After all, he told himself, it was not really his fault.

"Instead, he walked into the large office to find the secretary—a youngish chap with thick spectacles—standing in front of Pulitzer's enormous and gleaming desk reading aloud from the Hearst publication.

" 'The headline is in red ink,' the secretary said. 'It's a banner with several decks.'

" 'Read them,' Pulitzer snapped. He stared straight ahead through his useless spectacles, which he wore out of habit.

" 'Yes, sir. It says: *Cuba's Joan of Arc*. Then, below that, it says: *Beautiful Girl Violated by Spanish Ravishers*. Then, below that, it says: *Freedom Fighter's Daughter Imprisoned, Abused*.'

"Gardener saw his boss's jaw tighten. Gardener winced. Then Pulitzer said, 'And the story?'

"The secretary read it aloud with enthusiasm. He seemed to very much enjoy this part of his otherwise thoroughly distasteful job. Davis had composed a rather long piece, given the time constraints under which he had suffered, and he had outdone himself with his typically florid style. As the young man read, Gardener deposited his considerable bulk in a chair in front of the old man's desk. Actually, Pulitzer was not an old man at all—certainly not from my current vantage point. He was just fifty, but with his gray-flecked beard, his high, wrinkled forehead, and his stooped posture, he seemed the very eyes of age. Then there was the blindness, of course. And the nervousness— the frightful nervousness.

"Gardener was a longtime Pulitzer hand. He had been with the eccentric Hungarian almost from the beginning, ever since the Pulitzer purchase of the moribund *St. Louis Post-Dispatch* nine years earlier. Pulitzer had been the wonder of St. Louis. He had come west in sixty-five to make his fortune after a tour in the Union army. He had begun as a reporter for a German-language newspaper, taken the bar exam, and then persuaded the owners to sell him part ownership. He promptly resold his share, and—as an example of the ruthlessness that came to make him so dreaded a figure in newspapering—had used the proceeds to purchase a competing German-language paper so he could ruin his former partners.

"He was shrewd, though, and he soon turned his acquisition into quite a going concern. He then bought the ailing *St. Louis Dispatch*, merged it with the ailing *Post*, and began to grow unspeakably rich. In a few years, the *Post-Dispatch* dominated the St. Louis newspaper market. Gardener, only a lowly copyreader on the *Dispatch* when

[69]

Pulitzer gobbled it up, found himself propelled like a bullet through the ranks of management. He was, of course, ecstatic. But he found there is always a price to pay for the largesse of a lunatic.

"Pulitzer was the oddest of men—odder by far than my Chief, who is merely too naive to entertain the prospect that anything can be impossible. Pulitzer was brilliant; there was no doubt about that. And his energy level was spectacular. But he was autocratic to a fault, and so nervous that spending any time in his presence was an ordeal. He was given to stalking back and forth like a caged animal, agitated, waving his arms and screaming at the top of his lungs. His normal tone of voice was a roar. For him, a snarl constituted whispering.

"Under normal circumstances, the man was a study in agitation. Then an incident took place that drove him completely out of control. Pulitzer's top editor at the time was a chap I knew slightly, John Cockerill. He was a disagreeable sort devoted to the proposition that anyone who choose to see the world through eyes that differed from Cockerill's was deserving of any pain that could be inflicted upon him. One who disagreed—politically, at least—was a St. Louis lawyer named Alonzo Slayback. So one day Cockerill shot him to death. A rather extreme response to political provocation, to be sure, but Cockerill was like that.

"He undoubtedly should have been jailed, but Pulitzer immediately brought to bear his not inconsiderable political influence in St. Louis. The case never came to trial, but it was a scandal of impressive proportions. The *Post-Dispatch* even lost circulation over it. Pulitzer was so distraught over the incident that friends, family, and business associates feared a total mental breakdown. They persuaded him to leave town for an extended period. So he went to New York and bought the *World*. And he brought in Gardener from St. Louis to run it for him.

"In New York, Pulitzer found that his formula of screaming headlines and heavy crime coverage made the *World* an instant success. He made money, had fun, and was even elected to Congress. He became a player in that strife of interests masquerading as a contest of principles. He took naturally to the conduct of public affairs for private advantage. In short, the man had never been happier.

"Only, it did not last.

"Pulitzer's vision, never particularly good, began to fail badly after his election to Congress. By eighty-seven, he was totally blind, and he resigned his office in despair. This development had done nothing to ease his incredible nervousness. Deprived of sight, he became unnaturally sensitive to noise. A single word spoken in even a normal tone caused him enormous agony. He retired to his luxurious yacht in New York Harbor to run his empire and to brood.

"Gardener found the imperious edicts of an absentee owner only a minor annoyance compared to his master's actual presence. The *World* was the city's most successful newspaper. It was a gold mine of revenue. It occupied an unassailable position of dominance in the nation's largest city.

"Then came Hearst.

"The Chief was a great fan of Pulitzer's. When he used his father's millions to buy the *Journal* in ninety-five, he paid Pulitzer the highest compliment imaginable—he imitated him. He out-Pulitzered Pulitzer. And, in so doing, The Chief posed a huge threat to the Pulitzer empire.

"The very presence of The Chief in New York sent the old man into a perpetual, foaming rage. The imperious orders from the yacht increased in number and frenzy. Worst of all, the old man began making regular visits to the office to, in his words, 'see what's going on'—even though, in the strictest sense, he could see nothing at all.

"Gardener abhorred the old man's visits. For days before they occurred, Gardener would spend nights gazing in wakefulness at his bedroom ceiling. This particular visit was the worst in Gardener's memory. The Chief's *Journal* had demolished the *World* on the Cuba story—a story in which the old man took genuine interest. Gardener had read Davis's story that morning, and now Pulitzer's secretary was on the very last paragraph. Gardener shuddered. He knew that this would be a very bad day, indeed.

" 'Is that all?' Pulitzer asked.

" 'It is, sir,' the secretary replied softly.

" 'Very well,' Pulitzer told him. 'You may leave.'

"The secretary slipped out soundlessly. Pulitzer sat motionless for a moment, staring sightlessly into space. Then he said, 'You're there, aren't you, Gardener?'

"Gardener blanched. 'I am, Mr. Pulitzer.'

"He then braced himself. He didn't have long to wait. The bellow built slowly, like a train whistle in the distance. Gardener felt rather than heard it as it came roaring out of the old man's throat.

" 'Why has God done this to me?' Pulitzer screamed. He pounded with one thin fist on his desk. 'Why has he cursed me so?'

"Gardener had anticipated the worst, but this exceeded even his expectations. He said, 'You must try to relax, sir. You know what the doctor said.'

"But Pulitzer would not be contained. He leapt to his feet, shrieking, 'Doctor? What can a doctor do? God himself is against me!'

[71]

"Then, in a flash, the old man was suddenly all business. He snapped quietly, 'What was today's circulation figure?'

"Gardener moaned inwardly. He knew better than to lie. He said, 'We were down fifteen thousand.'

" 'And what was Hearst's figure, please?' Pulitzer asked politely.

" 'He was up eighteen thousand, Mr. Pulitzer.'

"The publisher's face turned a fetching shade of bright purple. Gardener could see the veins pop out like ropes on his forehead.

" 'Eighteen thousand?' Pulitzer howled. 'Up eighteen thousand?'

"Pulitzer sank into his chair and buried his face in his hands. His voice emerged as a plaintive whine from between his fingers.

"He said, 'What have I done, dear God, that you should afflict me so? Why hast thou forsaken me?'

Gardener slumped back in his chair, vicariously exhausted from his master's soaring and swooping of moods. He said, 'It's only a temporary situation, sir. When this Cuba situation blows over—'

"Pulitzer leapt instantly to his feet again. He screamed, 'Blows over? This Cuban Joan of Arc is the most discussed topic in New York—the most discussed topic in the country since the Associated Press picked up Hearst's story. And they did pick it up, didn't they?'

"They had, but Gardener was afraid to respond. Pulitzer needed no response in any event. He merely kept on bellowing, 'And that upstart Hearst has a reporter in Cuba. Why don't we, Gardener? Isn't it enough that God, in his inscrutable wisdom, has seen fit to deprive me of my sight? Must he also reduce my circulation? Must he burden me with incompetents of the lowest order?'

"The tantrum was all Gardener had feared and more. He made a mental note to stop at a liquor store on his way home that night. He would have to do some heavy drinking to get to sleep.

" 'Mr. Pulitzer,' Gardener said as soothingly as he could manage, 'we haven't been able to get a reporter into Cuba. The Spanish government is outraged by the stance taken by the American press toward the revolution down there. They've been most uncooperative.'

" 'Hearst has a man there,' Pulitzer replied in a feral snarl. 'He has two men—a reporter and that damned artist, Remington. Why didn't you hire Remington, Gardener? This young upstart from California is doing us real damage. He's using his father's money to take our readers—MY READERS!'

"Suddenly, to Gardener's shock, tears began gushing like geysers from the publisher's sightless eyes.

" 'I'm just a poor blind man,' Pulitzer sobbed. 'I'm only trying to make my way in this vale of tears, and you've been sent to torment me, Gardener. You've been sent by God to afflict me in my time of travail.'

"Gardener was truly shaken by this. He had endured hysterical fits and even catatonic trances from this lunatic who paid his salary. But never had he seen Pulitzer collapse into an uncontrollable emotional heap until this very moment. In a surge of genuine concern, he leapt to his feet, rounded the desk, and laid a comforting arm around his master's shoulder.

" 'Mr. Pulitzer,' he promised, 'we'll have a man in Cuba before the week is out. I promise you that—before the week ends, sir.'

"Pulitzer lifted his head, his face and glasses sopping with tears. But the sobbing, pitiful heap he'd been only a heartbeat before had vanished.

" 'I hope so,' he told his editor with quiet menace, 'for your sake, Gardener.' "

NINE

Frederic Remington
Cuba, 1897

We enjoyed no rest the balance of that day or night, Bierce. None whatever.

Gonzales was determined to put distance between us and the troop of massacred Spanish soldiers. Other patrols, he knew, would be along directly. As darkness fell, we continued our trek through the endless cane fields. Two of our party lagged behind as rear scouts, obliterating our trail by wiping out our tracks with ragged stalks of sugar cane.

Just before dawn, the skies opened up once again. The already softened ground became a slippery slide of mud. I fell several times before I realized that the way was growing steeper. As dawn peeked over the eastern horizon, I glanced back over the route we'd traversed to find that we'd climbed a considerable distance. Before us loomed a mountain—only one of a wall of towering hills, curved hummocks, and great heaps of jungle vegetation piled thousands of feet high to soaring, barren summits.

I was soaked from the rain and exhausted from the drenching heat but willing to continue. Davis, however, was near the breaking point. He scrambled to catch up with Gonzales, who was climbing effortlessly.

"I take it," Davis said, "that the rest of the trip will be uphill. For God's sake, how much farther, Gonzales?"

Gonzales turned to him casually. Davis wiped a river of sweat off his brow and swatted carelessly at the cloud of biting insects that swarmed everywhere.

"Is the warmth of Cuba troubling you, Rooster?" Gonzales asked. "Are you not impressed with the beauty of our land?"

His mockery was so broad that it produced from me a chuckle. The sound of laughter seemed to ease the tension slightly. Davis, less antagonistic now, said, "I'll be honest, Gonzales. It hardly seems worth fighting for. How much longer?"

Gonzales remained Gonzales, however—abrasive by his very nature. He replied, "We are nearing the headquarters of General Gomez.

I must caution you to remain silent. The area is heavy with Spanish patrols."

"How about them?" Davis demanded, gesturing toward the braying, protesting burros. "They make enough noise to attract every Spaniard on the island."

"True," Gonzales conceded, "but they are dumb animals, señor, and their noise is unavoidable. Besides, they carry guns. They are useful."

Davis bristled and was about to say something harsh, but I stepped in to quell the clash. I said to Gonzales, "What's the name of this mountain?"

"This mountain has no name," he told me as we resumed climbing. "Cuba is more than forty thousand miles square, and it has too many mountains for each one to have a name. We are entering what is known as the Sierra de Trinidad. It is one of several mountain ranges on our island. They are convenient places for Insurrecto forces. The Spanish like to say that if we had no mountains we would have no revolution. But, of course, we do have the mountains—a vast profusion of them. We have the Sierra de Trinidad, the Sierra de los Organos, the Sierra del Rosario, all of them offering shelter to patriots. God has been helpful to the cause of liberty in Cuba, Señor Artista."

Davis said, "You don't strike me as a religious man, Gonzales. Do you believe in God?"

The Cuban shrugged. "Perhaps I could believe in him with more devotion if he owned a newspaper in *los Estados Unidos*."

"The newspapers are that important to you?" I asked.

Gonzales nodded. "We cannot win a clear victory over the Spanish without the help of America. We can worry them, destroy the economy, perhaps make them so sick of Cuba that one day they may leave in disgust. But that would take a long time, and we have already been fighting for twenty-five years, on and off. We must have an end to it. The American newspapers can give it to us."

Davis shook his head wearily. "I can't imagine a war going on for twenty-five years."

Gonzales said, "This war, you realize, began when you were but a small child."

"I hope it ends before I die," Davis shot back immediately.

Gonzales actually laughed. Then he stepped up the pace.

By midday, the vegetation had begun to thin out in the higher altitudes. And, thankfully, even with the sun at its zenith the thinner air was cooler than down below. The swarms of bugs were thinner, too, the trees smaller and more generously spaced, and the path rockier and more rugged. I found this topography more congenial than the lowlands. I grew up in the Adirondacks, you know, Bierce, and I've always had a special affection for mountains.

At about three thousand feet, we began going down again. Then up. Then down. We were moving from mountain ᷍ ᷍ mountain along a thin, almost invisible trail. It was tough going, and by midafternoon even the tireless Gonzales had begun to drag. After nearly twenty-four uninterrupted hours of hard travel, he finally called a halt. We all collapsed where we stood. I fell asleep in seconds and came awake in darkness with Davis shaking me. I fought my way to alertness with great difficulty. The smell of cooking meat wafted into my nostrils. I realized that Davis was presenting me with a rude, wooden bowl of stew. I took it and watched him dig gleefully with his fingers into his own meal.

"Eat it," he said cheerily through a full mouth. "It's good."

I normally eat several times my own weight every day, Bierce, like a shrew. But I was still too weary for hunger to animate me. I reached into the bowl and pulled out a bit of meat. I put it into my mouth and chewed dully. Then my digestive system did its duty. It reminded me that I was starving. I came completely awake and ripped into the meaty stew, shoveling it down my throat in seconds. Immediately, I felt the glow of nourishment warm my middle. I licked the bowl clean, set it aside, and lay back down, utterly content for the first time since Key West.

"That," I told Davis, "was the best meal I ever consumed. Rabbit?"

Davis shook his head. "Hutia," he said.

I was puzzled. "What?"

"Hutia," Davis repeated. "They dug a colony of them out of a hole while you were sleeping. The beasts are rodents."

Alarm bells went off in my head. "Rodents? Like a rat?"

Davis nodded. "They look quite a bit like rats, actually. A bit larger, though."

I could feel my recently acquired meal threatening to exit its new home, but I managed to hold it down until I fell back asleep. In the morning, after two cups of that fierce Cuban coffee, I felt better than I'd felt in days. As we continued our march, I found Cosio at my side.

"Good morning, Mr. Cosio," I said.

"*Buenos días*," he told me, seemingly none the worse for wear after this ordeal despite his relatively advanced age. The man had to be near sixty.

I asked him, "How close are we now to Gomez?"

"We are close," he told me. "When we enter a deep canyon, then we will be there."

The canyon came up within no more than a mile or two. The trail we followed led directly into it. First there was a small opening, barely wide enough to admit a single man or a crate-laden burro. Then the trail fanned out into a long, dry streambed lined with high, naked rocks on either side. Even to my unpracticed eye, this canyon seemed a perfect ambush site. Along either side of the raised rim loomed huge boulders. Behind any of them, I realized, a regiment could hide.

There was, however, only Julio Un Ojo.

Julio, I later learned, was hardly a regiment—although, given his skill with a rifle, his fearlessness, and his intense hatred of the Spanish, he was almost worth a regiment under congenial circumstances.

From the top of his boulder, a vantage point that gave him a clear view over nearly a quarter mile of the canyon floor, he could have spotted our party coming long before we might have spotted him. Julio's great virtue, however, was his uncanny hearing, and he heard us long before he saw us.

When the sound of marching men and animals reached his incredibly keen ears, Julio scrambled down from his perch and pulled a small, wooden cage from its hiding place beneath a shrub. Inside the cage were two doves, cooing and dozing. He pulled out one of the pigeons with a gentle touch incongruous in one with such a visage.

Julio's face was a horror. His nose was mashed flat across his cheeks—the mark of a Spanish rifle butt. His upper front teeth had been broken to jagged edges, courtesy of the same gun butt. His left eye was no more than an open socket, courtesy of the soldier who'd wielded the rifle. Hence Julio's nickname—*Un Ojo*. It translates to One Eye.

Sometime after sustaining the injuries to his face, Julio had enjoyed the pleasure of roasting his assailant alive. But that had done nothing to restore his appearance, and he'd never grown quite accustomed to the expression of loathing he inspired in women. Julio hoped with all his murderous heart that the sounds he heard were being made by an approaching party of Spanish soldiers.

He carefully tied a scrap of blue cloth to the pigeon's foot and tossed it aloft. The bird caught flight and immediately flapped off down the canyon. The blue cloth would tell the encampment that a party of some size was approaching. Unless the first pigeon was followed within a matter of minutes by the second—this one adorned with a bit of red cloth—the walls of the canyon would soon be alive with guns to fire on whoever had prevented Julio from releasing the second pigeon.

Julio checked his rifle, an ancient percussion cap weapon of mid-century vintage. He tested the edge of his machete. He then crossed himself, climbed back up the rock, and flattened himself against its flat top. Within minutes, a party of men and animals rounded a bend many hundreds of yards away.

With only his one eye, Julio had problems with depth perception. Had he spotted us in an open field, he would have had difficulty determining how close, or how far away, we were. But he knew his little patch of canyon intimately. And he could see, as we rounded the bend, that we weren't Spanish soldiers. When he saw faces he recognized, he slipped off his rock still undetected and released his second pigeon.

I'd moved to the head of the caravan next to Gonzales when I saw the pigeon flap overhead with a scrap of red cloth affixed to one leg. Davis, who walked beside us, squinted at the creature as it disappeared around a bend of the canyon ahead.

"I'd always thought of pigeons as city birds," he said.

"That was a rebel pigeon," Gonzales explained. "He flies to tell Gomez of our arrival. We should soon encounter a reception party."

Davis asked, "I hope we can count on them to greet us in friendly fashion—instead of shooting first and asking questions later, as you did with that Spanish patrol in the cane fields."

"One can never tell, señor," Gonzales said solemnly. "These rebels—they are a bloody band."

I was somewhat entertained by Gonzales's feeble attempt at humor, but Davis was genuinely concerned about the greeting we might encounter. In another ten minutes, however, the nature of that greeting was made known to us. From various outcroppings of rock—not unlike the one Julio Un Ojo called his own—figures began to emerge. Like the rebels in our own party, they wore undyed cotton garments and wide-brimmed straw hats. Most were barefoot. All carried or openly brandished machetes, and more than a few bore rifles and wore bandoliers. They showed themselves openly—black- and olive-skinned men wearing harsh expressions, saying nothing and merely gazing down from their outposts in curiosity.

Finally, as we rounded still another bend in the canyon that snaked through the mountains, one of the rebels in our party raised a fist high above his head.

"*Cuba Libre!*" he shouted.

Instantly, the rocks surrounding us were alive with men. There were hundreds of them, Bierce. And, from their throats, we all heard that same cry reverberating off the rocks. "*Cuba Libre! Cuba Libre!*"

Our march through the canyon, so frightening at first, had suddenly turned into a triumphant parade. Gonzales strode next to me with a studied air of nonchalance, but I could tell that even he was touched by the warmth of his reception. He waved only once or twice

[78]

to the growing mob of men in the rocks. Finally, as we rounded still another bend, we came face-to-face with our reception party.

The canyon had grown much wider by this point, and the line of rebels stretched all the way across its floor. They bristled with machetes, knives, stolen Spanish weapons, and ancient firearms of all descriptions.

Davis nudged me. "So this is the Free Army of Cuba," he whispered. "They look more like a mob of mountain cutthroats."

Gonzales raised one arm and pointed. "There's your general. Did I not say he was heroic?"

Gomez was in the middle of the line. He was a tall, bulky man of perhaps fifty. He carried most of his weight in his shoulders and barrel chest, but he bore a noteworthy roll of fat around his middle. His eyes were black, and his stubble of beard was largely gray. He was dark, even for a Cuban, and he wore a tattered and dusty uniform jacket of navy blue, amply adorned with gold braid. On his head perched a tan campaign cap. High, military-style boots covered his feet and legs up to the knee.

Gomez also boasted a saber hanging from his hip. It was a duplicate of the one I'd seen in the Spanish officer's hand. Presumably, it had been taken from an equally unfortunate Spanish swordsman. Protruding conspicuously from the general's belt were two ugly revolvers.

Gonzales led us directly up to Gomez. As we drew near, I noticed something about Gomez I found profoundly unsettling. This man could kill you with just his eyes, Bierce. If Gonzales possessed eyes that burned with a fierce inner rage—and he did, believe me—then Gomez had eyes of black ice. They were dead and flat like the marble of a tomb.

Gonzales suddenly raised his hand, and our caravan skidded to an abrupt halt. There was a moment of awful silence as Gomez took in Gonzales, Davis and myself, and our party of rebels and heavily laden burros. Then, in a heartbeat, those dead black eyes came alight with mirth. Gomez broke into a broad grin, threw open his arms, and flung them about Gonzales, slapping him fiercely on the back in good fellowship.

"Jorge!" Gomez boomed, then launched into a monologue of rapid Spanish I couldn't decipher.

Gonzales favored his commander with one of his rare smiles. Then he turned and gestured to us. "Maximo, I have brought you two fearless *periodistas* from *los Estados Unidos*."

I stayed my ground, but Davis—ever the personality boy—stepped instantly forward and stuck out his hand. "General Gomez, sir. How do you do? I'm Richard Harding Davis of the *New York Journal*."

Gomez gave Gonzales a blank look.

Gonzales shrugged. "From Señor Hearst. They came with the rifles. What was I to do?"

Gomez's face lit up. He pushed right by Davis's outstretched hand. In the next moment, Davis found himself caught in an embrace that would have crushed a bear.

"Ah," Gomez said. *"Buenos dias."*

There was nothing Davis would have liked to have done more than respond to this startling and unexpected show of comradeship. Unfortunately, his eyes were bulging out of his head, and he had no breath left with which to speak. Gomez, feeling playful, honored him with a bone-shattering slap on the back. I was sure several of Davis's ribs had cracked from the impact. Then Gomez released him—partially, at least. Retaining an iron grip on Davis's arms, the general looked him squarely in the face and smiled broadly.

"And what have you brought me from the fine Señor Hearst?" he laughed. "Something very fine, no?"

Davis broke free as politely as he could manage, his arms numb. He moved back a step or two. This was, he'd decided, the proper moment for a bit of theatrics. He placed his right hand on the hilt of the sword I'd refused to even touch since that confrontation in the cane field.

"This, General," he said.

Then, with a brave flourish, Davis whipped the sword from its scabbard, laid the blade gallantly over his left arm, and presented the thing to Gomez. The big general gazed at the weapon in open astonishment. He reached out with one horny hand and examined it closely.

"Some nicks in the blade," he observed, "but it is very beautiful." Gomez glanced over Davis's shoulder. "And where are my guns?"

"The guns are on the burros, Maximo," Gonzales told him.

Without a word, Gomez passed by Davis, drove the point of the sword into the ground beside a burro to free both hands, and ripped open the heavy wooden crate attached to the animal's back as though it were made of paper. He pulled out a greasy rifle and hefted it, putting it to his shoulder and sighting along it toward the canyon's rim. Then he turned to Gonzales and bared his yellow teeth in a broad smile of appreciation.

"You have done well, Jorge," he said. Gomez swirled and roared to his men, *"Compañeros! Fusiles!"*

A triumphant cheer erupted from the throats of the hundreds of rebels lining the canyon. In just a moment, they were swarming over the burros, breaking open cases of rifles and cartridges in a frenzy of laughter and excitement. Gomez emerged from the mob with his own rifle held high, as a trophy.

"*Fiesta!*" he bellowed, and stalked off down the canyon.

Davis immediately darted into the raucous mob around the bewildered lead burro and retrieved the sword stuck into the dry earth of the canyon floor. He sprinted with it to Gomez's side and said, "General, you forgot this."

Gomez never slowed. He merely reached out with his free hand and grabbed the bejeweled weapon from the reporter's hand. Then, with the sword tucked carelessly under one arm, he marched off at the head of his shouting, gleeful men. The rebels streamed down from the rocks in a human avalanche to grab rifles and to follow their general back to camp. Davis fought free of the crowd and made his way to my side. His face was flushed with embarrassment and anger.

He growled, "Just draw something from your imagination, Remington."

TEN

The headquarters of the Free Army of Cuba was a shabby collection of grass-thatched huts—called *hohios*—and tents obviously stolen from Spanish bivouacs. The tents were generously ventilated by bullet holes and machete rents. Perhaps three hundred of these feeble structures carpeted the canyon floor where it broadened into a respectable plain at its eastern end. The high canyon walls loomed in the bright, tropical sky nearly four thousand feet above sea level.

To my amateur's eye, the stronghold seemed virtually impregnable. It was reachable only one way—through the narrow portal where Julio stood guard, and thus could be defended by a bare handful of men.

"It is like the story of Samson," Cosio explained. "Samson was able to slay so many enemies with the jawbone of an ass because he backed into a crevice in a canyon, not unlike this one, where only one soldier at a time could reach him. He killed a thousand of them because he could fight them one at a time. So, too, it is here. The Spanish, if they found this place in the vastness of La Sierra de Trinidad, would be forced to approach us only a few at a time, and this they will not do."

I glanced up at the towering canyon walls. "What if they managed to get up there—above you?"

"They cannot bring their horses up the outside of the canyon," Cosio assured me. "They cannot pull up their big guns without horses. And if they come by foot, we will see them and fire down on them as they climb."

"Could they starve you out?" I inquired.

Cosio shrugged. "In time, perhaps. But," he added, motioning to a vast herd of goats penned near the camp's rearmost wall, "it would take considerable time. By the time our food ran out, many nights would have passed. And, over the course of those nights, most of us could sneak down the mountain past the lines of Spanish sentries whom God seems to have cursed with an inability to see or hear properly. This is as fine a stronghold as an army of ragtag farmers and fishermen can expect. If it were to fall, it would have to be the will of God, since the will of men would not be sufficient."

I studied the topography and said, "If you're telling me that we're relatively safe here, then it's welcome news. I haven't felt safe since I left Key West."

Cosio laughed. "If your safety matters so much, then why are you here?"

Money, I almost said. Instead, I told the old man the truth. I said, "I suppose my primary motivation was a search for excitement. The intensity of the adventure my father experienced in our civil war thirty years ago sustained him for the rest of his days. I guess I was looking for what he found. Now I've found it, too."

"Adventure," Cosio told me gravely, "is a luxury for those who lead safe and comfortable lives."

I said, "Gonzales seems to consider Davis and me foolish for coming here. Do you agree?"

"No," he said gently. "I can understand how a man enjoying an excess of comfort would be moved to seek adventure. For myself, I have had too much adventure, and comfort would be a welcome change. But, sadly, this is not to be—not for me and not for my poor Evangelina, God help her."

He was saddened by thoughts of his imprisoned daughter, so I left him with his grief and toured the camp. I hadn't realized how crucial the guns were to these people until I saw the weapons with which they'd been fending off Spanish troops. While the party that had accompanied us had been relatively well armed, most of this main body of the rebel army made do only with machetes. Their few rifles had been stolen from Spanish dead. Or they were hunting and fowling pieces fired with percussion caps and so ancient that the stocks were rotting away.

The rebels had no artillery, only a single Gatling gun stolen from the Spanish and lacking ammunition sufficient to be of much use. The rifles we'd dragged here from the coast brought the Free Army only a hint of parity with the well-equipped European force they faced, but their arrival was the occasion for a huge celebration. I had the impression that these sunny people were prone to stage parties at the slightest provocation.

The festivities began with the slaughter of a dozen goats. They were mounted on spits, and by nightfall the smell of roasting meat filled the camp with an aroma I found irresistible in the crisp mountain air. Around the camp, fires were started in front of every tent and *hohio*. Guitars were broken out. Soon, music floated through the camp.

Davis and I had been more or less ignored since our arrival, as Gonzales and the other leaders of the force had retired to a larger tent to plot strategy. Finally, as night fell, we saw Gonzales and Gomez emerge from their council and take positions around one of the fires. We immediately joined them. Each carried a wooden cup and smoked a large, black cigar. Just outside the circle of the fire, leaning against a small tree, was an evil-looking fellow strumming a guitar.

As we sat, I realized that both Gonzales and Gomez teetered on the brink of drunkenness. Apparently, the council had consumed a considerable ration of alcoholic beverage as it plotted against the Spanish. Gomez saw us coming and motioned to a heavy, middle-aged woman who stood nearby. She ducked into a tent and emerged with two more wooden cups and a jug. As we soaked up the fire's warmth, Gomez took the jug from the woman and poured a dark liquid into the cups.

"Drink," the general instructed.

We did. Davis coughed violently. I managed to maintain my dignity, Bierce, but I felt as though I'd swallowed a slug of molten steel.

"What is this?" I managed to get out.

Gomez laughed. "Rum. This is what makes my men so ferocious."

I took another sip. The stuff was brutal. I said, "I thought rum was clear. This is the color of coffee."

In a thick voice, Gonzales said, "The rum you drink in America is made from refined sugar. Hence it has no color or character. This is made from good, dark, Cuban brown sugar. It is a more substantial beverage."

He took another sip from his own cup and turned to Gomez. "I have missed this, *compadre*," Gomez said, his words falling about one of his rare laughs.

I watched as Davis swallowed a few more drops. Like me, he could feel a large, warm ball growing inside him, spreading rapidly from his middle to his extremities. At first, the fiery liquid had numbed his vocal cords, leaving him speechless, but he was growing visibly more relaxed.

"It sort of grows on you," he admitted in a choked voice.

Gomez said, "Sometimes we are lucky enough to have truly fine rum to drink—from the manor houses of the great sugar plantations. But lately we have been too short of weapons to venture far out of our mountains. And every day more patriots leave their homes and families to join us here. We needed the guns very badly, and now we have them."

Gonzales nodded and abruptly raised his cup. "*Salud!*" he bellowed.

The sight of these two extraordinary faces illuminated by the flickering fire caught my artist's eye. I produced my sketch pad and a bit of charcoal and began to capture them as we spoke. That seemed to remind Davis of why we were here.

He said, "I must have a way to get my dispatches back to New York. How do I do that?"

Gonzales told him, "We have a constant stream of runners traveling between this stronghold and Havana. The Spanish call them spies and very much enjoy hanging them, but they catch very few. We shall take your dispatches to our friends in Havana, and they will see that they make their way to New York."

Davis raised his eyebrows. "Why don't you just cable them?"

Gomez shook his head. "Who is going to go into the cable office with material which clearly came from the Free Army? And even if you were in Havana and could cable your dispatches, the Spanish would censor your reporting. But when you are with the Free Army, your stories will be smuggled out with the greatest of skill just as you write them. We are very hospitable, no?"

"I take it," I broke in, "that you have quite an extensive smuggling operation?"

The heavy woman came up behind Gomez and handed him a chicken leg. The general set aside his cigar and commenced to gnaw on the poultry.

"It is sufficient, Señor Artista," he said. "It is not an easy thing to avoid the patrol boats, as Jorge tells me you are already aware. But we do it."

Gomez stopped to belch contentedly.

"Supplies from outside Cuba," he went on, "are our lifeline, and it takes money to pay smugglers. So we raise the money in Nueva York and pay the smugglers to bring it in. Then we pay other smugglers to take it out again and buy supplies, which they smuggle in, for which they are paid. It is a complicated arrangement."

"Who are the smugglers?" Davis asked. "Where do you get them?"

"American seamen, mostly," said Cosio, who had joined us by the fire. "You Americans are the most expensive, but you are also the most efficient. Your William McDonald, the *capitán* of the sailing freighter *Seneca*, he is very good. He has never even come close to being caught. But he costs much money."

"Perhaps," Gomez said through a mouthful of chicken, "when you go to Havana you could speak to Capitán McDonald. He might listen to you about his prices. You can see how poor we are."

Davis nodded. "When I get to Havana. But, frankly, I hope to stay here awhile—to report on the actual fighting."

Gomez swallowed. "Very well. You may stay. But you must not

write in your newspaper that the American sailors are smuggling for us. The Spanish consul in Washington will read it, and then we will have no more American seamen."

"Don't worry, General," I assured him. "The last thing we want is to have our line to New York cut off. We have to have a way to get our stories and artwork out. When does your next runner leave?"

"When do you want him to leave?" Gomez asked.

"In the morning?" Davis asked hopefully.

"It is done, then," the general assured us, tossing aside the naked chicken bone and pouring both our glasses full of the harsh, brown rum. "Drink," he ordered. "The night is often cold here."

I took my cup and downed another healthy slug of the stuff. As I swallowed, my eyes caught a shadow on the far side of the fire, and I glanced up. There, the firelight flickering over her face, was a woman. I guessed her to be in her early twenties. Her hair was long and black and heavily curled, hanging down her neck in an inky cascade. Her lips were full with the generosity of Africa and painted a deep, ruby red that shone brightly against her olive skin. Her eyes, I noted, were slanted in almost an Oriental cast. And her body, Bierce—she was as lush as the Cuban jungle.

This was a stunningly lovely woman with an earthy beauty that almost made me squirm as I sat on the cold mountain soil. She peered at me over the flames for a moment, then rattled off something to Gomez in Spanish too rapid for me to capture. Gomez nodded to her.

"This is Delores," he said. I nodded formally to the woman, who smiled slightly. "She would like to dance for the famous *artista* from Neuva York."

I was somewhat taken aback. I said, "I'm most flattered, General."

Gomez shrugged. "Who can understand the minds of women?"

"Indeed," Davis added, eliciting from me a most annoyed glare.

I was about to respond, but then the villainous-looking guitarist was next to me, his fingers flying nimbly over the strings of his instrument.

I'd seen Spanish-style dancing before—in Arizona when I traveled with the cavalry and even in a club in New York, where we have a bit of everything. But I'd never seen anything precisely like the dance Delores performed that night in a canyon high in the mountains of inland Cuba.

She danced barefoot, so the stomping, clicking heels of the traditional Spanish dance were missing. In their place, she substituted a savage, sullen, swaying motion of her hips and torso that melded the haughty Spanish dance with the sultry heat of the tropics. Her dance combined the delicate grace of the Orient with the heat of the Congo—

the quick, structured steps of flamenco with the free, animal passions of the Caribbean.

As the guitar strummed out its proud chords, I watched with eyes that surely were the size of dinner plates. I found my head spinning from the rum and the night air and my general exhaustion. And from the sensuous, arousing undulations of this spectacular woman.

The dance lasted only a few moments. Delores never took her eyes from me. When it ended in a flurry of swirling skirts and triumphant rhythms from the guitar, I found myself still mesmerized. I was unable to move as I continued to gaze at her. Her face was a dark, beautiful mask against the blackness of the night sky. The rest of them broke into appreciative applause while I sat motionless, still amazed. Then, coming to my senses at last, I managed a few halfhearted claps. It hardly seemed enough.

She favored me with a slow, appealing smile and then a curtsy. Then she was gone, into the darkness. I shook my clouded head vigorously and continued to gaze dumbly at the spot where she'd vanished. There was nothing now but blackness beyond the fire. I turned to Davis.

"Have you ever seen anything like that?" I whispered.

And, for once, the patented Davis cynicism was absent. "No," he told me gravely, "never."

We sat about the fire consuming rum well into the night. Finally, Cosio rose and staggered off to his *hohio*. Gonzales was next, departing like a ghost into the night. Gomez opened another jug and poured cup after cup. When Davis initiated a spirited effort to teach the commander of the Free Army of Cuba "The Whiffenpoof Song," I made my way unsteadily to my feet.

"Where do I sleep, General?" I inquired with a distinct slur to my voice.

Gomez motioned absently to a nearby row of stolen Spanish tents. "Take any one. Be careful, though, Señor Artista, if you select one that is occupied, one of my fighters might slice open your throat."

As I staggered off toward the tents, the general's injunction struck me as sound advice. I timidly stuck my head into one tent to be greeted by a ripe Spanish curse involving my mother, who surely would have been shocked to hear it. I prudently moved on. A mighty roar of snoring issued from the next tent, so I didn't try that one. The third I lurched by completely and decided it wasn't worth the effort to struggle back. In my state, turning completely about would have presented serious difficulties.

At the fourth tent, I peered inside, seeing only blackness. I pondered the wisdom of entering, considering the possibility that I might end up treading on a machete-wielding occupant. What if I coughed politely, first? I did, then waited.

"So," a woman's voice said, "it is you."

My mind was working slowly, so I followed the voice with no real thought. As I ducked unsteadily into the tent, the interior was bathed in light. Delores had lit a candle.

She was lying on the ground, wrapped in a maroon blanket of woven goat hair. I stared uncomprehendingly at her. Immediately, my head began to spin. I dropped unceremoniously to my buttocks in the dirt. She sat up, holding the blanket close to her chin.

"How did you find me?" she asked.

"By accident, I guess. I can leave, if you prefer."

She smiled at me—a dazzling smile, Bierce, even if I'd been sober.

"Do you want to leave?" she inquired.

I told her honestly, "I'm not certain I'm capable of getting back up, if you want the truth. But I'll try to leave if you want me to."

My eyes fixed on her face. The light from the candle bounced off all its captivating angles and hollows.

"No," she told me. "You may stay."

Then she leaned over, blew out the candle, Bierce, and reached for me in the darkness.

ELEVEN

"Why me?" I asked her the following day as we sat atop the mountain's crest.

Delores wore a dark shawl of home-woven cloth against the wind blowing ceaselessly across the summit. Her hair, which had flown free and wild the night before, was drawn back into a severe bun. She gazed out across the majestic expanse of La Sierra de Trinidad, at the taller mountain tops encased in clouds, at the immense vault of the sky.

"Perhaps because you are different," she said at last. "You are so large and so fair. Your eyes are not hard, like those of my *compañeros.*"

"Not hard?" I asked, baffled.

"I can tell from your eyes," she said. "You have not killed, have you?"

I shook my head.

"I could tell also by your eyes that you see the world in ways different than other men. You see it new and fresh each day, like a child."

I wasn't sure what to make of that. Yes, I do see the world differently. That's why I can reproduce it in paint. But like a child, indeed. I told her, "I haven't been a child in some time. I'm at least ten years your senior, I'd venture."

"I am sixteen," she told me.

I was astounded, Bierce. It wasn't bad enough that I'd drunk too much and committed adultery. That had happened before. Missie has never asked me, but she's not a foolish woman. She knows that I'm far from the perfect husband. My only excuse this time was that we were in a time and place of war, when passions are more intense, and I'd been openly lured.

But a child of sixteen?

She saw the amazement on my face, and she smiled. "We grow old quickly in Cuba, Señor Artista. No matter how old you may be, I am older. Believe me when I tell you this."

I took her small hand and clutched it gently. I told her honestly, "You fascinate me."

She told me, "You are easily fascinated."

"I mean it. Your hair, your eyes. You're a genuine beauty, Delores. You look—I don't know—almost Oriental."

"I am, in part. My mother's mother was Chinese."

"I didn't realize there were Chinese in Cuba."

She laughed. "There is everything in Cuba. I know little of the world, but Profesor Cosio is a learned man, and he can tell you of our people and our history."

"It's your history I'm concerned with," I told her.

"My history is unremarkable. The camp is full of women who could tell the same story."

"Tell me yours anyway," I pressed. "Why aren't you in your parents' house, breaking the hearts of striplings? How did you end up living on a mountaintop with five hundred armed men?"

Delores looked down on the camp far below us. It buzzed with activity—wandering chickens and goats and men and women lying in the sun or chatting. Except for the military-style tents studding the canyon floor, this could have been any mountain village.

As she gazed down silently, I studied her. In the light of day, armed with the information she'd just given me, I could see how young she was. I committed her features to memory, Bierce. One day I'll call up that image from the inner recesses of my mind and paint her as she looked that morning—a beautiful, exotic child-woman with the mountain sunlight splashing over her. I would have done it already, but Missie might recognize the image for what it is, and that's a problem I would rather not confront until I'm fully prepared.

Finally, she said, "Have you ever heard of Elia?"

I shook my head.

"It is a small city to the east. I lived in a village called la Mira not too far from Elia, this place of which you have never heard. My mother died at my birth of the childbirth fever. My father was a blacksmith. My brother was his apprentice."

She paused. I prodded, "Go on."

"The Insurrecto was quite strong in the east at that time," she said, her eyes ranging blankly over the mountains. She might have been talking to herself. Her manner was almost trancelike. "Many young men would leave the villages from time to time to join the rebels. Then they would come home again to tend to their shops and fields."

"An irregular army," I said. "That's what our army was like during the American Revolution."

"The Spanish could never find the rebels because those in the Insurrecto were home one day and at war the next. So what the Spanish would do when they found a known rebel hiding in a village was to burn that village to the ground. We were forbidden to offer shelter to our fathers and sons and brothers. Of course, we ignored such an impossible order. So, one day the Spanish came to la Mira. They were looking for a rebel soldier who had been recognized in an attack on a plantation. He was my brother, and they found him."

"What did they do to him?" I asked.

"They dragged him from the blacksmith's shop and beat him about the face with their rifles. They were led by a big sergeant, and he hit my brother in the face several times with a rifle butt. When my father tried to stop them, he was shot dead. Then the soldiers burned the village, and the Spanish soldiers killed many men and raped all the women who were not too young or too old."

I said nothing. I didn't want to ask the question. I didn't need to.

She met my gaze evenly. "There were twenty-one soldiers in that party. I counted them as they climbed upon me."

Her gaze was firm, and I shuddered at its cold hatred. I asked, "When was this?"

"When I was twelve," she told me.

"Then what?" I got out in no more than a rasp. My throat was very dry.

"They thought they had killed my brother with their gun butts, but he was very strong, and he survived. When he could travel, we came together into the mountains to find the Free Army. We have been here ever since."

"Where's your brother?" I asked.

"He guards the trail," she told me. "He is known as Julio Un Ojo."

I was sickened by what I'd heard. These were the stories Davis should have been writing—the agony of the Cuban people under occupation. I made a mental note to ask him to speak to Delores, although I suspected she would tell him none of what she'd just told me. After only one night together, she and I enjoyed a relationship of some intimacy.

I asked her, "How have you lived in this place, Delores? What have you done to survive?"

She said, "I have lived as every women lives in the midst of such an army. I found a man to care for me."

A disturbing thought crossed my mind at that news. I immediately asked, "And where's that man at this precise moment?"

"He is dead," she said, and I felt a surge of relief. "His name was Ernesto. He died on the journey that brought you to these mountains."

I told her, "I remember Ernesto. He was a brave man."

"He was a monster," she said simply. "Had he not been a monster, he would not have survived so long." Her eyes met mine and locked onto them. I was struck by the naked pride in her voice when she said, "Ernesto fought the Spanish every day for two years before they managed to kill him."

I asked her, "Did you love him?"

"He did not beat me," she replied.

"Did you love him?" I pressed.

She merely shook her head, as Gonzales did when asked what he considered foolish questions. "How little you understand of us," she said.

I leaned back against the rocks. I was silent for a moment, digesting what she'd told me, before I said, "What happens to you with Ernesto dead?"

She shrugged. "Before Ernesto there was Pablo, who left the Insurrecto to return to his family in Villa Clara. Now there is you. When you leave, there will be someone else."

I stared at the rocks. I said to her, "Delores, perhaps I could get you out of here—maybe to Havana or even to America."

She turned to me with an expression of outrage. "This is my place," she told me indignantly. "I am a patriot."

Then I became indignant. With a sudden surge of anger, I said, "You're right. I don't understand you people at all. All you live for is the pleasure of killing or dying for the Insurrecto."

She snapped back, "For us, there is nothing else, Señor Artista."

I rose, preparing to storm back down the mountain, but she reached out a slim, graceful hand and caught my trouser leg. I stopped, and she rose to stand next to me. When she spoke, her voice was gentle.

"And for us," she told me, "for you and me, there is only a heartbeat—a moment. And then you will be gone, and I will be here with the Insurrecto."

I was still angry, and I started to break free, but then she was in my arms, and she was saying, "But while you are here . . ."

We stayed in the mountains nearly a month. Davis spent his days interviewing rebel soldiers, and I spent mine creating sketches. Several times during that period, we accompanied raiding parties to the lowlands to ambush small bands of Spanish soldiers and to engage in the Free Army's favorite recreation—trying to derail the trains that hurtled at breakneck speeds through the cane fields. The trains were always heavily guarded, but the Free Army made life miserable for the engineers. The poor fellows never knew when a storm of bullets from a cane field might come whistling into the cab of the locomotive.

At night, I was with Delores. We didn't fool ourselves. We weren't in love, certainly. The differences in age and background were far too profound. I couldn't imagine more than a temporary stay on that detestable mountaintop, and there could be no life for Delores in New York even if I'd been inclined to leave Missie—which, of course, I was not. Ours hasn't been a perfect marriage, Bierce—largely my fault, I suppose—but it has grown into a vast common ground of shared experience. If Missie doesn't exactly admire every facet of my character, she understands them and finds it all a tolerable package. No other woman of value, I fear, could bear me for a lifetime. It would be nice if I possessed the ability to alter my temperament, but if I managed it I probably couldn't paint.

And Delores, too, viewed me as only a temporary diversion. More than a meal ticket, perhaps, but not much more. I sometimes had the feeling that she considered herself my emotional elder. That attitude had its annoying aspects.

I told the girl, "I've dined with governors and presidents. I've ducked arrows from Sioux and Apache. I've been shot at. In just the past few weeks, I've had a chap try to skewer me with a sword. I've eaten rats and made love to an exotic, beautiful woman on a mile-high mountaintop during a Latin American revolution. I am, by definition, a man of the world. Don't behave as though you're the worldly woman and I'm but a boy."

She only laughed, a pleasant tinkling sound, and there was no cruelty in her voice when she said, "You will be forever naive, Señor Artista, and it becomes you. A man of the world is cynical and jaded and not very appealing except to the most innocent of women. And, most of all, I am not that."

I'd become aware by that point that the Insurrecto was little more than a nuisance to the Spanish. The Free Army was only moderately effective as a fighting force, since it was so badly outnumbered and outgunned. And it held no ground of strategic value. It was able to hold the mountains only because the Spanish didn't care about them. The Spanish had firm control of the cities and the cane fields, which is all they wanted from Cuba. I couldn't see how the Free Army could ever hope to dislodge them. One night, over a meal with Davis, Gomez, Gonzales, and Cosio, I expressed those misgivings.

"General," I asked, "precisely how long have you been on this mountaintop?"

Gomez put down the chicken bone he'd been gnawing on and

[93]

counted on his greasy fingers. *"Uno, dos . . ."* three years." He picked up the leg and resumed eating.

"Isn't that a rather long time?" I asked him.

Gonzales looked up, his eyes flashing as he began to catch the drift of my questions. He snapped, "A revolution does not happen in a day, Señor Artista."

I merely nodded. Gonzales was prickly on the topic of the Free Army's effectiveness. I'd come to realize that his primary motivation for opposing my presence here—and Davis's, of course—was his mortal fear that we'd put something into the *New York Journal* that would denigrate the rebel forces and harm their fund-raising efforts. Davis noted Gonzales's defensiveness.

"Still," the reporter said, "three years . . ."

"We need more guns." Gomez shrugged. "Tell the fine Señor Hearst that."

"If we had proper arms," Gonzales broke in curtly, "we could drive the Spanish into the sea. If we had the sort of support in the United States that we deserve . . ."

"There are those in America," Davis observed, "who believe we should avoid foreign entanglements—that this is your war, not ours."

"The cause of justice belongs to everyone," Gonzales hissed. It was only then that we realized the true depth of his anger with the line of questioning. Luckily, the presence of the others prevented further trouble. Gonzales dropped his forkful of food on his metal plate and stood up, glaring at us. "Excuse me, jefe," he told Gomez, and disappeared into the night of the camp.

Gomez watched him go. Then he turned to us. "I fear you have offended Jorge."

"I find it difficult not to offend Jorge," Davis said. "He's a touchy man."

"He is," Gomez agreed. "Revolutionaries are often like Jorge, very serious. They do not laugh except in mockery."

"You seem far better natured, General," I pointed out.

Gomez shrugged. "Perhaps that is why I am the general and Jorge is the colonel. Yet, he is most valuable. Without him, Palma would be lost."

He was speaking, Bierce, of Tomas Estrada Palma, the silver-haired former schoolteacher who headed the Insurrecto's fund-raising efforts in New York. Davis knew the chap quite well. Palma lived humbly on Bleecker Street and used the office of Horatio Rubens, a lawyer sympathetic to the rebel cause, as the center of his activities.

"Palma," Gomez went on, "is a great talker—a diplomat much more valuable than the other we sent to Washington as our revolutionary chargé d'affaires. But Gonzalo de Quesada knows of military matters, of which Palma knows nothing. And it is in these matters that Palma relies on Jorge when questions are asked about the effectiveness of our army."

"What does Jorge say when he's asked about the army?" Davis asked casually.

A twinkle appeared in Gomez's eye, then he laughed. "Jorge lies, of course. But he lies very convincingly. Were he not so convincing, we would have far less weaponry than we have today."

The lies, I'd come to realize, were nothing less than stupendous in scope. Until our arrival with the Free Army, it had been nearly impossible for Americans to get news directly from Cuba. Everything written by English-speaking journalists had been rigidly censored by the Spanish. James Creelman of Pulitzer's *World* had been rudely ejected from the country based only on a rather innocuous story or two he'd written from Havana. He'd never even been permitted to enter the field with the Spanish. Operating without the contacts The Chief had built up with the politicians of the Insurrecto, the Pulitzer reporter had no means to reach rebel forces either.

As a result, the New York newspapers were filled with what I now knew had been utterly fraudulent reports of rebel victories and Spanish atrocities—all supplied from Palma's office on Broadway. Before I'd signed on with The Chief, I'd personally read several stories about Free Army forces supposedly capturing major cities, including Havana, and then having beaten "strategic retreats." Having seen what I'd seen, I now knew those stories to have been completely false. Gomez and his men, quite clearly, had never gotten within a hundred miles of Havana.

"I take it, then," I said, "that it was Jorge who concocted the story about the strip search."

Gomez burst out laughing, which confirmed my suspicions.

You must recall the incident, Bierce. The story had appeared exclusively in The Chief's *Journal* before being picked up by the Associated Press and transmitted across the nation, creating one hell of a stir.

It had related the tale of three pretty Cuban girls who'd boarded a ship in Havana Harbor bound for New York. Just before the ship sailed, the story went, Spanish soldiers had swarmed on the boat and rudely searched the women for rebel dispatches. All this supposedly took place over the vehement objections of the American captain of the vessel, the *Olivette*. The women had supposedly been left stark naked on the deck of the ship, and no rebel dispatches had been found.

The *Journal*'s story had been accompanied by an imaginative drawing rather startlingly explicit for a newspaper. The public and the

Congress had been outraged until the *World*, flogged into action by Pulitzer's wrath at having been beaten on the story, checked the facts of the incident and set the record straight.

The young women, it turned out, had been searched in quite proper fashion by a matron in a closed cabin. The *World*'s story had run under a headline something like, *"The Unclothed Women Searched by Men Was an Invention of a New York Newspaper."* I recall the stir it all caused. I now knew whose fault that lie was.

"So," Gomez laughed, "Jorge exaggerated a bit. But he did so with much elegance."

Davis said, "Gonzales told us he was a Spanish officer. Is that true?"

Gomez nodded, his expression suddenly solemn.

"How did he come to fight for the Free Army?" I inquired.

Gomez turned to Cosio. "You tell the story, *Profesor*."

Cosio said, "Jorge is Cuban by birth, from a very fine family. He was the second son, and his older brother was to inherit. So Jorge joined the army. It is not uncommon among us for the second son to become a soldier or a priest. There is little difference between them, after all. Jorge was sent to Madrid to train. There he discovered that the Spanish nobility viewed him—viewed all Cubans, in fact—as peasants and barbarians. The Spanish nobles were haughty. Jorge was deeply offended by their behavior."

I said, "I can see where he would be the sort of man to view a snub with disfavor."

"When he returned home for duty," Cosio went on, "the Insurrecto had begun again. After it had run for some years, Jorge was captured by a Free Army unit—one of a force led by General Antonio Maceo, who commanded the Insurrecto forces in the eastern portion of Cuba until he was killed last year. They did not kill Jorge. They held him for a ransom of guns."

"What happened then?" Davis asked.

"Jorge escaped," Gomez broke in. "But when he got back to his unit, he discovered that the Spanish had decided that he must have joined our army willingly. They had imprisoned his family as accomplices, and the Crown had confiscated the family lands."

"Why did they conclude that he'd defected?" Davis demanded. "He was one of them."

"This is the point, señor," Gomez told Davis. "He was not really one of them. Jorge is a Cuban, not a Spaniard. So they thought the worst of him."

"And then?" I asked.

"Then he escaped from them and joined us," Gomez said. "And a good thing, too. Jorge is a man most dangerous."

"I've seen that," Davis said grimly. He turned to Cosio. "And you, Professor? How did you end up with the Insurrecto?"

"I taught at the University of Camagüey," Cosio explained. "I spoke against the monarchy. I was jailed. When they let me out, I spoke more boldly. Then they accused me of trying to form a regiment for the Free Army. They arrested me and send me to the Isle of Pines."

"Were you guilty?" I asked. "Were you trying to form a Free Army regiment?"

Cosio blinked in puzzlement. "Of course."

Gomez leaned over and filled my cup and Davis's with that dark rum he so favored. "Drink," he advised. "It will keep away the night's chill."

He took some of his own advice while I eyed him carefully. With Gonzales no longer present, it seemed an opportune moment to ask directly the question at which Davis and I'd been hinting.

I said, "General, how do you expect to win this revolution if you're forever hiding up here in these mountains?"

Gomez, his cup to his lips, launched immediately into a coughing fit. He glared at me, his eyes bulging, as he cleared his windpipe and wiped the excess rum off his bristly chin.

"We are not hiding," the general told me indignantly. "We go out to fight all the time."

"You go out to burn cane fields," Davis pointed out.

"This is fighting," Gomez argued. "The Spanish guard the cane fields."

"But you haven't chased them away," I pressed. "You have no artillery, relatively few modern rifles, little in the way of explosives—"

"The Americans must help," Gomez broke in.

"And if America doesn't help?" Davis demanded.

This time it was the scholarly Cosio who responded. He said quietly, "For twenty-five years, the Cuban people have fought against Spanish rule. So, if the Americans do not help, we will fight for another twenty-five years—or another one hundred, if necessary. Sooner or later, the Spanish will lose heart and go home. The mothers of Barcelona and Castile will tire of losing their sons in a strange land so far across the sea. In time, the Spanish politicians will have no choice but to heed the cries of their people and put an end to this. And when that happens, as it must, we will have won. All we have to do between then and now is to avoid losing."

Davis nodded. "Perhaps. Meanwhile, what'll you do if they just drag their weapons up these mountains and blast you out?"

Gomez leaned forward, the fire glinting off his black eyes. His voice was low, and I must confess to having been struck by the sheer strength of purpose it contained.

He said, "They have come many times. And when they do, we fade into the mountains and regroup and make them pay in blood as they go back down to their soft and comfortable barracks in the cities. They may attack us again, any day. And we will evade them, worry them, kill them in small groups. And someday God will give us victory."

Gomez then crossed himself, sat back, and sipped his rum. "God would find this chore less troublesome, however," he added, "if the Americans would come in and fight alongside us. Put that in your newspaper, Señor Periodista."

AMBROSE BIERCE
MEXICO, 1914

The water Small Maria has brought to bathe the sweat from my fading body is warm and oily. It possesses an odor most foul. While I shall be clean for the arrival of death's baby carriage, the hearse, I shall also be slightly pungent.

She bids me drink some of the stuff, but I demur. I have always found water palatable only when suffering intolerably from thirst, for which it is undeniably a medicine. Upon nothing, however, has mankind's great and diligent ingenuity been brought to bear as upon the invention of substitutes for water.

"You must drink, Señor Bierce," my angel-whore tells me. "You are sweating your body dry. I pray for you, señor."

"My thanks, child," I respond, "that you would plead for the laws of the universe to be annulled on behalf of a petitioner so confessedly unworthy."

But I do not drink.

Maria frowns and pulls back the single light blanket that shrouds my bony frame. She wipes my gray-thatched nakedness with a wet rag. My heart thumps with no less labor, but the moisture of the rag induces relief from the heat. I suspect I might survive another day or two—another pair of disappointments to be accommodated. Small Maria scrubs at me with zeal, that nervous disorder so afflicting the young and inexperienced.

"Speak to me, señor," she orders, for such have her requests become. "Speak to me of your friend and of the Insurrecto. You must continue to talk."

How can any man so helpless refuse the entreaty of a woman whose strong young hands are separated from his most vulnerable parts by only a thin, damp rag? Immediately, I say:

"Remington was on his mountaintop, Small Maria—secure in the arms of his own waiflike angel—while a war of sorts erupted sporadically in the cane fields below. At about that same time, one of the field marshals of the vastly more vicious war raging in New York was confronting his most beleaguered minion.

"Pulitzer sat in the darkness and ordered, 'What's in it, Gardener?'

"Our friend Gardener unfolded the copy of The Chief's *Journal* that he had brought with him to Pulitzer's town house. He could hardly see the page. Pulitzer, in robe and slippers in midafternoon, kept the thick drapes to his study shut tightly against the intrusion of East Fifty-fifth Street. Only the dimmest hint of sun entered through a narrow crack in the drapes, since Pulitzer found light of no particular use. Unlike his master, Gardener required it, but he was afraid to open the publisher's drapes.

" 'I'm waiting, Gardener,' Pulitzer said impatiently.

"Gardener solved this problem by the expedient of striking a match and holding it over the newspaper. He said shakily, 'Well, sir, the front page contains a pen-and-ink drawing of a dashing young man and a middle-aged soldier in a somewhat ragged uniform. The younger man is handing the soldier a saber.'

" 'The headline,' Pulitzer snapped. 'Read me the headline.'

" '*Rebel Hero Accepts Sword of Liberty from Journal Reporter.* The story is by this fellow, Davis. It goes like this—'

" 'Never mind. I'll have it read to me later. What were today's circulation figures?'

"Gardener sighed. 'The *Journal* was up thirty-six thousand, Mr. Pulitzer.'

"The publisher said nothing. He was merely awaiting the drop of the other shoe.

" 'And we were down thirty-two,' Gardener blurted out.

"Pulitzer began to quiver. Even in the semidarkness, Gardener could see the man shake. Then the match burned down to Gardener's fingertips. He hurriedly dropped it, stamped it out, and thrust his stung fingers into his mouth. He could see nothing again, but he could most assuredly hear Pulitzer. The publisher's voice was an anguished howl.

" 'Hearst has a reporter and an artist with the goddamned rebel army!' he screeched. 'Where's our reporter and our artist with the rebel army, Gardener? Where?'

" 'We sent a man for a visa, sir,' Gardener explained hurriedly to the vibrating presence in the darkness across the desk, 'but the Spanish said no.'

" 'A visa?' screamed the voice. 'A visa? This, O Lord, is the tribulation you visit upon me, that my efforts be thwarted for want of a visa? For want of an editor with brains sufficient to get a man into

Cuba without a visa? Did Hearst's men have visas, Gardener? Did that stop Hearst?'

"Poor Gardener was totally unnerved. Such a scene was disturbing enough in the publisher's office in the *World* building—that gold-domed skyscraper Pulitzer was so fond of and visited, thank God, so rarely. The publisher's profane rages were difficult enough to endure amid the palatial luxury of Pulitzer's yacht, the *Liberty*. But here, in the near-stygian darkness of the great man's home, Gardener felt caught up in a nightmare.

" 'Mr. Pulitzer,' he said, his own voice rising in his panic, 'it's quite impossible to get into Cuba without the permission of the Spanish government.'

" 'It wasn't impossible for Hearst,' Pulitzer bellowed. 'That young pup from California got his men in. Why can't we get our men in? Who was it you sent for a visa?'

" 'Creelman, sir. He was there before.'

" 'Bad choice,' Pulitzer snapped, and Gardener realized that the hysteria had left the press baron's voice. It had been replaced by the cold, hard tone of reason that signaled that Pulitzer was ready to do business. Gardener relaxed, but only slightly, and a torrent of sweat ran down his sides from his armpits. He was very much aware that the madman could return in a flash—and probably would.

" 'Creelman let them throw him out in the first place,' Pulitzer pointed out. 'Why didn't you send Peatam down there to bully the Spaniards into giving him a visa? The man is a remarkable bully, is he not?'

"It was, Gardener reflected, an apt description of Peatam.

" 'Peatam,' the editor explained, 'is in jail, sir. He struck a police captain who refused to cooperate on that love triangle story.'

" 'Well, that's what I'm talking about,' Pulitzer snarled impatiently, as though dealing with a dim-witted child. 'Peatam is our man. He's the sort who'll stop at nothing. Get him out.'

"*Get him out!* Gardener was stupefied. Did Pulitzer have any appreciation of what would be involved in springing from jail a reporter who'd broken the jaw of a New York City police captain? Better Peatam had punched the mayor.

" 'Sir,' Gardener began, 'getting Peatam out might present some problems. You see, this lunatic who heads up the police board, this Roosevelt fellow, he doesn't look kindly on people punching police captains—'

" 'I don't care what Roosevelt likes or dislikes,' came the shriek from the darkness. 'You get Peatam into Cuba. Do it! *Do it, Gardener!*'

"Over the screams, Gardener heard a heavy, crashing, thumping sound. It came once, twice, three times. He then realized what it was. Pulitzer had drawn himself to his full six feet, two inches in the darkness and was pounding a heavy fist on the desk as he bellowed his orders. The madman was back. Gardener did the only thing possible.

" 'Yes, sir,' he whimpered.

TWELVE

Frederic Remington
Cuba, 1897

It wasn't until somewhat later, Bierce, after extensive conversations with some of the men who'd participated in the operation, that Davis and I were able to reconstruct how it had taken place.

Julio Un Ojo, the embittered brother of my only slightly less embittered mistress, heard the horses. He would have recognized the hoofbeats of only a few animals, and he might naturally have concluded that a rich landowner—or perhaps a careless contingent of Spanish cavalry—was missing some horseflesh.

Julio nonetheless slid down from his boulder, reached into the shrubbery, fastened a bit of blue cloth to the leg of one of his gurgling, cooing pigeons, and set it free. Then he clambered back up the rock to his vantage point on its crown.

Where Sergeant Ramos killed him.

Ramos was the lead scout for the attacking Spanish force. Ranging far ahead of the main party, he'd taken one look at the narrow canyon entrance, such a perfect spot for an ambush, and his blood had frozen. It had been only with some difficulty that Ramos had convinced his superiors to halt the advance until he could explore the canyon that had so disturbed him.

He'd crawled along the canyon's lip like a squirrel. Ramos was a small, wiry man of no more than twenty-five. He reminded me considerably of Ernesto. I never cease to marvel, Ambrose, at the extent to which deadly enemies so often resemble one another.

Ramos was a knife fighter from the streets of Barcelona, a veteran of six bloody years in Cuba. He knew how troublesome the Free Army could be in guerrilla engagements, so he moved with great care. In late afternoon, he spotted Julio atop his rock. Julio had not been looking up. What would have been the point of that? The rim of the canyon was so narrow that no force of any size could move along it. Julio was, instead, gazing down on the canyon floor. Ramos pondered only briefly the wisdom of shooting him at that moment. He decided to pass him by and scout on farther ahead.

The Spaniard found the Free Army's encampment at dusk, as the fires were being started up. From his hiding place on the canyon's rim, he noted the tents, the huts, the flocks of goats and chickens and concluded that this was a more or less permanent headquarters for the rebel forces. He concluded also, from the topography of the site, that this wasn't a bad place for such a facility. An infantry force could squeeze through the canyon entrance only with difficulty, and a cavalry charge would have been out of the question. He also knew, however, that with the equipment carried by the force for which he scouted, this would be like shooting fish in a barrel.

After nightfall, Ramos carefully backtracked, bypassing Julio. Near dawn, the sergeant found his main party and reported what he'd seen. His boss, a Captain Alvarez, was pleased with his report.

"There is no way out for them?" he asked.

Ramos only shrugged. "They must climb up and out over the rim of the canyon. They cannot take much in the way of food or arms. Even if we do not kill them all, we can scatter them all through La Sierra de Trinidad."

The Spanish force was on the march within the hour, just as the sun rose. They were preceded by Ramos, who ranged far ahead on foot, responsible for silencing sentries. He was followed most closely by a small contingent of cavalry. The main force, of necessity, moved much more slowly behind.

Ramos again climbed the outside of the canyon and scampered along the edge of the rim. When he spotted Julio, he crawled on his stomach for an acceptable rifle shot. He didn't want to miss.

He was only a short distance from Julio's rock when he heard the hoofbeats outside the canyon entrance. Ramos cursed silently. The cavalry were moving too quickly and far too carelessly. He saw Julio cup his ear toward the sound and then slide off his rock and down its far side. When Julio did that, Ramos was down the side of the canyon in a flash, running toward the rock with his rifle ready. At point-blank range, he dropped to one knee and sighted. In only a few seconds, he saw Julio's head as the sentry climbed back atop his vantage point. Ramos squeezed off his shot.

He told me later that the bullet blew off the top of Julio's head in an explosion of red and gray fragments. Julio hit the ground like a sack of sugar, sending up a cloud of dust. Ramos sprinted to the still figure and drove his bayonet into the man's back, just to be sure. He pulled out the bayonet, stuck a foot under the corpse, and rolled his victim over. He gazed down on Julio's ruined face. His bullet, Ramos said, had done this poor man a great favor.

As Ramos stood over his prize, three Spanish cavalry troopers came through the entrance in single file. He was almost aghast at their stupidity. Had Julio been alive, he could have picked them off with indolent ease. Spanish cavalrymen were like that, Ramos told me later—foolhardy to the point of lunacy. Their officers were mainly aristocrats. He despised them.

"Where are the rest?" the scout demanded of the horsemen.

"No more than twenty minutes behind," one of the troopers told him. "And the main party is moving with more speed than one would think possible."

"Tell Alvarez," Ramos said, "that the main encampment is close enough to this spot that we can begin the bombardment from just outside the canyon."

The trooper nodded. "You are the scout."

We were in the camp, drinking coffee and chatting.

Delores, sitting in the morning sunlight, said to Cosio, "*Profesor*, tell the *artista* about the Chinese."

Cosio glanced my way. "How is it," he inquired, "that you wish to know so much about us? Is it because we are such an interesting people?"

I squeezed Delores's hand. "I find this one interesting. Tell me why she looks as she does—why there's so much of the Oriental in her face?"

The old man sipped his strong coffee. He was preparing for a lecture, I could see. He loved to teach, and there was so little opportunity for that here.

"In the beginning," he told me, "there were only Indians in Cuba. They had come, we suppose, from the mainland of South America, since they were similar in many ways to the Indian peoples there. The Guanahatabey lived in the far west of our island, and the Ciboney spread throughout Cuba. They lived mostly, however, in the islands to the south of the big island. There were many Ciboney on the Isle of Pines, with which I have a nodding acquaintance."

I was impressed at the old man's ability to make jokes about his imprisonment. I doubted I would have the same capacity.

"Eventually," the old man went on, "these tribes were overcome by the Taino, who came from God knows where and eventually came to dominate not only Cuba but the rest of the Greater Antilles as well. And the Bahamas also. When Cristóbal Colón claimed Cuba for Spain, the Taino dominated the Indian population."

"But the Chinese?" I pressed.

"I am coming to that," Cosio scolded. "You *norteamericanos* are always in such a great rush."

"Not in all matters," Delores giggled.

I was embarrassed. I urged the professor, "Ignore her, please. Go on."

Cosio, a man of some dignity, pretended he hadn't heard her remark. He said, "When the Spanish came, there were perhaps one hundred and fifty thousand Indians in Cuba. Fifty years later, there were fewer than five thousand. They died in the gold mines, in the fields, as slaves and, most especially, of European diseases—smallpox and venereal disease in particular. Then came the Africans."

"The Chinese, Professor?" I said, almost pleading.

Cosio held up a disapproving hand. "Patience, Señor Artista. True knowledge, like true liberty, does not come in an eyeblink."

I sighed wearily, surrendering.

Cosio said, "The Africans were mostly from the Yoruba and Bantu tribes. All in all, the Spanish brought in eight times as many Africans as there had been Indians before the Spanish invasion. They were brought in to work the sugar plantations, and—as you can see from our forces here—have become a substantial part of our population."

"How substantial?" I asked. "And, please, what about the Chinese?"

"The Spanish government has estimated that perhaps fifteen percent of our population is of African descent and that at least that many are part African—mestizos. We are, the Cuban people, a happy blend of Indian and Spanish and African. It is for that reason as much as any other than the Spaniards do not like us."

"Not to mention Chinese," I said, giving it one more try.

The old man's eyes twinkled. "That, too. Fifty years ago, the landowners were desperate, as always, for field hands. They could bring in no more African slaves, and they had killed off all but a few of the Indians, so they brought in nearly one hundred and twenty-five thousand Chinese from Canton as indentured servants."

"And one of these," Delores broke in, "was my grandmother."

"Ah," I said, enlightened at last.

Just as the word passed my lips, we saw the pigeon fluttering in from down the canyon to her roost. Her red, ratlike feet—one adorned with a bit of blue cloth—clutched the wooden bar. The moment she landed she began to preen herself. The rebel lounging closest to the roost leaped immediately to his feet and sprinted for the tent of Gomez. Delores tugged at my hand, and we excused ourselves from the company of Professor Cosio.

She led me toward the general's tent just as he emerged with the golden sword at his hip and his expression solemn. He began a rapid chatter with his aides. Despite my many weeks in the encampment, I still found that Spanish delivered by too many voices at once and with too much speed remained gibberish to me. As Gomez and his officers babbled, I asked Delores to translate.

"The bird with the blue cloth," she explained. "Someone is coming. We must wait for the next bird, the one with the red cloth. If she does not arrive shortly, that means the Spanish are here."

There was, however, little time to wait. It was only moments later that the first shell came whistling into camp. It was high, striking the far wall of the canyon with an ear-splitting roar. It showered considerable dirt and bits of rock down on us.

Instantly, the rebel camp was bedlam. Women screamed and men cursed. For my part, I grabbed Delores and hit the dirt with her. The second shell was better aimed. It landed squarely in the goat flock. I tell you, Bierce, even from the other side of the camp, I could hear the terrified bleats of the poor creatures.

Still holding Delores in the dirt, I turned my head to see Davis sprinting my way. His face was wine red, and he was furious, as though he'd been personally betrayed. He slid into the dirt beside us as another shell struck somewhere in the vicinity.

"Artillery," Davis shouted at me. "How the hell did the Spanish get big guns all the way up into these mountains?"

I had no sensible response. I said only, "It must have meant a great deal to them."

Around us, the rebel camp was in disarray. I was overwhelmed by a sense of mass panic—of hundreds of people running, horses neighing, goats bawling in terror. The sudden, frenzied movement of so many living things had churned up the dust of the canyon floor in a matter of seconds, with visibility extending barely a few feet.

I kept a tight grip on Delores as I said to Davis, "What now?"

As the words passed my lips, two more shells came whistling squarely into the middle of the encampment. Clearly, the Spaniards had spotters on the canyon rim signaling the range. Their accuracy was improving, and the screaming of the animals was suddenly drowned out by the screaming of human beings. Through the dust cloud, I could spy groups of rebels clambering up those canyon walls in a mad attempt to break out of the trap.

"It's a rout," Davis told me, demonstrating his incomparable grasp of the obvious. "There's no way they can stand up to firepower like this."

Then, without warning, he leapt to his feet and grabbed my collar. "Come on," he said. "We've got to get the hell out of here."

I staggered up, pulling Delores with me. I was confused, Bierce. I make no apology for it. Occupying the target zone of an artillery barrage can be a most disorienting experience. Davis was grabbing at me and pointing toward a slight cleft in the canyon wall.

"That's our best bet," he shouted.

At that moment, I lost my grip on Delores. It was no accident. She'd picked that moment to deliberately pull free.

I shouted her name, desperate to keep her with me and to employ whatever meager powers I might have possessed to protect her, but she would have none of it. She backed away, into the swirling clouds of dust.

"Our time is ended," she called out. "Go with God, Frederic."

Then she was gone into the mist. I was bereft, Bierce, and I went staggering after her only to have Davis grab my arm and shout into my face, "She's right, Remington. We've got to get out of this canyon."

I could only nod more or less dumbly, and then we were working our way through the madness of the camp, running along in crouches. In my short stay there, I'd learned every inch of the campground. As the smoke and dust swirled ever thicker, I found I was leading Davis. I made my way toward the cleft with him in tow.

I called out, "Do you think there's any chance the Free Army can hold them off?"

"Not a chance in hell," came the reply. "You heard Gomez. This is strictly a hit-and-run operation. They won't even try."

By this time, the canyon floor was an untidy collection of craters and corpses, some animal and some human. We wove our way around them as we strained for the canyon wall. All the while, shells were whistling in, assailing us with their terrifying noise. Then, as we neared the wall, the smoke cleared in that spot, and I felt Davis's hand on my shoulder.

"Look!" he called out, pointing.

Barely twenty-five yards away, we spied Gonzales sprinting across the canyon floor, rifle in hand, barking rapid orders in Spanish. He stopped and pulled a wounded man to his feet and pushed him rudely toward the canyon wall. As the man staggered off, Gonzales stood erect, surveying the scene with the same careless courage he'd demonstrated on the deck of the *Vamoose*. We were watching as his luck ran out. A shell struck not fifteen yards away. Gonzales went down in a shower of dirt, rocks, shrapnel, and smoke. As the smoke cleared, we could then see Gonzales rolling in the dust, blood pouring liberally from his mouth, nose, and ears.

I immediately shook off Davis's grasp and was off across the canyon floor. I hurdled bodies and dodged craters. Then I was at Gonzales's side, lifting him with remarkable ease. I imagine the excitement had lent me even greater strength than usual. In any event,

I found that I was able to move at almost a full run with that dead weight on my shoulder. At the wall, however, my legs began to fail me. I slipped to the earth behind a sheltering boulder, and Gonzales fell from my shoulder to land with a thump. I was struggling to regain my breath, my heart pounding like a wild thing. It took me a moment to realize that Davis was with me again, and the two of us were bending over the Cuban searching for signs of life.

Gonzales's eyes flickered open. He gazed blankly up at both of us. He recognized Davis first.

"Run, Señor Rooster," he said. "The Spanish infantry will be here soon."

"Run where?" I demanded.

"Over the canyon rim and then down the mountain," he choked out. "You can make your way back through the forest to the coast. Then head west, toward Havana."

For all the annoyance I periodically felt toward Davis, I must admit, Bierce, that the fellow indeed had his moments. He looked down on our sometimes friend and said, "Not without you, Gonzales. Believe it or not, I've grown rather attached to you."

It took both of us to drag Gonzales up the canyon wall. He was coughing blood continually, and I knew from my time with the cavalry in Arizona that that surely indicated a lung wound. Gonzales had taken shrapnel in the torso and was probably bleeding internally. None of this boded well for his long-term health in this climate, but we had no time to consider that. The thing for us to do was to get out of that canyon. The shells were now falling at the rate of one every ten seconds or so. Somewhere, far down the canyon, some Spanish gunnery officer was having a field day. It was a textbook bombardment, and its effects were devastating.

At the top of the canyon wall, I stopped for a moment to gaze back on the scene. Oh, the carnage, Bierce. The sheer bloodiness of it. I was looking for Delores, but I saw no sign of her through the smoke. I had to assume that she'd scampered up and over the canyon wall. I did see Cosio, moving with Gomez and several of the general's other officers, disappearing over the top of the canyon well off to our right. I was glad to see that the general and the old man had evaded harm. Now they had to slip past Spanish lines to safety, but I had no doubt they could manage that. I was certain that Gomez had a personal plan of escape firmly worked out in advance.

The rim of the canyon was no more than a few feet wide. We scrambled over it, felt a moment of unsettling vulnerability as we were silhouetted against the sun, and then we were sliding unceremoniously down the loose dirt of the summit. We scrambled nearly a half mile before we found adequate cover. We could see rebels fading into the boulders and sparse greenery all around us. We followed their lead, moving ever downward, dragging the bleeding Gonzales with us.

By midafternoon, Davis and I were so exhausted that our pace had slowed to a crawl. Drenched in sweat and coated in dirt, we stumbled into a thicket protected by high grass and an outcropping of sharp, gray rocks. We lay there, chests heaving, too weary for speech. After perhaps twenty minutes, I heard an unmistakable and chilling sound—footsteps, and they were coming from only a short distance away. I crawled to my knees, moved warily to the edge of the thicket, and peered through the greenery. A Spanish patrol, heavily armed, was moving down the mountainside. I scuttled back into my hiding place and motioned to Davis to remain silent. I held my breath as we heard the patrol continue past our refuge and move on down the rough mountain trail we'd been following.

I waited a few moments until I was sure they'd gone. I turned to Davis and said, "We can't stay here."

"You're right," Davis replied, uttering words that seldom passed his lips. "The Spanish infantry must have moved into the Free Army camp, cleared it out, and is now combing the mountainside for stragglers."

I turned to pull the bloodied Gonzales to my shoulder once again, but he mustered all his strength to confound my efforts to lift him.

"I can go no farther," he said weakly.

Davis and I exchanged hurried glances. Gonzales was pale, the color of day-old milk. Davis reached down and grabbed the wounded man's wrist.

"You're just a little under the weather, Gonzales," he said with forced cheerfulness. "You're going to be fine when we can get you somewhere where there's some rum."

Between the two of us, we managed to raise the protesting Cuban to Davis's shoulder. We emerged from the thicket, Davis wearily staggering under Gonzales's weight. I led the way down the mountain, into thicker and thicker brush. After a while, I took my shift carrying Gonzales, but I maintained the lead even with my load. Davis was almost done in, but I was getting my second wind. All those years of football and boxing had taught me about second winds. You never know what you have left, Bierce, until you think you've expended everything.

I was edging around the bole of a tree that grew at a sharp angle on the slippery slope when I felt Davis's hand on my shoulder. I turned to face him, and his expression was ghastly.

"You can put him down now," Davis told me, his voice no more than a whisper. "I think he's dead."

I lowered Gonzales off my shoulder and deposited him on the mountainside as gently as I could manage. He was motionless, staring blankly up at the sun. I checked for a pulse. I could find nothing.

"His eyes," Davis rasped out. "I saw the light in them go out just a moment ago."

I gazed down at the dead face of the angry revolutionary, Jorge Gonzales. I said sadly, "He burned very brightly."

Davis was also moved by Gonzales's death. He said, "I was getting so I rather liked him."

I sighed and said brusquely, "None of that does much good now. Come on, we've got to get out of here."

Davis lifted his eyes from the corpse and looked past me. He said quietly, "Too late now."

It took me a moment to grasp the significance of his words. When I spun about, I found myself squarely in the sights of a dozen Spanish army rifles.

There was no point in resisting. The roughest part was climbing back up the mountain we'd just clambered down, but at least this time there was no Gonzales to carry. The Spanish left his corpse where it lay.

It took what seemed like forever to reach the lip of the canyon. It was hours of climbing, at any rate. Once over the rim, we slid down the inner wall at gunpoint and were tightly bound before we were permitted to walk on the level ground. Completely spent, we nonetheless managed to stagger down the canyon, several miles from the devastated site of the Free Army encampment. I saw the corpses of many men I'd come to know.

Finally, just beyond the narrow entrance to what had been the rebel stronghold, we reached a neat, sprawling camp of Spanish soldiers and enormous field pieces. There were hundreds of men and dozens of guns on their mule-drawn caissons. We were marched through the rows of tents and cannon, and I couldn't help but marvel at the contrast between this meticulously maintained campsite and the squalor of the rebel stronghold, with goats and chickens wandering freely about the gaily disorganized company.

At last, we were brought to a tent much larger than the others. Realizing that our journey was at its end, I merely slumped to my knees in the soft dirt. Davis collapsed beside me. We were both encrusted with filth and stank, I'm sure, far worse than the mules.

For a long moment, we could do no more than grovel in the soil, our chests burning and our breath coming in deep, irregular gulps.

Then the flap of the tent opened, and an officer stepped out into the fading afternoon sunlight.

In contrast to the fairly ragged Spanish foot soldiers who'd brought us in, this man was attired in an ornate uniform. A pistol in a gleaming holster hung on his right hip. On his left, a saber hung carelessly in its shining steel scabbard. He was not a particularly tall man. As I observed his bristling gray mustache and salt-and-pepper sideburns, I surmised him to be well into his fifties. The man was compactly built, with a deep chest and broad shoulders. He placed his white-gloved hands on his hips.

"Who are you?" he demanded.

Davis found his breath before I. He replied, "We're representatives of the *New York Journal*. We're American citizens, and your government is going to hear about the rough treatment we've been accorded."

The Spanish officer's expression sharpened. He said, "You're the writer, Davis?"

Startled, Davis said, "I am."

The officer turned immediately to me. "And you must be Señor Frederic Remington, the noted artist."

I nodded. "And who might you be, sir?"

The barest hint of a smile began to play about the officer's lips. It was not, I can assure you, Bierce, a nice smile. He said, "I am General Valeriano Weyler of the Royal Army of Spain, governor-general and commander-in-chief of all her majesty's forces in the colony of Cuba. Tell me, Señor Artista—to your practiced eye, so flawlessly trained in painting and sculpture—do I look like a butcher to you?"

For only a moment, Bierce, my throat failed me. I felt it close in fear, and my heart began to beat wildly. I spun my head about to look down the barrels of two dozen Spanish rifles. I turned back to the man The Chief had dubbed "The Butcher of Cuba." Weyler's thin-lipped smile appeared the very essence of cruelty.

I said quickly, "Not really, General. In fact, you look to me like a rather pleasant chap."

THIRTEEN

"General," Davis said, "I'm afraid I still don't understand."

Weyler leaned back in the leather seat of his carriage and favored my colleague with a jovial smile. He'd been smiling precisely that way at every question for the past three days.

"Then I have failed to communicate with appropriate clarity, Señor Davis," he replied graciously.

Without doubt, Weyler was a gentleman—if not to the manor born then an accomplished master at affecting the gracious manner of Old World nobility. He looked so completely at home in the elegant carriage in which the three of us rode that you could just see him rolling down Fifth Avenue with the other swells in their fancy rigs. Of course, such a picture would have been ruined completely had Weyler been accompanied, as he was at that moment, by nearly eight hundred cavalry, infantry, and artillery troopers.

We were proceeding at a crisp pace through a rolling sea of cane. We'd reached the flatlands only after several days of laboriously dragging Weyler's big guns back down the steep slopes of La Sierra de Trinidad. During that time, Davis and I had been treated as honored guests, granted every courtesy after Weyler had apparently decided that shooting us would constitute a diplomatic blunder of unacceptable magnitude. During our journey, he'd permitted us periodically to ride with him in his carriage. The Spanish had even supplied Davis with pencil and paper and me with bits of charcoal so we might carry on with our journalistic duties.

Moreover, the governor-general had answered each of our queries without hesitation. We hadn't yet, however, broached the question of whether we would be permitted to send our work back to New York without censorship, so we had no idea at that moment whether our efforts would be of any particular benefit to the readers of the *Journal*.

"What I don't understand," Davis said, "is this: It's one thing to characterize the Free Army as an undisciplined rabble. I've seen them, and I can't quarrel with that assessment. What hasn't yet been made

[113]

clear to me is Spain's moral justification for refusing to permit Cuba independence."

"Because," Weyler responded, "we have an obligation to the people of Cuba. They are not yet ready for independence. You must not try, señor, to apply your American standards of democracy to these people. Most of the rebels are illiterate peasants who have no conception of their obligations in a democracy. If they found themselves on the losing end of a vote, they would simply seek to impose their will on the majority by force. And the majority in Cuba is loyal to the Crown. Were they not, we could never seek to hold this island."

Davis scribbled as Weyler spoke. "Go on, General," he said.

Weyler slowed his rate of speech, to be certain Davis was getting every word. "Let me put it this way: My government has been autocratic, it is true, but we have not been oppressive. And, morality aside, Spain needs the revenue Cuba produces from tobacco and, more important, sugar. Do you know much of the affairs of my nation, señor?"

"Not as much as I should, I suppose," Davis replied.

"My country," Weyler said gravely, "has undergone grave hardship in my lifetime. Our empire has shrunk until we have only Cuba and Puerto Rico as colonies in the Americas. Cuba has been a most vexing problem. We were forced more than a quarter century ago to send in one hundred thousand troops to keep the Cuban rebels from slaughtering loyal subjects of the Crown. This is most expensive, maintaining so many troops so far from home."

I broke in. "The Free Army people told us that you have at least twice that many troops on the island, General."

Weyler nodded. "Keeping the peace has been most costly in recent years, Señor Remington, and the sugar revenues are lower than ever. This has great impact on domestic politics in my country. The monarchy faces serious opposition."

"That means what, General? That your country may throw out its king?"

He shook his head. "King Alfonso has been dead for some years now. His widow, the good queen regent Maria Christina, rules today. But she does so only with the cooperation of the political leaders who control the ballot boxes and who ensure that the parliamentary system supports the monarchy. In the past few years, the Cuban Insurrecto has begun to drain the royal coffers. Now, more than ever, a peaceful, prosperous Cuba is essential to the stability of Spain and perhaps to all of Europe. To suddenly tell the Cubans that they are an independent nation, that they no longer have to pay Spain taxes on sugar revenues, this would be ruinous, señor. And it will not happen. Maria Christina will not permit Spain to fall into bankruptcy."

Davis said, "None of what you're telling me, though, addresses the questions raised by the leaders of the Free Army. It addresses only the problems of Spain."

Weyler's eyebrows rose. "And with whose problems should Spain be more concerned? This rebellion has been inspired only to a small degree by economic problems here in Cuba. These people are admittedly very poor, Señor Davis, but it has been mostly the work of revolutionists in New York who have the ears of your misguided Señor Hearst and other important *norteamericanos*. So, the rebel forces have money from *los Estados Unidos,* and here they have some small measure of support only because of the rebel decree."

"What's that?" I asked as I sketched.

Weyler smiled slightly beneath his mustache. "They did not mention that, did they, your friends in the mountains? The rebel decree is a most interesting document. It says that any Cuban who does not aid the rebels is to be considered an enemy of the Insurrecto and an ally of Spain. This document, issued by the bandits who call themselves the Free Army of Cuba, Señor Remington, states that all enemies of the revolution—or allies of Spain; take your pick—are to meet the same fate."

"Which is?" I inquired.

Weyler shrugged. "Hanging if they are lucky; disembowelment with machetes if they are not. The rebel strategy, such as it is, is to swoop down from the mountains we just left and wreak havoc on the sugar plantations and railroads that are Cuba's economic lifeblood. And also to terrorize those who oppose them—that is to say, those who do not actively assist them. So, when our queen regent decided that my predecessor, Martinez Campos—who was a fine politician but not so fine a soldier—was unable to deal with the Insurrecto after the issuance of the rebel decree, I was sent here to defend Cuba. This revolution must be put down, señors, and put it down I shall."

It was beginning to dawn on me, Bierce, that there perhaps had been a gap or two in the story Davis and I'd been told in the rebel camp on the revolution's history. Still, my sympathies continued to lie with Delores, who'd been so victimized. Davis's loyalties continued to lie with the man who was paying us.

"Your version," he told the general, "makes it sound as though the Insurrecto is made up simply of bandits and vandals."

"A most apt description," Weyler responded. "You were with them. Can you doubt that?"

"Well," Davis said rather lamely, "equipment and manpower problems seem to leave them little choice in their tactics."

"Nonsense," Weyler shot back. "Do you know what they did after

I arrived here to replace Campos? They tried to blow up the governor-general's palace in Havana. Instead, they managed to blow up only my downstairs toilet."

Davis fought unsuccessfully to stifle a grin. "I take it you weren't using it at the time."

Weyler chuckled. "Luckily, no. These are the men your newspaper is supporting, señor—vandals with American dynamite. You know, I spent some years in America. I was military attaché at the Spanish legation during your civil war. I accompanied General Sherman on his march through Georgia. Sherman did, indeed, burn Georgia to the ground. He left a path of scorched earth such as the world has not seen since the Romans leveled Carthage."

Then Weyler leaned across the small space in the carriage that divided us, and added, "But Sherman always spared the toilets, señors. He was a soldier and a gentleman and a respecter of civilization—not a vandal like these brigands of the Cuban Insurrecto."

I wasn't sure that Weyler was entirely serious with this observation. The man seemed inordinately amused with his own remark.

"I never looked at it that way, General," I told him.

Weyler merely shook his head and grew more serious. He said, "I do not understand the way you American *periodistas* insist on looking upon this rebellion. I find I am fighting the Cubans openly and the Americans secretly. Your newspapers poison everything with false-hood. As a result, all *norteamericanos* seem to believe the Spanish government is composed of murderers and rapists. Do American readers know of the poverty the rebels have caused by so maiming the sugar industry here? Do they know of the famine—that thousands of Cuban children starve because of this pointless destruction of the sugar facilities? No, they know only that Valeriano Weyler is a butcher. And how do they know this? Because Señor Hearst has told them this lie over and over again in the columns of his great newspapers."

Weyler frowned deeply. He seemed, during this last outburst, to have undergone a transformation from genial host to wounded politician. Clearly, he was sick of being called names in the American press.

Davis pressed on. He said, "That's all well and good, General, but what about your reconcentration order? The rebels told us a lot about that one. Are you trying to say that hasn't contributed to the starvation?"

Weyler sighed wearily. "The reconcentration order was necessary, Señor Davis. It says merely this: Because so many people in the interior were aiding the Insurrecto out of fear, they must move behind Spanish lines where they can be protected. This order has saved many loyal Cubans from death at the hands of the bloodthirsty rebels."

Davis nodded, but his expression was skeptical. "And after you ordered them out of their homes, you burned every village in the interior. That's what the rebels say, General."

For a moment, I feared that Davis had gone too far. A flash of anger glinted in Weyler's dark eyes. Then, his voice fiercely controlled, he said, "The rebels had to be starved out. They have dared not meet me upon the battlefield, and they must be compelled to fight. So now they live in the mountains on chickens and goats—if they can find any left after our attack. And when they run out of chickens and goats, they must either break up or come down and fight like men. There was no other way to accomplish this, Señor Davis. Warfare with honor requires two honorable antagonists."

Davis, I realized, could keep up such a debate all day. He already had enough material for a half-dozen stories, and I had more sketches of Weyler than I could ever use. I wanted answers to more immediate questions.

I said, "Well, General, what happens to us? You have three choices, as I see it. You can toss us in jail when we get back to Havana, but it doesn't look as though you're going to do that. You can throw us out of the country. Or, you can let us stay and report honestly on the revolution—both sides of the conflict, fairly. That, of course, is what we'd prefer."

Weyler smiled slightly. And coldly. "I could also have you hanged, Señor Remington. You neglected to mention that option."

I'm sure I paled visibly beneath my tan, Bierce. I told him, "I was hoping that wouldn't occur to you."

Weyler laughed aloud. It was a reasonably good-humored laugh, for which I was exceedingly grateful. He said, "I will not hang you, señor. Nor am I foolish enough to jail American journalists, as Campos had an unfortunate habit of doing. But I might yet eject you from the country. You are, after all, here without visas, and I can only speculate on how you arrived upon our shores—probably on a smuggler's craft. You would not care to illuminate me on that matter, I would imagine."

Davis said, "I suppose we could be persuaded to do so, if you were to put your mind to it, General. But we'd prefer not to."

"No matter," Weyler said curtly. "You may stay in Havana. You may wire your Señor Hearst for money, if you require it. And you may write stories and make drawings of our little war here to your hearts' content. You may not, however, return to the rebel forces. And your dispatches will, of course, be subjected to military review—some light censorship."

"That part troubles me," said Davis, pressing as ever.

Weyler raised his palms in supplication. "I said light censorship,

Señor Davis. Nothing you could send from Havana could be worse than the lies your newspaper is already printing, based on lies they are told by the Insurrecto's representatives in New York. I ask only that you keep your promise and explain—in some small measure, at least—the difficulty of the Spanish position here."

Davis nodded. "General, you have my word that as soon as we get to Havana I'll send back a story on my interviews with you—and Remington will send back his sketches of what he's seen."

I took the opportunity to turn around the sketchbook and display it to the governor-general. "Acceptable likenesses, I trust," I said.

Weyler leaned forward and peered at the sketches. I'd caught him speaking in his animated style in more than a dozen roughs. He seemed quite pleased with the work. He asked me to sign one and then stuffed it into his tunic.

"For my wife," he told me gratefully. "She is a great admirer of your work, Señor Remington." The general then eyed both of us sternly. "I depend upon you, gentlemen, to provide Spain a fair hearing in your newspaper."

Davis reached out and shook the officer's gloved hand.

"You can count on that, General," the reporter pledged.

"Indeed, sir," I added grandly.

Little did we know, Bierce.

FOURTEEN

T.R. could jabber so, Bierce. You could never shut the fellow up. He's much worse, I'm certain, now that he's in the Executive Mansion. Can you imagine the agony of serving in his cabinet? John Hay so loves to talk, and I'm certain the poor fellow never gets in a word.

Nonetheless, every once in a while T.R. says something worthwhile. One such rare nugget of value came tumbling from his lips during the return trip I made to Cuba after the United States finally intervened. It came only a day or two before he led that glorious charge up San Juan Hill, the one that made him so famous.

He was bivouacked with his Rough Riders, all of them knee-deep in mud. I was living in a tent just behind the lines while scrambling to find new images to commit to paper for the pages of The Chief's publication. T.R. came upon me one morning as I was sketching and insisted on a boisterous reunion. I reluctantly accompanied him to his tent, where we uncorked a bottle of something abominable while he overwhelmed me with the relentless force of his personality and the usual torrent of words.

Then, in and amongst the flood of verbiage in which I struggled to stay afloat, I heard a magic word. The word, Bierce, was "Peatam."

I said, "Slow down a bit, T.R. Now, what's all this about Peatam?"

And he said, "I got the bugger into Cuba, you know. He'd never even have seen this wretched place, had it not been for me. Belting a New York City police captain is the best possible ticket to jail, Frederic, and this Peatam chap hadn't just belted one; he'd broken the poor fellow's jaw.

"As it was presented to me, the incident began when a society matron returned unexpectedly to her home on East Seventy-fourth Street and found her husband abed with a woman of easy virtue. She'd responded with predictable irritation. She'd gone to the poor fellow's study, taken his pistol from his desk, and returned to the bedroom, where the ill-fated couple was hurriedly dressing. The outraged lady fired a total of six shots. He got four; she two. Both were quite dead when my chaps arrived. The corpses were being removed when this fellow Peatam, with a photographer in tow, appeared on the scene on behalf of the *World*. An incident like that made the yellow sheets positively drool.

"Peatam was an extraordinarily pushy sort, even for a reporter. When he tried to delay the removal of the bodies while his photographer set up all his complicated, newfangled equipment to make a photograph of the victims, the precinct captain intervened. The routine bribe offer was ignored—something of a miracle, when you consider it—and one thing led to another. This Peatam chap, I'm told, was the proud possessor of a left fabled in press bars all across town. The captain hit the sidewalk outside the brownstone mansion as though he'd been struck by lightning. It took four of my officers, all snarling and swearing in thick brogues, to bring Peatam down.

"This Peatam fellow hadn't been hurt in the brawl—probably because the officers were loath to inflict injury on a chap who'd just done to their captain what each of them had been so often tempted to do. They did, however, take the chap into custody, and an unforgiving police-court judge sentenced him to three full months for assault and battery on an officer of the law. This was a judge with a grudge against the Pulitzer organization. Not that Peatam didn't have it coming, mind you.

"For the first few weeks of his incarceration, I'm told, Peatam spent his time vengefully gathering material for an exposé of the New York City prison system. After that initial period, however, the time surely began to weigh heavily on him. I'm certain he viewed it with a certain measure of relief when the guards came to his cell in the Tombs and offered him the opportunity to bathe, shave, and dress in his own clothing. He was then loaded into a paddy wagon and deposited—in chains, of course—in the outer office of my lair at Police Board headquarters in city hall. They told me the chap seemed quite taken with my decorations—the stuffed heads of a few mountain goats and a black bear I'd happened across in Manitoba. Remind me to tell you about that bear some time, Frederic. A bully adventure, that.

"I'd been out and about my duties. He was sitting there, seemingly captivated with my cape buffalo trophy. I'd never met the man, but I'd sent for him, and the sight of a fellow in a business suit and chains left no doubt as to who he had to be. I ordered him brought into the inner office. Then I closed the door, and just the two of us were there for our conversation.

"I said, 'So, you're the chap who delights in beating up my captains, are you?'

" 'He had it coming,' Peatam told me. He is, as you well know, a brassy sort.

" 'Oh?' I replied. 'And why's that?'

"And he said, 'Your captain was interfering with the constitution-ally protected gathering of the news. Besides that, he was the sort who needed beating up. I understand you've felt the need to carry out similar chores with some of the other members of New York City's esteemed police department.'

"Well, Frederic, I enjoyed a hearty laugh at that. I knew precisely the incident to which Peatam was making reference.

"Those Irish coppers reviled me. A Harvard-educated Protestant from Oyster Bay—a chap with spectacles at that? Not their sort of fellow at all. They didn't figure I was hardy enough to be police commissioner, and I was determined to put that canard to rest. As soon as I was appointed, I'd started prowling the streets. One night I spotted one of my coppers on Forty-second Street sneaking a mug of beer from the side door of a saloon. I came up on the chap from the shadows and ordered, 'Officer, give me that glass.'

"The officer rather carelessly shook loose his truncheon to deal with the annoyance. Then he recognized who was addressing him. He immediately dropped the mug to the sidewalk and fled like a deer. I ran him down inside of thirty yards. When the chap resisted me, I subdued him thoroughly with my fists and had him hauled up on departmental charges the very next day. The incident ended up on the front pages not only of the yellows but of the more sedate sheets, like the *Sun* and the *Herald*, as well. After that, I was no more popular with my coppers, but they damned well understood that I would tolerate no nonsense.

"So I was still chuckling at Peatam's remark as I settled into the wooden chair behind my desk. I studied him closely. He struck me as a well-set-up chap—burly, bearded, thirty-five or so. A solid-looking sort with a considerable store of grit, but with a bit of meanness in him, I surmised.

"I said to him, 'So, they seem to think I should let you loose, Mr. Peatam—despite your nasty habit of bashing in the heads of my senior officers.'

"Peatam immediately demanded, 'Who are they?'

"I told him honestly, 'The people I'm counting on to make me an assistant secretary of the navy in a few months. It seems that your superiors at the *World* realize that I don't give a hoot in hell for what these local politicians think about you or anything else, so they went a little higher to find people whose arguments on your behalf I might find compelling. Now, it has been hinted to me that a favor to the

Pulitzer organization might further my goals with regard to the naval department post. The question I confront is whether I want the job badly enough to let a ruffian like you back on the streets.'

"He said, 'And are you going to, sir?'

"I told him, 'I'm not at all sure. It would seem to be in my interest to go along. But in my interest to what degree? That's the question.'

"This fellow Peatam was a cool customer, Frederic. He merely gazed at me and replied, 'Only you can answer that.'

" 'Not quite,' I told him. 'You can help me make up my mind. My understanding is that the Pulitzer people plan to send you to Cuba.'

"Peatam shrugged. 'I have no idea, Commissioner. I go where I'm sent.'

" 'I have a special interest in Cuba,' I told the chap. 'I tend to believe that an American intervention there would be in our country's best interests. Do you agree, Mr. Peatam?'

"Clearly, the fellow couldn't have cared less, but he had the good sense to concur with my view. I told him, 'A war with Spain could bring the United States some pretty valuable real estate in this hemisphere and elsewhere. Have you considered that, Mr. Peatam?'

"Obviously, he hadn't, but he demonstrated the judgment to say he had. So I went on to say, 'A reporter for an influential newspaper, reporting properly on events in Cuba, could have a powerful influence on public opinion here in America. The Hearst press seems to have the right idea on Cuba, Mr. Peatam, but Hearst more or less dislikes me. He's never said so directly, but I suspect he sees me as an aristocrat with too little in common with the ordinary people who read his newspaper. He's right on Cuba and wrong on me.'

"Peatam said, 'I can hardly help you with Hearst, Commissioner.'

"I told him, 'Nor do I expect you to. On the other hand, if you're in Cuba you'll be in a position to help me through the auspices of the Pulitzer organization, and that'll be quite help enough, I suspect. You seem an aggressive sort, Mr. Peatam. I would certainly hope that if I were to let you go, and if you went to Cuba, you might decide to do some aggressive reporting—perhaps even some stories on the threat posed by a Spanish naval presence to American shipping, that sort of thing. If I let you go—and if you go to Cuba—do you think that's likely to happen?'

"Peatam said, 'I can't say for certain what I might find.'

"Then I told him, 'Let me put it another way, sir. Your conviction for assaulting an officer is not being dropped. You're simply being permitted an unofficial furlough. Were you to return to New York having distinguished yourself journalistically in Cuba, I suppose that someone in a position of authority might be able to have your conviction expunged from city records. On the other hand, that same person could have you taken into custody and returned to the Tombs to finish your sentence. Now, let me ask the question again, sir: Do you think that you might be able to accomplish some aggressive reporting from Cuba if I let you go?'

" 'Without a doubt, Commissioner.'

"I reached into my vest pocket. The fellow's eyes virtually danced when they fell on the handcuff key I pulled out.

" 'Bully,' I told him."

FIFTEEN

You've never seen anything quite like Havana's Hotel Inglaterra, Bierce.

It was the city's pride, and justifiably so. It stood, white and proud and elegant, on a meadow of meticulously manicured green grass on the waterfront. Its guests were an international collection of business-men, indolent millionaires, military men, and a few European journal-ists in town to do a story or two on the rebellion on their way to or from South America. Among the guests, too, were the usual high-stakes gamblers and expensive prostitutes who frequent the grand international hotels.

Those for whom such pleasures of the flesh held little appeal enjoyed ample opportunity to stroll the beach and gaze at the rolling azure sea. The water surrounding Cuba almost glows from within, not at all like our forbidding northern ocean. That's how I occupied myself Christmas Day, the first I'd ever spent away from Missie. I cabled her my warmest regards, just as Davis cabled his mother, but it wasn't really the same. I was growing homesick, Bierce. And fat, too.

The food was marvelous. The cuisine was a combination of Cuban, Spanish, Italian, and German—all of it quite good and quite expensive. Not that Davis and I cared about expense. The Chief had wired us an almost unconscionable amount of money. Then, as always, he seemed not to understand its worth—at least, not in the same sense it's understood by us common folk whose supply of the stuff requires constant replenishment.

From a recreational standpoint, the hotel was ideal. It was only a few blocks from the city's finer restaurants on one side and Havana's famed and seamy underbelly on the other. There one could find spectacularly explicit live sex shows in dim, smoke-filled club rooms that were at once the shame of the Caribbean and its wonder. Shortly after we'd settled ourselves into the hotel, my curiosity prompted me to drag Davis to one such show in which a huge, splendidly endowed Negro performed with no fewer than four winsome and willing white women. Davis, the self-styled man of the world, found it all rather shocking—mostly, I'm sure, because of the miscegenation.

From a business standpoint, the hotel was also convenient. Nearby was Casa Nueva, the luxurious office building that housed the American consulate, which was supervised by the gracious consul-general, Fitzhugh Lee. He was a portly southern gentleman in the old tradition. He was a nephew of Robert E. Lee and a former governor of Virginia. He would regularly drop by the hotel to discuss with foreign journalists and businessmen the role of the United States with regard to the revolution. Consul-General Lee made no secret of his sympathy for the rebel cause, and when he discovered that the hotel housed two Hearstlings he sought us out and bowed low in greeting.

"Suhs," Lee said, "Ah am but a servant of our gov'ment, and Ah wish to be of all pos'ble assistance to yo fahne oh-gan-eye-zation."

Davis asked rather quickly, "Can you get our dispatches out without censorship?"

General Lee shook his white-maned head. "Sadly, suh, Ah cannot. No one cay-un—legally, thay-ut is."

So, after sending for money, we were forced to wire New York and explain the delay in sending out stories and sketches. When they came back from the Spanish censors, we were delighted to find accompanying them a polite memo from the officer in charge mandating only a few small changes. We were told by the European journalists that the office was seldom so lenient in its censorship, so we concluded that our favored treatment was the result of Weyler's direct intervention.

The governor-general had liked my sketches of him, and Davis's stories were less strident than what the *Journal* had been running based on information from the Insurrecto's New York spokesmen. Davis had portrayed Weyler as a stern but essentially fair man, as his earlier stories from the mountains had described the courage of the rebels in a conflict with a vastly superior force. It was Davis's goal that neither side emerge as villains, and neither side be portrayed without blemish. In their totality, the stories were to draw a vivid portrait of Cuba as we'd seen it.

Because the stories required my sketches, it was pointless to wire them. We had to send them to New York by boat. We were in the hotel lobby one morning just after the new year began, looking for a messenger to accomplish just that chore, when I noticed that Davis's jaw had dropped down to about his knees. He was staring directly at a man at the registration desk, a rugged, bearded fellow in a New York–style suit and derby. The bearded man noticed us at just about the moment we noticed him.

"Davis," he said with a grin. "Well, fancy meeting you here."

Davis's face was dark. He said. "Hello there, Peatam. I'd heard you were in jail."

"I was striking a blow for freedom of the press," Peatam laughed.

"A blow against a police captain, as I recall," Davis said.

The bearded fellow just shrugged. "Tyranny takes many forms, Davis." He turned to me and stuck out a hand. "You must be Remington. I'm Peatam, of the *World*."

I took his hand and was beginning to utter a suitably polite greeting when Davis grabbed me by the elbow and virtually dragged me away. Peatam scurried after us.

He said, "What's the matter, Davis? Surely you don't object to a little competition. After all, Hearst has enjoyed something of a monopoly on this little war, hasn't he, old man?"

Clearly, Davis loathed the fellow. He said, "Don't 'old man' me, Peatam. Since you're so eager to strike blows for freedom of the press, I suggest you unlimber your fabled fists against a Spanish officer or two. They appreciate a good fighting man here, Peatam. They wouldn't mind at all, really."

I had no idea what was behind this display of animosity. At that early juncture, Peatam had struck me as a rather good-natured sort. I'd forgotten that Davis had served a short stint on the *World* before moving to *Harper's*.

Peatam said, "Now Davis, you're not still angry over that Klausman business, are you? That was just part of your initiation into the robust world of New York newspapering."

"Oh, really. Just part of the initiation to tell that man—a butcher at that, with all those knives—that I was the man who'd strangled his daughter?" Then Davis's voice slipped into a startling faithful imitation of Peatam's deeper tones. " 'You mustn't be angry, sir. This fellow Davis is mentally ill. When they let him out of Bellevue in a week or two, he'll be just heartbroken over what he's done.' "

Peatam didn't even bother to stifle his raucous laughter. This must have been one of his favorite pranks. Davis, fuming, said grimly, "That damned butcher almost split my skull with his meat cleaver."

"Well," Peatam laughed, "what are you complaining about? You got away, didn't you?"

Davis wasn't at all amused. "Just how did you manage to get out of jail, Peatam?"

The Pulitzer man's wolfish grin was beginning to annoy even me at that point, and I didn't even know the fellow. Peatam said, "I got out through resourcefulness, Davis—the same way I'm going to take over this splendid little war down here. See you around, old man. Nice to meet you, Remington."

It took me a good hour to restore Davis to his normal humor even after we got off our dispatch to New York. I know you've always gotten on with Peatam, Bierce. You have an unfortunate affection for the brash and amusing regardless of their other failings. But Jim Peatam got on my nerves almost from the very beginning. I've never warmed up to him, and Davis simply couldn't abide the man.

Not even when they'd been on the same side.

Ambrose Bierce
Mexico, 1914

The chills. Oh, the damnable chills.

They took me captive at midday, swathing me in an embrace of ice. I shiver alone. Small Maria—whom I now suspect to be more angel than whore—departed as I slept. I presume she will return. Ultimately, it is a matter of minimal consequence. As I make this arduous journey between sin and punishment, I mind not at all the solitude and opportunity for reflection it provides.

I find I cling to life with an unfortunate tenacity previously exhibited in my character only in relation to the coin of the realm. I have enjoyed success in that area—success being an unpardonable sin against one's fellows. Little good it does me now. Money is a blessing of no advantage to us excepting when we part with it. Unless one chooses to employ it as a passport to polite society, that is, which was never one of my goals.

Oh, the chills. I pray that Hell is as warm as it is portrayed in the sacred books of Christianity—as distinguished from the false and profane writings upon which all other faiths are based. Anything to drive away this infernal cold.

A shadow falls upon me. My eyes focus and capture the image of Small Maria's angelic face.

"You shiver, Señor Bierce," she observes.

I offer no response to this proclamation of the obvious. I merely continue my shivering, so as not to make the lady a liar. In only a moment, Small Maria lies beside me, encasing my icy body in her soft, silky warmth. She lies almost atop me, and her flesh radiates heat. Under other circumstances, I should attempt to explore that flesh in greater detail. Now, however, I gratefully partake of the warmth for all it can be for me at this stage—salvation instead of temptation.

"Does this feel better?" she asks.

"Much better," I tell her truthfully. "I am a man of the highest order of unworth, Small Maria. I can never compensate you for your kindness."

She lies against me, warming me from ankle to chin and, after a while, providing the rare and agreeable sensation of communion with another soul. It has been my lifelong curse to see things as they are, not as they ought to be. That has been my burden from the idiocy of infancy through the folly of youth to the sin of manhood and the remorse of old age. Still, there are moments, this being one, when what is can be gratifying. My longevity has been no more than an extension of the fear of death, but it had lent me a proper appreciation for those uncommon instances when human contact can be rewarding instead of annoying.

"I love you, Señor Bierce," this guileless child tells me.

I am startled by this confession. I tell her, "Small Maria, love is no more than a temporary insanity curable almost instantly by marriage—or, in my case, by the removal of the patient from the circumstances under which she incurred the disorder. I shall soon be but a memory, and your illness will depart shortly thereafter."

"You know so much," she says. "Just speaking to you has made me curious."

"Curiosity is an objectionable quality in the female mind," I caution her. "The danger of curiosity is that you will ultimately learn that which you wish to know and suffer from disappointment forever after."

"Talk to me," she urges. "Tell me more of your story."

I say, "You will remain here next to me as I speak? You will warm me as I spin my lies?"

"Is it a lie?" she asks.

I tell her, "A lie is only a version of events shaped by the listener's beliefs. The truth is the same. In that sense, there's little difference between the two. Certainly, there wasn't to Sam Chamberlain."

"Chamberlain?" she asks.

"You have forgotten," I scold. "He was the managing editor of the *New York Journal*. He told me this part of the story himself at T.R.'s first inaugural. We were drinking to the nation's luck, under the presumption that the nation would indeed need it.

"Chamberlain told of being at his desk, directing the affairs of the newspaper, when the most recent dispatch from Davis and Remington arrived. It was delivered to him by a clerk as Chamberlain labored over the layout of a front page. He was a master of Hearstian layout—if not the architect of the style then its most prodigious practitioner. The clerk deposited the packet before him. Chamberlain, his concentration disturbed, glanced up in annoyance.

" 'What's this?' he demanded. The youthful clerk had the good grace to be properly terrified at all times in the presence of the managing editor.

" 'It just arrived from Cuba, sir,' the clerk quavered.

"Chamberlain ripped open the package and brought out a Remington sketch of a sober, dignified man in a flashy military uniform. Chamberlain studied it in puzzlement.

" 'Who the hell is that?' he mumbled to himself.

"He set aside the drawing and dug deeper into the packet, coming out with a thick sheaf of paper covered with line after line of Davis's hurried scrawl. Chamberlain scanned the first page, then the second, then glanced up at the clerk and smiled broadly.

" 'Well, well,' he said. 'What we have here is an interview with none other than Governor-General Valeriano Weyler.'

" 'The butcher, sir?' asked the clerk.

" 'The very same,' Chamberlain said, studying Davis's writing, 'although you'd never know it from this story. My God, this actually borders on the sympathetic.'

"Chamberlain scanned the pages rapidly, reading at that effortlessly breakneck pace so common to men who work daily with language and so uncommon among the lip-moving masses who stumble over every trisyllabic word. He digested and judged each page in only a matter of moments. Then he handed the story to the clerk.

"Frowning, he said, 'This stuff is quite a bit softer, I think, than The Chief would care for. Take this to Reed, over on the city desk. Tell him I said it's all right, but too dull. I want one of the rewritemen to dress it up. He should go to the clips and make Davis's stories more consistent with the tone of our past stories on Weyler.'

"The clerk nodded. 'Yes, Mr. Chamberlain. I understand.'

"Chamberlain dug through Remington's sketches, holding them out at arm's length and appraising them with care. 'These could use a little work, too,' he said. 'Take them to the art department. Let's get more of a scowl on this fellow's face.'

"Chamberlain passed the packet in its entirety to the clerk. 'One more thing. Our friend Davis seems to have been taken in a bit by this Weyler fellow. That's what happens when you hire outsiders instead of having a staffer do the work. The Chief has strong feelings about this Cuba business, and we're not going to go soft in our coverage. Get off a letter in my name to Davis and tell him we want more on that girl—that Cuban Joan of Arc he wrote about earlier. The Chief was very pleased with that story.'

" 'Very good, Mr. Chamberlain,' the clerk said.

" 'Also,' Chamberlain added, his mind working furiously, as always, 'it would be marvelous if this girl were to escape from prison.

You might suggest to Davis in the letter that The Chief would look quite fondly on a story like that.'

"Then the clerk was gone, and Chamberlain was back to laboring over his front page. He was a fine managing editor, Small Maria, and he was determined to have stories in his paper that told his readers the truth—as he understood it, that is."

Small Maria has listened to this story rather more attentively than to prior installments of the tale. My chills lessening now, I find myself sufficiently distracted from their torment to become intrigued by her response. Her expression exudes bafflement.

"What troubles you, child?" I inquire.

"Señor Bierce," my childish angel asks, "what was the truth? Was it the words written by this Señor Davis or the changes in the words desired by this Señor Chamberlain?"

I tell her, "Truth is what you make of it. Have I told you the story of the blind men and the elephant?"

She shakes her head.

"Three blind men were in the forest one day and came upon an elephant. One of them reached out and grabbed the trunk. 'What sort of beast is this?' he inquired. 'Is this a snake?' The second blind man reached out and felt the animal's side. 'No,' he replied. 'It is a cow.' The third blind man reached out and touched the elephant's tusk. He said, 'No, this is the tooth of a great lion.' All spoke the truth as they knew it, Small Maria. That is what journalists do. Their work reflects only their understanding of events."

She says nothing. She is engaged, perhaps for the first time in her life, in the act of thinking. This is a dangerous habit to instill in a woman, but I know that my time with her will be short. The wages of the sin I commit by stirring her to thought will be borne by some other sinner.

"Tell me more," she says finally.

I huddle closer to the warmth, both physical and spiritual, that she provides me. In gratitude I comply with her wishes.

I say, "I'll tell you now of Peatam. Remington was right. I've always harbored a fondness for Peatam. I've been intrigued by the ruthless enthusiasm of his enterprise, by his bottomless capacity for conflict, and by his cruel but outrageous wit. A flawed man, Small Maria, often is drawn to flawed friends.

"In any event, he later told me of his first encounter with Weyler. Peatam had gone from the Hotel Inglaterra directly to the governor-general's palace and presented his card, demanding an audience. To Peatam's shock, Weyler received him grandly. The governor-general had been badly buffeted by the New York press, and apparently he was determined to do what he could to blunt the criticism.

"Peatam was ushered into Weyler's spacious ground-floor office. The governor-general offered him a cigar, which Peatam lit and savored with appreciation. Then Weyler said, 'What might I do to be of service to you?'

" 'That's not the right question, General,' Peatam told him.

"Weyler's eyebrows shot up. He said, 'No? I would have thought that was exactly the question. What question would you prefer?'

"Peatam leaned over the delicate, Louis the Fourteenth desk that separated him from the governor-general and said, 'The question is, General, what we might do together to be of service to one another.'

"Weyler's lips, beneath the mustache, twisted into a half-smile. He was intrigued with Peatam, who has the talent to inspire such emotion almost at will. He's a most compelling man, albeit one devoid of all principle, which is why I'm so fond of him.

"Weyler said, 'Would you care to be more specific?'

"Peatam said, 'Well, General, I'll just ramble on for a bit here, and you feel free to stop me when I say something that interests you. Now, you have a war to fight, and I have stories to write. We each have a problem in carrying out our respective duties, and it's the same problem. The problem's name is William Randolph Hearst.'

"Weyler said, 'Already you have said something that interests me.'

"Peatam merely smiled and winked. 'General, your problem with Hearst and my problem with Hearst aren't really all that different. You want to keep—well, let's call it adverse publicity—out of the *New York Journal*, and I want to keep anything at all on this war out of the *New York Journal*. I think we can work together.'

"Weyler simply listened. Peatam said, 'Here's my proposition. I'll keep an eye on Davis and Remington, and you'll freeze them out completely, giving me and the *World* whatever information I ask for— within reason, of course. In return, I'll tell you what those two are up to, who they're seeing, what I hear them saying around the hotel.'

"Weyler said nothing, but he appeared thoughtful.

"Peatam plowed forward. 'I'll need day-to-day reports, General. I'll need hard facts—where the rebels are, where your troops are, casualty counts, that sort of thing. I'll need to know, in detail, what's going on at the front. I'd even like to make some trips out into the field—with Davis and Remington suitably restricted to Havana, of course. So, what do you say? Can we do business, General?'

"Weyler digested the offer. Then he responded, 'An interesting proposition, but such a bargain would be of no value to me. I can, at my whim, ship Señor Davis and Señor Remington right back to New

York—as I can you, Señor Peatam, if I find you bothersome. What need do I have of the services you offer?'

"Peatam had expected a response along those lines, and he had his answer ready. He told Weyler, 'Whatever the *Journal* prints with Davis and Remington in Cuba, it would mean even worse publicity in Hearst's papers if you threw them out. Once again, Hearst's only sources of information would be the Insurrecto's mouthpieces in New York, and you've already had a taste of what that might mean for the Spanish position with the American public. What you need, General, are stories in the *New York World* that'll illustrate to the American people just how strong the Spanish forces here are and just how weak the rebels are. If you can accomplish that, then you might—just might, that is—succeed in keeping America from walking in and relieving Spain of this little island. And you and I both know that the United States could do that anytime McKinley decided it was politically necessary.'

"Weyler said not a word. There was no need. They both knew Peatam was speaking nothing more than the naked truth.

" 'My solution,' Peatam went on, 'would keep you posted on the activities of Davis and Remington, on who they're seeing and talking to. Hell, you might even pick up a few high-ranking rebels with my help. I'm sure you've toyed with the idea of putting some Spanish agents on their trail, but if they spot your boys, they might shy away from reporting that could endanger their rebel friends. But if they spot me sniffing around, that'll just make them more aggressive.'

"Peatam then shut up. He knew he'd made a good case, and he was wise enough to avoid damaging it with unnecessary and possibly careless reiteration. So he merely smoked his cigar, watching the gears and wheels turn in the governor-general's head.

"Finally, Weyler said, 'Isn't this . . . forgive me, my English fails me . . . isn't this a bit of a dirty trick to play on colleagues, Señor Peatam. I recall from my years in your country that you Americans always seemed to place an inordinate value on what you called fair play.'

"Peatam merely laughed—roared, actually. He said, 'General, I never play fair.' "

I turn to Small Maria, who is lying with her head on my shoulder on the rude mattress of cornhusks. I say, "And what do you think of this part of my story, small one?"

She is silent for a long moment. Then she says softly, "I will tell you a story of my own making, Señor Bierce. It is not unlike your story of the blind men and the elephant."

I am intrigued. "Please," I entreat her.

Small Maria says, "A rabbit and a rattlesnake, each sightless since birth, bump into one another in the desert. The rattlesnake says, 'What sort of animal are you?' And the rabbit replies, 'I do not know. I have never seen myself.' The rattlesnake says, 'I, too, know not what I am. Let us rub our bodies together to see if we can help one another determine our species.' When they have touched intimately, the rattlesnake says, 'You are round and furry, with large ears. You must be a rabbit. But what am I?' And the rabbit says, 'You are cold and scaly with beady eyes and no balls. Your chest is too small for much of a heart. You must be a journalist.' "

SIXTEEN
Frederic Remington
Cuba, 1898

Davis and I daily sent Diego, one of the hotel bellboys, to meet the steamships that docked in Havana Harbor. His instructions were to ask for any mail addressed to us. For a considerable period, he came back every day empty-handed.

One January morning as Davis and I were just coming awake in our spacious second-floor room overlooking the sea, Diego appeared at our door with a packet from New York. Inside were several copies of the *Journal* and a letter in a *Journal* envelope.

Our journalistic egos being what they were, we set the letter aside and went immediately to the newspapers to see how our work had been displayed. I must tell you, Bierce, Davis and I were utterly aghast at what we saw.

There, on the front page, was my best sketch of Weyler, four columns wide. But the man's somber expression had been not so subtly altered by some finger-painting specialist in the *Journal*'s art department into a glare of menace. His brows had been thickened and arched, his expressive eyes narrowed to tiny slits, and his benign mouth turned downward into an angry scowl. This monstrosity occupied the center of the page under a gigantic headline in red ink. It read: *Butcher Weyler: I do what I must!*

Beneath the drawing and the headline was Davis's story, more skillfully reworked. His narrative remained intact, but detailed descriptions had been trimmed to tighten up the piece to the detriment of reality. Weyler, his quotes cut severely, came across as a hard, vicious fellow possessed of a blind, unflagging dedication to Spanish imperialism.

"Those idiots in New York," Davis moaned. "Editors, they call themselves."

I was furious, Bierce. I said, "Cobblers, is more like it."

Davis sighed and said, "Well, that's life on the yellows, Remington. They tighten and punch up stories beyond all recognition. There's no room for subtlety, as we enjoyed at *Harper's*—no room to adequately explore all sides of an issue. And if a story cuts against the grain, then the reporter had better be on hand to defend it. We weren't around when the editors got their hands on this. And you know the definition of an editor, Remington—someone who separates the wheat from the chaff and shepherds the chaff into print."

I was so angry I could hardly speak. I said, "When Weyler sees this, he'll throw us right out—if he doesn't hang us. It'll just be more of the same, as far as he's concerned. What fool could have done this?"

Davis reached for the letter. "Let's see if this might tell us."

It did, more or less. It was signed by Chamberlain, although clearly scribbled in the handwriting of some underling. It commended us for our enterprise thus far and urged us to continue the fine work. It also added, needlessly, that some editing of our work had been required to "maintain the continuity of coverage expected by readers of the *New York Journal*."

"There's your answer," Davis said. "The managing editor himself did it."

"Mangling editor, is what I'd call him," I fumed. At a later date, Bierce, Sam and I became fast friends, but if he'd been within reach of me that day . . .

"They were very good with our stories out of the Free Army camp," Davis pointed out. "I have to presume that Chamberlain took one look at the Weyler piece and did what he figured The Chief would want."

"It's not what The Chief told us he wanted," I said.

"There's more to this," Davis told me as he studied the letter. "There's a paragraph at the end commending us on the earlier stuff on Cosio's daughter. Listen to this, Remington: 'Mr. Hearst has ordered that we in New York get a petition to the queen regent of Spain for this girl's pardon. We are enlisting the women of America to sign the petition, the important ones first. The petition and all names will be cabled to the queen regent. We want to make a national issue of this case. Mr. Hearst feels it will do more to open the eyes of the country than a thousand editorials or correspondents. Mr. Hearst says the Spanish minister can attack the newspapers, but we'll see if he can face the women of America when they take up the fight. The girl must be saved even if we have to take her out of prison by force.' "

I was at the window, glaring out at the sea, when Davis read those last few words. My anger instantly was replaced by an amazement too profound to describe. I said, "Does that mean what I think it means?"

Davis put down the letter and looked at me in amazement. He said, "It sounds as though they expect us to break her out of prison."

I felt my stomach knot.

"All of us?" I said to Davis.

SEVENTEEN

To appreciate the character of Evangelina Cosio y Cisneros, Bierce, you should understand the conditions under which she'd lived and the mechanisms she'd developed to deal with them.

Recojidas Prison occupied the better part of an entire block near the Havana docks. It had no outer walls, as such. The structure had been built like a good many Spanish-style buildings in the Americas, around a great courtyard. Many of its cells faced out on the streets below, and prisoners could avail themselves of the dubious pleasure of observing through thickly barred windows the world from which they were segregated.

Evangelina, we were to learn, occupied a cell on the third floor of the five-story prison. Her abode while awaiting trial on sedition charges was perhaps ten feet square. Contained in that space were a rusted steel-framed bed with a straw mattress, a table with a dented metal washbasin, and a chamber pot.

Once daily she was permitted to travel, under the watchful eyes of a burly matron, to the community lavatory at the end of the hall. There, she would be allowed to wash out her chamber pot, replace the water in her washbasin, and—if she so chose—take a few moments to undress and wash all over, especially her hair. Prison authorities permitted this as a means of controlling pestilence.

She told us later that the shimmering cascade of inky hair we'd seen in the likeness in her father's locket had quickly proven a handicap in prison. Despite her best efforts, it soon became a haven for lice. She asked for scissors, and—as the matrons looked on—cut it to a length just below her ears. The loss of her long black hair, of which she'd always been quite proud, had inspired her to tears, but Evangelina had contained herself. She would not let them see her cry.

Because of the political nature of her offense, she was kept apart from the other prisoners, lest her radical attitudes infect them. Initially, this didn't trouble her because she knew what the other prisoners would be like. There's no scum in the Americas, Bierce, to rival the scum of Havana. The other female prisoners were, for the most part, prostitutes, and their relationships with one another were on the level of the jungle. Evangelina had no idea how long she might be imprisoned, but she preferred her own company to that of her fellow inmates.

You recall that she'd been captured on the Isle of Pines. Some of the details of that story I mentioned earlier, and she'd come to Recojidas convinced that Professor Cosio had been drowned in that failed effort. Her mother was long dead, so she viewed herself as an orphan alone in the most hostile of worlds.

She spent hours peering through her barred windows into Obispo Street. From her solitary vantage point, she came to know virtually everyone who walked the street regularly—from the whores who practiced their trade on the docks to the priests and nuns from the church and convent a few blocks away. It was a busy street, especially in the early morning when the waterfront workers headed to their jobs. Evangelina took pleasure in watching the street's routine, but she was painfully aware that she wasn't living life, only observing it from a barred window three flights up. At one point, she realized that she hadn't uttered a word—not a single word, Bierce—in several weeks.

In the early days of her imprisonment, she'd wept bitter tears of despair, heartbreak, and hopelessness. But she'd permitted herself this indulgence only when the matrons had stepped away and she was able to grieve privately. While they watched her, she maintained a steely composure. Sometimes she could hear the matrons outside in the corridor, chatting about their charges. Evangelina realized she'd earned a nickname. They called her *La Virgen de Hielo*—the Ice Maiden. She took a perverse pride in the name because it was evidence that she could stand them off—that she could protect and maintain her inner self. Her body they might have, she told herself. After all, how difficult is it to imprison another human being, or even to kill one? But her soul, the essential Evangelina, would remain her property alone. That was her pledge to herself.

Slowly, over months of confinement, she learned to deal with the solitude. No bars could hold her mind. With immense concentration, she began painstakingly to recall as much of her life as she could summon up. She dug deeply into her memory, from the earliest, blurry images of awareness to those last, marvelous days in Camagüey before the Spanish had arrested her father. From the deepest recesses of her mind, she called forth her childhood—dolls she'd loved, pets and friends, the warm moments with her mother before that woman's untimely death. She recalled the faces of her teachers, how they'd dressed and spoken. She remembered favorite dresses, long since outgrown or worn out. She dredged up her first childish blush of love, with a rough-and-tumble ten-year-old named Carlos, who'd pulled her hair and smacked her bottom while she'd reveled, red-faced and secretly thrilled, in his attentions.

In her mind, Evangelina plunged once again into the sunlit surf, reclined on the white sand, and rode with careless abandon over the plains of Camagüey, through the cane fields and the villages.

Slowly, time lost meaning. As her imprisonment dragged on, she spent hour after hour peering out her window, traveling backward in her mind to better times, never speaking and never, ever betraying emotion to her captors. She was *La Virgen de Hielo*, and they would never break her.

The first day Davis and I went to visit her, the guards placed us in a small room with a battered table and three chairs arranged around it. We waited in silence while Señorita Cosio was led down from her third-floor cell. The moment the matron led her into the room, Bierce, I realized I was in enormous trouble.

Even in her dull prison dress, with her hair chopped short and without the aid of cosmetics, Evangelina Cosio y Cisneros was a stunning vision of womanhood. Her features were smooth and fair, her eyes large, brown, and lustrous. I heard a sharp intake of breath from Davis, and I glanced instantly in his direction.

The man was absolutely thunderstruck. I recalled how he'd reacted to only the small photograph of Evangelina that her father had shown us that day on the *Vamoose*. Davis had gotten all misty-eyed over just that. Now, the sight of the same women in the flesh successfully robbed him of what little sense he might have possessed only the moment before.

We'd gone there only to get an interview with her, a few quick sketches, and get all that back to New York along with a letter to the effect that it would be impossible to break her out of prison. The task still seemed impossible to me, but I could tell from Davis's expression that the very sight of Evangelina had changed everything.

Whether I cooperated or not, he would be certain to try something foolhardy. And, whether I cooperated or not, I realized that whatever fate befell Davis was certain to befall me as well. To the Spanish, we were an inseparable duo. When I saw Davis's face, I could only shake my head and offer a silent prayer for luck. We were, from that moment on, embarked upon a course totally different from the one we'd been sent to Cuba to negotiate.

"My name is Richard Harding Davis," he told her, "of the *New York Journal*."

She stared at us blankly.

I said, "I'm Frederic Remington. I'm also with the *Journal*. We've seen the professor."

Instantly, she came alive. She reached out and clutched at my hand.

"You have seen my father?" she said, almost in a whisper.

"Yes," Davis told her. "In the mountains with the Free Army. He was fine when we saw him last, although he was running from an advancing Spanish force, as were we all."

She turned back to me, her luminous eyes shining. "This is true?"

"*Es verdad*," I assured her.

Evangelina released a grateful sigh. As we sat beside her, tears rolled down her smooth cheeks.

"You cannot know how happy you have made me," she said. "I was certain he was dead."

I was deeply touched, but Davis was almost absurd in his response. He sat beside her and almost immediately dropped his role as journalist. Instead, he promptly adopted that of protector.

"How're you being treated?" he demanded, almost angrily.

The girl wiped away her tears and fought to regain her composure. She said, "Prison is prison, señor. But I am a patriot. I will endure—just as the Cuban people endure."

Wonderful, I thought. Another fanatic like my warlike Delores, at whose fate I could only guess. I recall something you once said, Bierce, that patriots are the dupes of statesmen—fodder for cannons when politicians' lies on behalf of their countries prove insufficient to the task of staving off war. That was Evangelina. She was a most willing victim to the lust of politicians to draw lines on maps. And Davis was no longer a mere chronicler of such disputes. Now he was a participant in their madness. Which meant I was as well.

In a low whisper, he confided to the girl, "We're going to get you out."

She was dumbfounded. "Going to get me out of what?" she demanded in a normal tone.

Davis and I both winced.

"*Sshhhhh!*" Davis hissed, cocking his head toward the surly-looking guard with a rifle standing at attention just beyond the open door. "Out of this prison," he added in a low voice.

Evangelina studied Davis's almost ludicrously earnest expression, and then behaved the only way a rational person could in the face of such an outlandish suggestion. She laughed aloud and said, "And how will you do this, señor? With your guns? With your great army?"

She made no attempt to keep her voice down, and if Davis seemed unperturbed with this, I was frantic. I whispered angrily, "Will you please be quiet, young woman, before we all end up in this place?"

Davis cast a hurried glance at the guard, who seemed thankfully unaware of the nature of our conversation. My colleague turned back to the girl, plastered a silly grin across his face, and said, "We don't have a plan yet, but we will. We'll come here every day to talk to you. What you have to do is tell us exactly where your cell is in this prison, what the guard shifts are like, every detail. You have to give us every piece of information you can think of to enable us to formulate an escape plan."

Evangelina took very little of this seriously. She said, "I can give you that now."

Davis shook his head. "They're watching us too closely today, but if Remington and I are here for several days in a row—or several weeks in a row, if necessary—they'll slacken off a bit and we can talk more freely."

As they spoke, I unlimbered my sketchbook and drew a few lines, getting the overall sense of the shape of her head and the placement of her features. She was a fine portrait subject, Bierce, even if her patriotism did indicate to me a certain level of emotional imbalance.

"This is very dangerous, señor," she told Davis, realizing he was serious. "And where am I to go if you succeed in freeing me?"

"On a boat to America," Davis said. "That's the easy part. We have a ship's captain to contact first."

"And my father?"

"He's where he wants to be," Davis said. "I know he'd feel better if he knew you were in America, safe from the Spanish."

Evangelina's lips pursed in thought. She said, "Assuming you can free me, which I doubt, I could not go to New York. My place is in Cuba, with my *compañeros*."

I frowned. I was beginning to understand what it was about this young woman that had so annoyed the Spanish.

I told her, "The revolution is kept alive by money from New York. Believe me, Miss Cosio, after the buildup you're likely to get in our newspaper, you're going to be the greatest fund-raiser the Insurrecto has ever had. If you want to help the revolution, you can be more effective in no other way."

She said, "What is the meaning of this word 'buildup'?"

"News stories," Davis explained. "Articles in the newspaper."

"And very fine drawings," I added, somewhat annoyed.

"Everybody in New York reads the yellows," Davis assured her.

"I'm going to do a five-part series on you, your role in the revolution, and your life in prison. And we're going to start right now. Tell me in your own words how you came to be arrested."

Evangelina only stared at the poised pencil for a long moment, collecting her thoughts. Then she began to talk. And what she said, Bierce, went more or less like this. . . .

Evangelina's Story

Colonel Jose Berriz was given to ferocious outbursts at the slightest provocation. So it was not surprising, when I went to his office on that last morning to continue my plea for improved conditions for my father, that Berriz responded at first by pounding angrily on his desk.

"No!" he roared at me. "Absolutely not."

I said merely, "Surely, Colonel, you cannot continue to treat my father like a common criminal. He is a political prisoner, and he is also a man of advanced years. All I ask is that he be allowed to visit my cottage one night a week so he may bathe and enjoy one decent meal every seven days. Surely this is—"

"This is out of the question," Berriz bellowed. "Why do you keep badgering me, señorita? We have been over this ground time and again."

This was true. I had been pleading with Berriz almost daily since I had arrived at the Isle of Pines some weeks earlier. I had rented a small cottage near the sea, and I had been in his office at the prison almost every morning, when the colonel's head was still throbbing from too much rum the night before.

I could read his thoughts on these occasions. Who could blame a man who drank too much on the Isle of Pines? What else was there to do on that barren spit of sand? What Berriz would not have given for a transfer to Havana, where there were women. So he numbed his brain with rum in the privacy of his quarters at night, and when I visited him each morning he always rudely rejected my suggestions and chased me away. I knew I had offended him by failing to offer him money, but I had none. I had only justice on my side.

Just about everything on the Isle of Pines set Berriz's teeth on edge, but I suspect I was the worst torment of all. I was the most exhausting, to be sure, because I would not give up. On this morning, he first tried to intimidate me. When that failed, he tried a new tack. He struggled to sound paternal, capable, and wise.

"Señorita," he said, "almost every day since you came here— against the advice of the government, I must add—you have been looking for me to give him special privileges. First, you want to do his cooking for him. Then you want to bring in your own physician to care for him. And now you want him removed from his cell and brought to your cottage for dinner as though he were not in prison at all. Surely you know these things are not possible. You have seen that the Isle of Pines is not a harsh prison. It is certainly far better than the penal colony in Africa where your father was originally to have been sent. Please, go home to Camagüey, señorita, and leave me in peace."

At the mention of Africa, I shuddered. The Spanish prison in Ceuta, Africa, is a place of unspeakable vileness. To be sent there means almost certain death. To survive there is far worse.

"I will not leave my father," I told Berriz. "He does not belong in this prison with thieves and murderers. He is a patriot."

Berriz said, "Your father, señorita, was convicted by a court of law—"

"A Spanish court of law," I pointed out.

He said wearily, "A Spanish court of law, as you will, of treason. It was only through the clemency of our good Governor-General Weyler that he was not executed or sent to Ceuta, as would have been more proper. Instead, he was sent here—to a gentle prison under the command of a just and fair man."

I said nothing. And when it became clear by my manner and expression that my vision of this place and this man differed from his, Berriz suddenly erupted into another rage. He shouted, "And here he will receive no special privileges. None of my prisoners receive special privileges. Is that clear, señorita? Is that finally clear to you?"

Then, with true menace in his voice, he said to me, "And if you continue to plague me so, I will have you removed from this island under military escort."

The time had come, I realized. When I had arrived on the island, with no plan for freeing my father, I had judged Berriz a bumbling buffoon assigned to run a prison rather than fight rebels because he was a drunkard. I had since discovered that my earlier assessment had been only partially correct. True, Berriz was not a towering intellect, but he did possess a certain cunning. And it was clear now that he could be pushed only so far. I could not take the chance that he would remove me from the island.

So, I permitted my lower lip to quiver. Then I began to tremble—perhaps a bit too dramatically, but I sensed that Berriz required a bit more emotion than would have been necessary with a more subtle man. I caused some large tears to roll down my cheeks. And, very quietly, I began to sob.

Berriz was astonished.

For weeks now, he had watched me as I had walked by his men and endured their remarks—words that would have reduced some of those soft Spanish gentlewomen to tears in an instant. I had fended off those pigs with careless disdain. Now, when he least expected it, I was crumbling, and he was feeling the surge of pity I had hoped my tears would instill in him. Berriz was thinking the thoughts I wanted him to think. *It is not the girl's fault that her father is a traitor. Is it so bad that she loves her father so deeply?* This is what was going through his tiny mind, I could tell.

He was most uncomfortable. He said, "Señorita, you must not carry on so. Surely you can see that I have no choice. I cannot permit your father outside these prison walls."

I merely sniffled and lowered my eyes. I said, "Colonel, I love my father more than I can say. I will make you a bargain. If you will permit my father to come to my cottage tonight—just once, for a decent meal and some conversation—then I will return to the main-land. And I will be most grateful, Colonel. More grateful, perhaps, than you can imagine."

He chuckled. So here it was—the bribe he had been seeking. The Spanish army is one of the poorest paid in Europe, and money routinely buys Cubans favored treatment. But how much? Immediately, he began to haggle.

He said, "Señorita, what need does a soldier stationed on a small, isolated island have of money?" He spread his hands expansively, indicating the meanness of this world. "What could I buy?"

I then clarified matters for him. I said, "I have no money to give you, Colonel. I was thinking of . . . well . . . a more personal expression of gratitude."

The pig's eyes glittered. He would rather have had money, of course, but he would take what he could get. He said, "I suppose some accommodation could be reached."

That night, Berriz and four soldiers marched my father to my cottage by the sea. They arrived as the sun was setting in the west, painting the clouds red and purple. I brought my father inside while Berriz's men began to play cards in the sand outside my front door.

Night fell quickly. Inside, I lit candles and oil lanterns throughout the house. After a while, I noted that Berriz was not participating in the game. These enlisted men were not his equals, and he did not socialize with them. His only companion after duty hours was his rum. He smoked a cigarro and stared out to sea, and I knew what he was thinking.

He was wondering if he should have forced me to submit before carrying out his end of this bargain. He knew, however, that I might not have gone along. Besides, he might want me more than once, and if he were to betray me by refusing to bring my father to my cottage—which he surely would have done had I submitted first—I would never have permitted him near me a second time no matter what he promised. He wanted my gratitude. I already had what I wanted—my father in my cottage.

It was hours before Berriz grew impatient. Finally, he burst into my cottage, where my father and I sat at the table over the remains of the meal I had prepared, and he said, "It is time to go, Cosio. Your escort awaits."

My father said, "I have just this moment lit my cigarro, Colonel. I would consider it a kindness if you would permit me a few more minutes."

Berriz snarled, "Now."

My father and I exchanged glances. I got immediately to my feet and said, "Colonel, before my father returns to his cell, may I have a word with you?"

He said, "We can talk later, señorita. Now I must—"

I gestured toward the bedroom in the rear of the house. "Could we talk in there while my father finishes his cigarro?"

Berriz was puzzled. Surely, I would not permit him to take me while my father waited in the next room. He glared at me. I met his gaze firmly. He glared at my father, who averted his eyes. Then he understood. My father was beaten. Anything for a few more minutes out of his cage. The colonel considered all this.

He said, "Of course. Your father must finish his cigarro."

We went into the bedroom. I closed the door and leaned against it. He smiled and said, "So, here we are, señorita."

I said, "Yes, Colonel. Here we are."

He crossed the few steps that separated us. As he reached to embrace me, I took a quick step forward. With a rapid movement, as I had been taught by my *compañeros* in the Insurrecto, I brought up my foot in a kick that caught this unsuspecting thing of filth squarely in his detestable private parts. It was a good kick, señors. I could hear it land with a satisfying *thud!*

At first, Berriz merely stood before me, transfixed with surprise. Then the fire in his crotch hit with a vengeance and rose up rapidly into his guts. A strange, low-pitched sound filled the room, and it took me a moment to realize it was issuing from his throat. His hands covered his legs where they joined, and he pitched forward to his knees. The impact when he struck the floor seemed to shake the entire building. It surely doubled his agony.

I immediately turned and opened the door. I whispered, "Papa!"

Slowly, my father took one last pull on his cigarro. He stubbed it out on his plate, rose, and walked slowly into the bedroom. He looked down at Berriz, who was still clutching his foul male organs and mouthing deep grunts of pain.

My father said, "My daughter is a very resourceful young woman, no, Colonel?"

I hurriedly shut the door behind us. I said, "We must hurry, Papa."

I reached inside my bodice and produced the set of brass knuckles I had been given by my *compañeros* in the Insurrecto. As I fitted this thing on my hand, Berriz realized what was coming. This son of a sow pleaded with me with his eyes. I struck his face with all my force. I heard the teeth on the left side of his mouth break. He toppled headlong to the floor, unmoving.

I said, "Now, Papa."

I had told my father during dinner of my plan. At first, he had tried to persuade me that our chances of success—of physically over-coming the enormous Berriz without alerting the others—were too slim. But I had been insistent, and he had agreed to let me try.

He had two reasons for this. First, my father knew I would never leave the Isle of Pines as long as he was a prisoner. He suspected also that I was fully capable of sleeping with Berriz, or an army of such beasts, if that activity would keep me close to him. He was not entirely wrong. I love my father very much, señors. And, two, my father did not want to return to the horrid little cell where he lived with rats. That he considered more cruel than hanging.

My plan was this: Each night, the fishermen of the Isle of Pines would carefully remove their sails and carry them back to their shacks, lest the sails be stolen. A fisherman without a sail was a fisherman who could not reach the deep waters where the big fish swim.

But one fisherman—his name was Manuel—was habitually care-less with his sail. Night after night, he left his sail in the bottom of his little fishing dinghy. He did this because the señorita from Camagüey had given him the last of her money to behave carelessly, and because she had promised him she would replace the sail if it were stolen before she had use for it.

And so we went out the rear door and ran down the beach toward the spot where the boats were kept—toward a boat with a sail that might, if we were lucky, carry us to the mainland. And, if it did not, would my father be worse off?

I knew we should have killed Berriz, but my father would have none of it. I had no choice but to give in because he would not have cooperated had I defied him on this. My father, señors, is too gentle a soul to be a revolutionary, and that has been his undoing.

As it was, I knew as we fled down the beach that the soldiers would soon be after us. It took only minutes, although it seemed like hours, for us to reach the boats. They were not much. The largest was only fourteen feet long—small enough for a man to sail alone yet large enough to contain a respectable load of *bonita*. The boats were made of cypress, and they all leaked. The fishermen dressed them with pitch from the scrub pines that dotted the island, but the pines were too small to yield much pitch, and the ocean's salt ate it away almost as quickly as it was applied.

We quickly felt each boat with our hands, searching for the one with the sail. At last we found it—canvas lying in a crumpled heap at the bottom of a rickety boat. My father and I shoved this worm-eaten craft into the pounding surf. True to his word, Manuel had left the sail, but there had been no mention of oars, and these he had prudently stowed in his shack. So we could get out only a short distance, and we struggled to raise the sail as the waves rocked the little boat.

Then, down the beach, I saw the light. The soldiers were coming, following our trail by the glow of the oil lanterns I had been forced to leave burning in the cottage.

It was a dark night with only a sliver of moon. To the soldiers, we must have been little more than a darker blotch against the black of the night sea and the flashing white of the surf. Still, they spotted us and began to fire. The first shot went far wide, and we hauled frantically on the sheet to raise the sail. Then there were more bullets splashing around us. My heart sank when I heard the dull thump of bullets strike the hull of our frail vessel. The water gushed in on us.

I shouted, "Papa, we're sinking."

We had the sail up by now, and the breeze from the island had us moving. Papa wrestled with the tiller, trying to guide us out to sea, but the water was already above our ankles. We exchanged glances, knowing now our quest was hopeless. The boat slowly sank beneath us. When the water splashed over the gunwales, we held hands for a brief moment, said good-bye to one another, and then dived into the sea.

As I slipped beneath the water, I opened my eyes. I saw only blackness, and the silence of the sea was all-consuming. There was no gunfire, no crashing surf. It was a peaceful world, and I would have been pleased to remain in it. Only my lungs craved air. I struggled upward, my chest bursting. Then I was popping up, gasping for the cold air, and the waves were breaking over me. I put down my feet, but I could feel no bottom. I spun about in the water in time to see the top of the mast on Manuel's boat slip beneath the waves. I could see no sign of my father. I called for him, but the wind and the waves and the gunfire drowned out my words.

Spinning about in the waves, buffeted by their force, I spotted the dim image of a soldier on shore stripping off his blouse and plunging into the surf. I tried to swim out to sea, but the waves caught me and hurled me back. I swallowed water and came up coughing, fighting for air. I felt the soldier's arms encase me tightly, pulling me back toward shore. As the Spaniards retrieved me, coughing and retching from the surf, I cast one last glance out to sea. There was no sign of the boat, no sign of Papa. There was only the blackness of the water meeting the blackness of the sky. Then rough hands were on me, and I was bound.

And dragged back into the evil shadows of the Isle of Pines.

Ill though I may be, alternating between episodes of burning and freezing, my heart no longer thumps with such a distressing threat of cessation. My breathing seems no more impaired than that of any citizen of London, where coal smoke is such an essential component of the atmosphere. In my improved state of health, quite possibly one of transitory nature, I weigh the possibility of bedding Small Maria.

Surely she would not deny me in my hour of greatest need. What kinder way to dispatch me if my heart proves inadequate to the task of coupling in animal lust? I ponder the prospect as I lie alone in the hut. She seems for no good reason to view me with a special reverence, that spiritual attitude of a man to a god and a dog to a man. I find I am confident of my chances of success, based on experiences garnered before my unfortunate ill fortune. I await her return with renewed anticipation.

Small Maria has gone to market, armed with some of the vast store of pesos in my purse. A Hearstian quantity of operating cash was forced upon me by The Chief in San Francisco. Surely it will come in handy when funeral expenses are added to the other outlays of living. Soon, Small Maria enters the hut with vegetables and cornmeal.

"Are you hungry, Señor Bierce?" she asks.

I risk it. "Not for food, Small Maria. But for you, indeed. Come to me, child."

She puts down her booty and approaches the bed. I reach for her, but she pushes my hands away.

"There is always time for this," she tells me. "First, tell me more of the Insurrecto in Cuba."

Small Maria has grown annoyingly entranced with my tale—that is, largely Remington's tale—of Cuba. Perhaps that is because of the revolution currently unfolding in her own country, a conflict in which she clearly sides with the insurrectionists. I have struggled, to no avail, to make plain that a successful revolution is nothing more than an abrupt change in government, after which all returns to normality.

I say, "The tale can wait."

She replies, "I must hear of this revolution."

I tell her, "Revolutions are always accompanied by considerable effusions of blood. They are accounted worth it, but this appraisement is invariably made by beneficiaries whose blood has not suffered the mischance to be shed. Then comes but another revolution, Small Maria. Peace is no more than a period of cheating between two intervals of mayhem. We can devise more entertaining methods of passing time."

I reach for her again, and again she catches my hands. I say, accusingly, "You deny me, then?"

She says, "Not if your story is well told, señor."

Thus inspired, I say, "Do you recall Curry? He was the military aide who attended President McKinley at that auspicious gathering at Andrew Carnegie's town house in New York. Curry is an interesting sort. He served with distinction in Cuba, retired a brigadier, and then had the misfortune to be elected to the California State Senate, an august body artfully engaged in the circumvention of moral propriety.

"One night not long before I left on this journey to Mexico, Curry and I shared a haunch of mutton in Sacramento. Our talk gravitated toward his service with McKinley and the war. He told me of a meeting in early 1898 with the President and George Cortelyou, McKinley's secretary. Cortelyou had come armed with a copy of a cable he had just dispatched to Consul-General Lee in Havana. Cortelyou told the President, 'I expect to hear from the consul-general, sir, before the day is out.'

"The President of the United States, staring out the window of the Oval Office at the broad expanse of the South Lawn, turned slowly, his brow furrowed with concern.

"He said, 'I hope we get better information from him this time than we've gotten in the past. If all I had to go by was this"—he grabbed a newspaper from his desk and held it up—"then I'd be forced to send the marines down there this afternoon. The Spanish minister is going to be fit to be tied.'

"McKinley threw the newspaper down on the desk. The President well understood that the fiery Spanish minister, Enrique Dupuy de Lôme, was almost out of his head with rage over press coverage of the Cuban civil war. The Spaniard had proclaimed on any number of occasions that he viewed the *New York Journal* as the greatest enemy of clearheaded American understanding of the Cuban situation. The startling disclosures in the latest editions of that newspaper could hardly have softened his judgment.

"Across the front page of that day's *Journal* was one of Remington's matchless drawings. This was a skillful rendering of a young woman, horribly thin and drawn, lines of care and distress creasing her lovely brow. Across the top of the page, in capital letters in vivid red ink, a headline screamed: *Cuba's Joan: I Fought for My Virtue.* Dupuy de Lôme would be beside himself.

"McKinley plopped his thick frame into his chair. He ran a hand over his forehead and brushed back a few strands of thinning hair. Congress had never been like this, and neither had Ohio, where he surely wished he was at that precise moment. Barely a year into his first term, he was being forced to confront what his predecessor, the avuncular Grover Cleveland, had managed to avoid. McKinley found himself in command of a boisterous young nation eager to flex its growing muscle, and the likeliest target for this bit of bullying was Spain. Cleveland hadn't minded the prospect. He had made clear in his conversations with McKinley before leaving office that he viewed war with Spain as inevitable.

"McKinley, however, had a different perspective. He had been a soldier as a young man, and he was all too aware that young men died horribly in wars to defend the self-righteous ideas of old men. Idealist that he was, he had never thought this quite fair, and he had done everything possible to avoid conflict with the Spanish.

"But The Chief was quickly making that impossible. Editorials calling for war with Spain thundered almost daily from the pages of the *Journal* and the *San Francisco Examiner*, my home base. And Davis's stories were being picked up by the Associated Press and transmitted even to the tiniest provincial newspapers around the nation. Political pressure was mounting on McKinley. And he was, like all politicians, responsive to the squeakiest wheel. He understood that, in politics, integrity is no substitute for support.

"The President snapped at Cortelyou, 'Just what's the consul-general doing down there, anyway? Why are we finding out about matters like this from the newspapers—and the yellow sheets at that?'

"Cortelyou made a gesture of helplessness. He replied, 'Mr. President, we mustn't exclude the possibility that the young woman is precisely where she belongs and the consul-general felt the matter unworthy of reporting.'

"McKinley shook his head angrily. 'Hearst is reporting it, and so are the rest of the New York newspapers. With the exception of the *New York Times*, that is, and no one reads that.'

"McKinley picked up the newspaper again, studied it, then tossed it aside once more. He said, 'This sort of thing creates enormous sympathy for the revolutionaries down there. I had a message yesterday from the party boys in Ohio. Did you know that the Youngstown

Chamber of Commerce is so riled up over this Cuba business that they've announced a boycott of the Spanish onion? Can you imagine that? And now, I suppose, when this catastrophic economic sanction—not one more Spanish onion purchased in Youngstown, by God—when that fails to bring the Spanish government to its knees, they'll expect me to do something about it.'

"My friend Curry had held silent until then. At that point, he interjected, 'Well, Mr. President, some action on your part might tend to put a lid on that young Turk you just put into the Naval Department—that loudmouthed Roosevelt fellow. He's been proclaiming loudly ever since he arrived in Washington that you have no more backbone than a piece of pastry, or some such thing.'

" 'A chocolate éclair,' McKinley corrected. 'I'll take care of the overly exuberant Mr. Roosevelt when the occasion arises. He wouldn't be within three hundred miles of Washington if I hadn't been forced to make certain concessions to certain people in New York for some support in Congress. Politics is the art of fishing tranquilly in troubled waters, Colonel—something Mr. Roosevelt hasn't yet discovered. And he'll learn that lesson painfully, if I have anything to say about it.'

"Curry replied, 'Be that as it may, sir, he's already making something of a name for himself. He's been on the Hill screaming at the top of his lungs for more money for the navy. He wants six more battleships, six more large cruisers, and seventy-five torpedo boats.'

" 'Good God!' McKinley cried. 'What do we need with all that? That would give us a navy bigger than Germany's. We need nothing of the sort for national defense.'

"Curry said, 'Roosevelt isn't interested in national defense, sir. He's an expansionist, pure and simple. He's a man looking for a fight. And, since Spain provides us with the likeliest prospect for a war, he wants a fight with Spain and the ships to fight it with.'

"McKinley shook his head wearily. 'Everybody wants me to go to war with Spain—this rich young lunatic, Roosevelt; that other rich young lunatic, Hearst. Politics is a demanding occupation, Colonel, but I've learned this much from the game—nothing is politically right that's morally wrong.'

"Curry served his master dutifully. And he saw his duty as providing the President with informed advice. In that regard, he said, 'I can't speak with any authority on the politics of the matter, sir. But, speaking purely as a military man, certain undeniable advantages would accrue to us if Spain were, for whatever reason, to depart the Caribbean. And I'm not talking just about Cuba.'

"McKinley leaned back in his chair. He'd heard the arguments before, but not from a man whose military advice he valued, and not from a trusted aide whose loyalty was without question. The President demanded, 'Explain yourself, Colonel.'

"Curry nodded submissively. Then he said, 'I'm talking, for one thing, about the canal through Panama that has been dreamed of for so many years. Such a canal wouldn't be secure to American shipping with a serious Spanish presence in those waters. From a military standpoint, it would be foolish to build such a thing unless the Spanish were cleared out.'

" 'That,' McKinley broke in, 'is if the damned thing can be built at all. It would be an engineering project of horrifying proportions.'

"Curry said, 'I can offer no advice on engineering, sir. I can, however, tell you that without a Spanish naval presence in those waters, Puerto Rico would be ours for the plucking. A Cuban naval base would also be of great advantage. And in the Pacific, a Spanish withdrawal would open the way for us to take over Guam, the Philippines, and perhaps even the Hawaiian Islands. We could extend the outer walls of Fortress America, Mr. President, well into each ocean. It would virtually assure that no power, from east or west, could reach our shores without unacceptably bitter naval warfare.'

"McKinley pondered the matter. He sat in a house that had been burned almost to the ground by the British only eighty-five years before, and Curry's vision had its appeal.

"That was when Cortelyou threw in his two cents. He felt compelled to add, 'Also, sir, the economic implications of such regional dominance would be of enormous appeal to the chambers of commerce in Youngstown and elsewhere. Annexation of Hawaii would provide us invaluable access to the markets of the Orient. In addition, Hawaii's sugar would be of great benefit—especially considering the havoc the rebellion in Cuba has wreaked on the sugar industry there.'

"Curry then weighed in with an even grander perspective. He said, 'We also can't ignore the fact, Mr. President, that the expulsion of Spain would make our military position in the Western Hemisphere vastly more influential. And we could extend that influence, without bloodshed, as far as Asia. It might well be that with all his foaming over Cuba just to sell a few newspapers in New York, this Hearst fellow is providing us the opportunity to do real good for our military posture in a rather large chunk of the world.'

"McKinley felt himself pushed and pulled in a great tide that was dragging his nation into war. He said, 'Yes, I've heard all that before, and it all has merit. America teeters on the brink of becoming a global power by virtue of the real estate we occupy. Still, gentlemen, I view it as my duty to avoid war. If we need to grow, then my duty is to accomplish growth through peaceful negotiation, just as Jefferson negotiated the Louisiana Purchase. Negotiation takes time, and it's not served by war fever whipped up by yellow journalists.'

"'Forgive me, Mr. President,' Curry replied, 'I'm not much of a political philosopher. I do believe, however, that moments crop up in history when a single man can alter the course of world affairs and the balance of power between great nations. It may well be, sir, that the yellow journalists of New York are forcing upon you such a moment. If so, then you must seize it.'

"McKinley's expression hardened. Curry, who ardently believed every word he had just uttered, wondered if he had gone too far. The President said, 'You too, Colonel? Are you urging me to use this girl—Cisneros, or whatever her name is—as a pretext to send troops to Cuba?'

"Curry shook his head. 'Not troops, sir. But I would suggest that you could blunt the force of this fellow Roosevelt's attack if you were to dispatch a naval vessel or two into the area as a show of force. That would guarantee an American military presence to protect our commercial interests, and it might ease pressure from the Hill.'

"McKinley rubbed his chin thoughtfully. 'It might shut up that maniac for a little while, and that would certainly be something.'

"Cortelyou said, 'It could be useful from a political standpoint, Mr. President. It would take the edge off this tripe Hearst is printing, and it would indicate genuine responsiveness on your part to the deeply felt sentiments expressed by the Youngstown Chamber of Commerce.'

"McKinley laughed aloud at that. He said, 'I suppose you're right, George. No Republican politician can eternally withstand the chambers of commerce—not even the president. All right, send a battleship or two down to Havana Harbor and have them just sit there. Just sit there, now—understand?'

"Curry clicked his heels like a Prussian corporal. He said, 'Very good, sir. The *Maine* is available. I'll have orders cut dispatching her to Havana.'

"The President leaned back in his chair and picked up a sheaf of papers on his desk. His aides, correctly viewing this as a dismissal, turned and headed for the door leading out of the Oval Office. As they did, McKinley called out, 'Colonel?'

"Curry said, 'Sir?'

"McKinley said evenly, 'If there's going to be a war, I don't want us starting it. I want that made clear to the captain of that vessel.'

"Curry nodded. 'I'll see to it, sir.'

"McKinley said, 'Very well, then. Thank you.'

"As Curry headed out the door, he heard the President's voice from behind him. McKinley was speaking quietly to himself. Curry strained to hear the words, and he caught them as the door closed behind him.

"The President was muttering, 'Chambers of commerce, indeed . . .' "

Small Maria has listened intently to my story. Her expression now is intensely serious. This is not at all the state of mind I had sought to induce.

I say to her, "I have offered you a rare window, child, on the doings of the mighty. Some women find such contemplation of power a potent aphrodisiac. I trust you are appropriately representative of your gender."

I reach for her once more. Once more she grasps my hands, more enthralled by my words than by my more tangible assets.

"You must continue talking, Señor Bierce," she orders brusquely. "I would know more."

For a long moment, I say nothing. I ponder the strange events unfolding in this hut. I fear that through my tale I am unwittingly committing a horror of almost uncontemplatable dimension. In all the universe, does there exist sufficient forgiveness for what I suspect I have created here?

A woman who has commenced to think.

EIGHTEEN

Frederic Remington
Cuba, 1898

We dared not submit our stories on Evangelina to censorship. Relying instead on the contacts of our resourceful bellman, Diego, we smuggled out dispatches on various boats bound for America. We had no idea how long we might be permitted to remain in Cuba once the Evangelina stories began running in the *Journal*, but it often took weeks before the New York newspapers made their way to Havana. Moreover, Weyler was in and out of the city, waging some sort of campaign against a regrouped Free Army in the east. If he'd happened to spy the fruits of our labors, he must have restrained his urge to expel us for breaking censorship. But he probably hadn't had time to study the American press—not with renewed military demands occupying his attention.

Regardless, Davis and I knew our time in Cuba was limited. At some point, some Spanish bureaucrat in Havana or Washington would erupt over the Evangelina story, and we would be on a steamer back to the United States. If we were going to help this girl escape from Recojidas Prison, we would have to work quickly.

Unfortunately, we still had no clue as to how we might go about such a perilous task. We visited her almost daily for the next week. I was somewhat surprised on one of those days to spot Peatam skulking about in Obispo Street behind us. I learned from one of the prison guards that Peatam had attempted to see the girl, but Davis and I'd already assured her that her best hope of salvation lay with the *Journal* and that she should speak to no other American reporters.

Evangelina was most interested in our adventures in Cuba prior to our contacting her. She was also, of course, interested in how her father and the other rebels had been living in the mountains. We told her what we could. At one point, Delores figured in one of the tales we recounted. Evangelina—like most Latin women, wiser than her years in such matters—asked me directly, "You were in love with this Delores?"

I told her honestly, "No. I have a wife in New York."

Evangelina only nodded. She said, "Do you think Delores survived the Spanish attack?"

"I don't know. My suspicion is that if anyone survived, it was Delores. I imagine she's still up there on that mile-high mountaintop with the Insurrecto."

"It is to be hoped," Evangelina said.

I never knew, Bierce. To this day. I have no idea what became of Delores. I would hope that by now, with the war over all these years, she's a placid matron with children to occupy her attention. She would be . . . let's see, now . . . twenty-seven or twenty-eight years old. I think of her often. Ah, well . . .

Evangelina also exhibited an intense curiosity about America—especially New York. Davis told her, "It's much bigger than Havana, many more people. It's full of restaurants and theaters and people rushing madly to get from place to place."

"What sort of places?" she asked. "And why do people rush so?"

"They just do," Davis said. "That's the way people are in New York."

"Then they are not much like Cubans," she observed.

Davis laughed. The woman amused him immensely. The poor fool was quite obviously lovesick. It was almost embarrassing to watch.

He told her, "They're more like Cubans than you know. New Yorkers and Cubans seem to have one crucial characteristic in common. Both peoples are always, at any given moment, expending enormous amounts of energy in demanding their rights."

I told her what the place was like physically and what she would first see when she arrived there. I said, "What you'll spy first, from the harbor, is the Statue of Liberty. That went up only a few years back, and it dominates the entrance to the city from the sea. The moment your boat comes in through The Narrows, you see it off to your left. You'll also see more boats than you can imagine, Evangelina—barges, ferry boats, freighters. They float like flotsam against a backdrop of red brick and granite, structures of brownstone and painted wood, church towers, and odd, contorted creations of stone rising from the landscape like obscene statuary."

"It's the finest city on earth," Davis assured her. "You can have a meal the equal of any in Paris, hear an opera of such quality that the Romans would weep, then walk in the wildness of Central Park and go for a swim in the Hudson. And maybe you could catch a sturgeon for breakfast. You can do it all in the same day—or anything else your fancy requires. That's the sort of place New York is."

She said, "Is New York not a place of unspeakable coldness?"

"We have winter," I admitted, "but it's positively balmy next to where I grew up in the Adirondack Mountains. And the change in seasons has a charm of its own."

She also told us how she came to be involved in the revolution. She said, "At first, I believed in the Insurrecto because I believed in my father. But as I came to know more, I also came to believe that it is not right for Cubans to be ruled by Spain, many thousands of miles away. There is an essential question of right and wrong involved in our Insurrecto, no?"

Davis merely shrugged. "You have your version of right; Governor-General Weyler has his. It must be nice to be so certain of one's ·onvictions."

The girl eyed Davis carefully. "And you are not so sure of yours? Tell me, what do you believe in, señor?"

"A front-page story every day," he responded truthfully, "and two on Sunday."

Evangelina gave him a blank look. I explained, "People have more time to read the newspaper on Sundays."

She shook her head slowly, her expression one of sadness. "And that is all? You believe in nothing more?"

"That's actually quite a bit," Davis said, "although foreigners tend not to appreciate it."

"Here," she told the reporter somewhat coldly, "you are the foreigner."

"Duly noted," Davis conceded. "But you should understand, se-ñorita, that the American press differs from newspapers here—and from newspapers in Europe as well. In Cuba, a newspaper prints nothing but political propaganda. In my country, newspapers print news."

"*Noticias*," she said.

"Yes," Davis said solemnly. "That's the Spanish word for the contents of a newspaper. But it doesn't translate perfectly. Your *noticias* means just that—notices. In English, 'news' has a vastly broader meaning."

"What meaning, then?" she demanded.

I sat back to observe this little exchange. It was made all the more intriguing by Davis's rather poorly disguised romantic interest in the girl. Perhaps she hadn't yet caught on to the fact that he was so enthralled with her, but I somehow suspected she had and hadn't yet decided if the situation pleased or troubled her. If she was attempting to bully him a bit, just to see how he might react, she would find herself disappointed. Whatever his other feelings or failings, his ego and his brashness, Davis's temperament wouldn't permit him to be bullied.

He said, almost condescendingly, "News is a made-up word. It stands for north, east, west, and south—N-E-W-S, news. It means everything that's happening everywhere, from all directions. In America, newspapers are dedicated to informing people accurately and completely. To people in my line of work, devotion to that chore is something akin to a religion."

She nodded, a slow flush working its way up her neck to her cheeks.

"And you never lie?" she said accusingly. "You never exaggerate?"

Davis coughed a bit nervously. He said, "Well, we try not to. There are occasions, like this war of yours down here, that test our ability to present the news dispassionately. Sometimes we can get a bit carried away, I suppose."

"That is yellow?" she asked.

"Yellow?" replied Davis.

Evangelina said, "You told me not long ago that your newspaper—and other newspapers—are yellows. What are yellow newspapers?"

I couldn't resist, Bierce. I said, "Tell her, Davis. And tell me, too, please."

He shot me a sharp glance. Then Davis turned back to Evangelina and said, "Well, there are many different sorts of newspapers in America. There's a newspaper like the *New York Post*, for example, which is read by intellectuals and has a very low circulation; that means not many readers. Then there are papers like the *New York World* and the paper we work for, the *New York Journal*, which are read by ordinary working people—many more readers than tonier sheets like the *Post*. We're a lot like the people of New York—brassy, bold, demanding. We're lively and we're fun, and we never whisper when we can shout."

She gazed at him blankly. "I still do not understand this yellow," she persisted.

"Well," Davis said, groping, "papers like the *World* and the *Journal* are called yellows because of the stories we play up big—human interest pieces, crime articles, the sort of things people are really interested in. A city council meeting is a *noticia*—the sort of thing your papers like to cover. At a yellow sheet, we'll take an ax murder over a city council meeting any day. And so will most New Yorkers."

"But this word yellow," she insisted. "Why not blue? Why not red?"

Davis glanced over at me, desperate for assistance. "You're the artist, Remington. Explain to her about Outcault."

Evangelina shifted her attention to me. I told her, "Yellow is just a name that caught on because the *World* used to run a cartoon called

'The Yellow Kid.' It was about a street urchin, of which we have more than a few in New York, and his rather colorful adventures. Our master, the illustrious Mr. Hearst, finally lured the artist who drew the cartoon to the *Journal*. He was a chap named R. F. Outcault. After a while, the cartoon became closely identified with the sort of paper that carried it, and people began to call papers like the *World* and the *Journal* yellows. It means . . . well, I suppose it means we're brighter and livelier."

"Precisely how are you brighter and livelier?" she inquired.

"Well," Davis said, "you're lively, Evangelina. Cuba is lively. That's why we're down here writing about you and your revolution."

She shot Davis a cold glance. "This is what our Insurrecto is to you, then? That is all? You do not believe in our cause?"

"We believe in our cause," he responded honestly. "And that cause, Evangelina, is to make sure that the American people know about your cause. It amounts to more or less the same thing."

She shook her head slowly. "I think not. I think your cause is much different, señor."

"Our ends are the same," Davis argued.

"No," she said. "Our end is liberty. Yours is profit. This is not the same. I do not think I like this yellow of yours."

Davis merely smiled in quasi-surrender. He told her, "That may be, pretty señorita, but the yellows certainly like you. And, to prove it, we're going to arrange your escape from this prison."

NINETEEN

While Davis and I were hanging around Havana figuring out how to stage a jailbreak, we came to develop rather cordial relations with Consul-General Lee. Davis had taken the prudent step of doing a rather flattering profile of the fellow for the *Journal*, insisting that I illustrate it with an even more flattering sketch. The result was that the consul-general became our fast friend.

And a source of useful information about what was happening at home and elsewhere.

Lee was a delightful old chap. He was the cagiest of politicians, and his slow, southern speech masked a first-rate mind. He spoke regularly with diplomats of other nations to augment the information the State Department made available to him, and several glasses of rum had a tendency to loosen his tongue.

It was he who explained to us the extent of the political pressure on President McKinley to intervene in the Cuban situation. And by that time, the pressure was truly enormous. McKinley was just about the only man in America who wasn't howling for war with the Spanish. Consul-General Lee also recounted for us a story he'd heard from a Dutch diplomat who'd been present at a meeting a week or two earlier in Madrid at which the Cuban situation had been discussed at the highest levels of the Spanish government.

It seems that the queen regent, Maria Christina, had erupted in a towering rage at General Carlos Castillo Montoya y Escoto, the commander in chief of the Spanish military, over the question of how a simple country girl like Evangelina had been capable of rousing so much American ire against Spain. Montoya had argued that it was all the fault of The Chief and those lying journalists he'd sent to Cuba—presumably, Davis and myself.

The queen had waved a sheaf of papers at Montoya. She told him it contained signatures from around the world demanding Evangelina's freedom. More than two thousand signatures had been collected in Britain alone, Bierce, after The Chief had asked Lady Rothschild to organize the effort there. And, in the States, The Chief had done even better. He'd collected God knew how many signatures. Among them were the names of the wife of Secretary of State Sherman and—you'll love this, Bierce—the President's mother. The Chief had actually persuaded McKinley's mother to sign a petition protesting the weakness of American policy with regard to Cuba.

The queen regent complained to Montoya that she'd received letters of complaint from the Sisters of Notre Dame and from the superior of the Order of Visitation—both powerful forces to array against a Catholic monarch. And she told Montoya that similar pressure had been brought to bear on Pope Leo XIII, who was now inquiring of the Spanish government about Evangelina.

"This horrid little newspaper!" the queen regent said to Montoya. "You have given this man Hearst ammunition to use against us with this furor over a silly girl. The people of America are outraged, and only McKinley holds them back. How much longer he can keep them from our throat in the Caribbean is a question I would prefer not to consider."

Montoya backed Weyler. He told the queen regent that Evangelina was a traitor and that Weyler was holding her for trial because she'd committed treason. He urged that the government support the governor-general, who was in such a difficult position in his attempt to maintain order. Any other course, Montoya suggested, could undermine Spanish authority in Cuba.

The queen regent had remained obdurate. "Undermine Spanish authority?" she shouted. "They are in armed rebellion against us! Does not Weyler consider our authority there already sufficiently undermined?"

Montoya had been a soldier for a half century, and he'd been in command of the Spanish military a good many years. In the end, the Dutch diplomat told Consul-General Lee, the general convinced the queen regent to permit Weyler to carry out his duties as he saw fit; but now looming in the air was the possibility of a royal pardon for Evangelina if the queen regent were to lose confidence in her military advisers. Given the tale of her anger, that didn't seem all that unlikely.

The moment we heard that story, Davis insisted on scurrying over to the prison to let Evangelina know.

"We now have some understanding of why Weyler hasn't thrown us out of the country despite the fact that he knows we're smuggling out uncensored dispatches. He's apparently afraid of the furor that would cause—in New York and, shortly thereafter, in Madrid. That's how effective our reporting has been in shaping public opinion. Our problem here, Evangelina, is that our reporting may have been too successful. We're told that you might be pardoned."

"This would be a bad thing?" she asked in mystification—a mystification, by the way, that I shared completely.

"It would be a disaster," Davis assured her. "The *New York Journal* has too big a stake in your case to permit a pardon to kill this story for us. If the Spaniards free you voluntarily, we might not get proper credit for your liberation in the eyes of the world. Also, a pardon will dramatically reduce your effectiveness as a fund-raiser for the Insurrecto. It just won't do, Evangelina, to have you set free as an example of Spanish civility. You must escape from this prison dramatically."

The girl said, "But how can you possibly break me out of here by force?"

"Yes," I broke in. "I'd like to hear the answer to that one myself, Davis."

"It won't be by force," Davis assured us. "It'll be by stealth. Here's what I've come up with: There's a small apartment house next door to the prison. Its roof is only a single story below the roof of the prison. The place is empty, unless you count rats, and the landlord was more than happy to rent me the top floor."

I was aghast. "You've already rented it? Why didn't you tell me?"

Davis said, "I was going to, Remington. But, knowing how cautious you are, I wanted to wait until I had a plan worked out solidly enough to satisfy even you. We can get to the prison roof from the roof of the apartment house. Then you can lower me down the side of the prison on a rope. You were heavyweight champion of Yale and all that. Surely you'll have no problem handling my paltry one hundred and seventy pounds at the end of a rope."

"That was a long time ago, Davis," I said, astounded at the man's brass. "If I can't hold you, you'll fall into the street."

"Then we'll find something on the roof to tie the rope to," he said almost casually. "We'll work it out. In any event, I'll be armed with a hacksaw. When I get to Evangelina's window, I'll simply saw her bars away and bring her out. Then we can climb back up the rope." He turned to the girl. "You'll have to tie a bit of cloth to the bars so I'll know what window to drop down to."

"Lunacy," I said.

"It's the only way," Davis argued. "We can't let them pardon her. It would ruin everything."

Evangelina seemed no more convinced of the wisdom of this plot than I. She said, "But even if you succeed in freeing me, what then? How would I get to America to raise funds for the Insurrecto?"

"We'd have to get you smuggled out by boat," Davis explained,

[167]

"but that shouldn't be difficult. Just about everything else you can imagine is smuggled in and out of Cuba almost daily. Our dispatches, for example."

"Dispatches are one thing," I pointed out. "She would be something else entirely."

Davis nodded. "You're right, Remington. Diego would be of no help in getting Evangelina out of the country. But do you recall Gomez telling us about the American sea captain on his payroll—that McDonald chap? I've put out the word that we want to see him at the hotel. As soon as we've connected with him, we can put this plan into motion."

I shook my head doubtfully, but Davis was paying no particular attention to me. He was fixated on Evangelina, and his manner toward the girl told me that his judgment had been badly impaired by his hormones.

He told her, "You have to remember to tie a bit of cloth to your bars every night, and to take it off just before dawn every morning. One of these nights, señorita, you'll find me outside your window, hanging like a spider, to take you to freedom."

She only gazed into his eyes. They were falling in love, Bierce, and it was clear that this situation was fraught with peril for a rational man like myself.

Davis told the girl, "I wouldn't do a crazy thing like this for just anybody."

TWENTY

The next day, Bierce—the very next day, by God—Davis's maniacal scenario went wildly awry.

We were lunching on the hotel veranda, arguing bitterly over the feasibility of the fantastic plan he'd concocted. Actually, this was but another installment of the argument that had begun the moment we'd left the prison the day before. The man had lost his mind, and I told him so.

It was one thing to develop plans to break Evangelina out of prison. I'd been reluctantly willing to explore the possible fruits of a well-placed bribe or two. But this? And especially when it appeared likely she would be free in the near future without any risk to us? Davis's argument that the *Journal* might not receive proper credit for her release in no way justified such a foolhardy scheme.

We were haggling back and forth over a meal of fresh fruit, boned chicken breast in some sort of spicy tomato sauce, and some rum and fruit juice when a squad of Spanish soldiers marched directly into the hotel lobby. They were led by an arrogant young officer, one strikingly similar in manner to the chap Gonzales had killed in the cane field. The officer grabbed one of the bellmen, asked him a question, and the bellman pointed directly at us. Followed by his men, the officer strode directly to our table and unloosed a burst of rapid Spanish.

I said to Davis, "What does this chap seem to want?"

Davis told me, "They're here to take us to Weyler. This young lieutenant here seems upset."

No one, however, could have been more upset than Weyler. We were dragged before him in his grand office in the governor-general's palace. His dark face was nearly purple with rage. When he informed us we were being ejected, however, he spoke in crisp, controlled tones.

"You can't do this, General," Davis moaned.

Weyler's eyes were flashing. He said, "You are quite wrong, Señor Davis. I can do precisely what I please on the forty thousand square miles of this island. I once told you that I am not foolish enough to jail any more American journalists, and that remains true. And I have been more than patient with you, permitting you to write the most outrageous lies and to smuggle them out for weeks now. But you have presumed on my tolerance too often. You and Señor Remington here will be on tomorrow's steamer for New York."

"General," Davis pleaded, "if you're angry about any of those stories, I can explain. You see, the editors in New York—"

Weyler raised a restraining hand. He snapped, "Forgive me, Señor Davis, but I find it difficult to distinguish between you and the newspaper you represent—this newspaper which has, in the past week, I might add, referred to me as the cruelest military dictator of the century."

So, that was it. He'd been pushed over the edge by a particularly spirited editorial that had appeared in the *Journal* earlier in the week. Given the elegant sharpness of its style, there could be no doubt that the author had been Sam Chamberlain, carrying out his chores for The Chief with characteristic vigor.

"Well," Davis said, "the editorial writers do get a little carried away now and then, General. That's not our doing."

Weyler opened a drawer in his desk and produced a copy of the *Journal*. On the front page was one of Davis's stories and what I must admit was one of my more skillfully rendered sketches of Evangelina. I had her at her prison window, pale and wan, peering out into Obispo Street below. I'd managed to do some interesting things with the lighting, Bierce, considering that I'd been working only in pen and ink.

Weyler said, "All right, we will blame those slanderous words on these mysterious editorial writers of whom you speak. Do you deny, señor, that these words are yours: 'This tenderly nurtured girl was imprisoned among the most depraved criminals in Cuba, and now she is about to be sent in mockery to spend twenty years in a servitude that will kill her within a year.' "

Davis squirmed a bit in his chair. Those were certainly his words. He'd read them aloud to me with some pride before smuggling them out to New York.

"And this," Weyler went on, his voice dripping with bitter sarcasm, " 'This girl—delicate, refined, sensitive, unused to hardship, absolutely ignorant of vice—has been thrust into a prison maintained for the vilest class of abandoned women in Cuba, and she has been shattered in health until she is threatened with early death.' "

Weyler looked up at us, his dark face even darker now. "I am told that you see Señorita Cosio almost daily, señor. Does she appear shattered in health to you?"

Davis made an awkward, futile gesture with his hands. "A little colorful writing, General. It's part of the trade—"

"He's right, General," I broke in. "It's just part of the personality of the yellows. It's certainly nothing to take personally."

Weyler threw the newspaper down on the desk and leapt to his feet. The suddenness of the movement startled us. I jumped in my chair, and Davis involuntarily shrank into his. The man's anger was terrible to behold, especially when you consider that he had the power to have us dragged out and hanged at his merest whim. But then the aging soldier took a deep breath, regained control, and settled slowly back into his chair. Quite suddenly, his mask of rage disappeared, and he became benevolent in manner. It was a startling transformation, and I wasn't sure what to make of it.

"I should not wish you to think me overly sensitive," the governor-general said.

Davis let go with a conspicuous sigh of relief. For whatever reason, Weyler's rage seemed to have vanished, and the reporter decided to press his advantage. He said, "Well, you were leaving that impression, General."

"Forgive me," Weyler said, leaning forward and opening a wooden box of cigars on his desk. "Please, have a cigarro. These are Cuba's finest."

Davis and I exchanged nervous glances. We leaned forward and each removed a long, thin cigar from the box. I bit the tip off mine and stuck it in my mouth. Davis ran his under his nose, savoring the ripe aroma of rich tobacco. He slipped the cigar in his coat pocket while I lit mine.

"General," Davis said, "I'm glad to see that you're taking a more realistic view of this. You're a man of the world, sir, and you understand how these matters work."

"I am being very realistic about this, Señor Davis," Weyler said softly. "And I do, indeed, know how such matters work." Then, in an instant, his brows flew together like a thunderclap. His face once again darkened dangerously, and his voice turned icy cold. "They work as I wish them to work. You may look upon these fine Cuban cigarros as souvenirs of your visit here. You are banished from Cuba." Weyler turned his head toward the soldiers at his office door. "Take them away," he snapped.

An instant later, we felt ourselves being lifted almost bodily from our chairs and dragged toward the door. Being acutely aware of the precariousness of our situation, I offered no resistance, but Davis broke free of his captor and glared at Weyler.

"I think you're being pretty thin-skinned about all this, General,"

[171]

he said, seeking to rekindle the debate. They grabbed him again and dragged us both from Weyler's lair.

Within the hour, Davis and I were back in our hotel room with an armed guard outside the door. No, we were told, we couldn't go to the prison. Yes, if we tried to leave we would be unceremoniously shot. Those were the direct orders of the governor-general.

We spent the afternoon—a strikingly lovely afternoon, by the way, as we could see from our window—packing our papers and the clothing we'd bought with The Chief's expense money. At sundown, a sumptuous meal was brought up to us from the dining room, but Davis left his food virtually untouched. I have to confess, Bierce, that I was delighted to be on my way back home to my Missie—and even more delighted that Davis hadn't managed to put his ludicrous escape plan for Evangelina into motion. He'd settled into the chair at the little desk in the corner, scribbling away at the story of our ejection, while I lay on the bed doodling in my sketchbook. I ripped off perhaps a dozen quick portraits of Weyler, highly stylized, some showing him with fangs, some with horns, some with both.

At one point, Davis looked up from his work and asked irritably, "What are you drawing there, Remington?"

"Nothing much," I replied. "Just playing."

Davis got up from his desk and began to pace the room. He was a vast reservoir of nervous energy. He said, "This isn't at all how I'd had our exit planned."

"Thank God for that," I said. "Now we go back to New York in a stateroom on a steamer instead of some filthy smuggler's hold—assuming we would have gotten that far. Nobody shoots us, at least."

"And we go back heroes, I suppose," Davis said. "The Chief might even give us bonuses."

I nodded in agreement. "We've certainly earned them. Stop moping around, Davis. I know what's bothering you, and it's foolish. The Spanish will let the girl go in a few weeks. With the pressure The Chief has been putting on them, they'll have no choice."

"I don't know," he said. "Weyler seemed pretty determined today."

I began to respond, but from the hallway outside our door we heard a muffled exchange of angry voices. Davis and I looked at one another in puzzlement. I went to the door, opened it, and peered out into the hallway.

I could see the armed soldier down the hallway a bit, his back to me. Standing directly in front of him was a smallish, bandy-legged man, clearly an American or a European, dressed in a seaman's cap and work clothes. He was arguing ferociously with our captor, who was barring his way. Davis poked his head out the door over my shoulder.

He said to me, "I'll bet I know who that is."

We watched for a moment. The conversation in the hall was a frantic babble of Spanish uttered in loud, impassioned voices. Finally, the sailor reached into his pocket and produced a wad of bills. The soldier guarding us immediately lowered his voice but kept on talking. Then, after a moment of thought, his hand went out. The sailor counted out five bills and placed them in the man's outstretched palm. The guard stuffed the bills into his tunic and let the man pass. We opened our door wide to admit him and closed it after him.

He was about forty years old, and as dark as leather from the sun. He said, "Mr. Remington and Mr. Davis?"

"That's us," I said.

"I'm Captain Bill McDonald, from the sloop *Seneca*. You left word you wanted to see me. I didn't expect to have to bribe my way past an armed guard."

"We're being ejected tomorrow," Davis told him.

"I guess I can figure out why," McDonald said, flashing a lopsided grin. "I've seen some of that stuff your paper has been running. Frankly, I'm surprised they waited this long to toss you out. So, what do you want with me? If it's smuggling, I do it. But it costs, gentlemen. These damned Spaniards aren't quite as polite with smugglers as they are with you fellows from the big New York newspapers."

"It was to be smuggling," I told him. "Now, it's all rather academic, I'm afraid."

McDonald shrugged. "No deal, then? Fair enough. Just give me the money I had to pay to get into this room, and I'll be on my way."

"Wait a minute!" Davis suddenly shouted. "We might still have some cargo for you, Captain. But first we have to get out of this room."

I felt my heart rise directly into my mouth, Bierce. I began to protest, but Davis merely ignored me. And McDonald was interested in the business. He paid me little mind as well. He said only, "Just that one guard out there?"

"He's the only one we've seen," Davis told him. "There might be more downstairs in the lobby, though."

"I didn't see any," McDonald said.

"There's a whole city full of them," I protested, futilely.

"If there's only one man," McDonald told Davis, "then there's no problem."

"There's an enormous problem," I said, seemingly pissing into the wind.

But McDonald was already opening the door and gesturing to the soldier.

"Señor," he called out.

The soldier approached cautiously. McDonald motioned again, and the man continued his wary approach. When he reached McDonald in the doorway, I was struck by the disparity in their sizes. The Spaniard was nearly six feet tall, no more than twenty years old, and solidly built. The top of McDonald's head came only to the guard's chin.

The sailor glanced over his shoulder at us, smiling. "Watch this," he said.

As the soldier moved to a position in front of the sailor, McDonald slowly raised both his hands. He held them palms outward. For the briefest of moments, the soldier's eyes fixed on them.

Which was when McDonald kicked him in the shin, hard. The soldier's mouth flew open in shock, and he made a sharp, high-pitched sound of utter surprise. He staggered from the blow, but by then McDonald had hauled off and delivered a second fearsome kick, this time to his other shin. The soldier hit the floor with a tremendous thump. As he struggled to a sitting position, McDonald moved back and drove still another ferocious kick directly into the guard's face. It was delivered with rather astonishing grace and economy of movement. The steel-toed work boot caught the poor fellow directly on the point of his chin. He fell over backward and didn't move another muscle. McDonald immediately bent over the chap, grabbed him by the ankles, and dragged him into the room, his rifle clattering along the tile floor.

"Where do you want him?" the sailor asked.

"The closet," Davis said.

I must confess to having witnessed this exhibition with considerable amazement. I said to McDonald, "I've never seen anything quite like that."

As he dragged the unconscious guard into the closet and closed the door on him, the sailor said, "Learned it from a French fellow in Marseilles. Them Frenchies, they like to fight with their feet. Most men figure if they're keeping an eye on your hands, they're pretty safe. But if you can get in that first kick, then you're in good shape. Now, what's your deal?"

Davis cast a nervous glance at the closet. "Is he likely to wake up?"

"Not for a while," the sailor said. "I've been doing this sort of thing for years, gentlemen. Trust me."

"Where's your boat?" Davis asked him.

[174]

"Tied up to the wharf at the foot of Obispo Street."

Davis was elated. "Wonderful," he said. "That's only a few blocks from the prison.

McDonald's eyes narrowed. "What's my cargo?" he demanded suspiciously.

"An escaped prisoner," Davis told him.

McDonald was silent for a long moment. "It's that woman, isn't it—that Joan of Arc girl?"

"That's right," Davis said. "And if you can see to it that she's delivered to William Randolph Hearst in New York City, you can name your own price, Captain."

"Along with us," I added hurriedly, now that we were into this demented thing despite my best efforts. "You have to deliver us as well—and in good health."

McDonald pondered the proposition for only a moment. You could almost see the phrase "name your own price" reverberating around inside the man's skull. "All right," he said. "I'll do it. When do you deliver her to my boat?"

"Tonight," Davis assured him. "We'll need some three-quarter-inch line from your vessel. And you probably ought to have some men in Obispo Street outside the prison to guide us to the wharf."

"She's still in prison?" McDonald demanded, truly astonished. "How the hell are you going to get her out?"

"We have a plan," Davis told the captain.

What he didn't tell him was that it was a plan devised by a madman.

TWENTY-ONE

We were gathering up our possessions. It pained me to leave behind the spectacular wardrobe of expensive tropical suits I'd bought at The Chief's expense, but there was no choice, and my attire was the very least of my problems. We were halfway down the stairs to the lobby when Davis suddenly snapped his fingers.

"I have to go back," he said. "I forgot my notebook."

"Get another one," I advised him.

He shook his head. "I've written a complete story in this one. I'll be right back."

"Hurry up," McDonald snarled.

Davis scurried back up the stairway. I said to McDonald, "I'm going back to make sure the fool doesn't dawdle."

When I reached the room, a startling sight greeted me. Davis was in the room, but so was Peatam. The Pulitzer man had the closet door open, and he was inspecting the still form of our sleeping guard.

Peatam was asking Davis, "Did you kill this man?"

"I don't think so," Davis told him coldly. "What are you doing in my room?"

Peatam merely shrugged. "I heard some noise in here, Davis. I thought perhaps you'd been injured somehow."

"I'm touched," Davis said.

Peatam flashed a broad smile. He said, "Well, since you're obviously all right, I'll just be on my way—if you'll move out of the way, that is."

Davis said, "Not a chance, Peatam. You'll go right to the Spanish. I've known you too long, and I know how you operate."

"Turn on a fellow American?" Peatam said in mock indignation. "I'm wounded, Davis, truly I am." Then his expression turned more sinister. He snapped, "You fool. Who do you think it was who talked Weyler into letting you stay as long as he did, despite all that garbage you were writing and smuggling out about that girl? Me, that's who."

Davis cocked his head. I was standing behind him in the hallway, just out of Peatam's line of sight. The comment had surprised me, but it carried with it the ring of truth somehow. Obviously, it struck Davis the same way.

"Why?" he asked softly.

Peatam snorted. "Competition, Davis. That's why. What's the point of having the best stories coming out of Cuba if there's no other American journalist in Cuba but me?"

Davis said, "In other words, you had to have somebody to beat. You can't be a winner unless someone else loses. Is that it, Peatam?"

"Something like that. But the game is over now. You wouldn't have jumped this poor fellow here unless you had some outrageous stunt in mind. And I can hazard a guess at what it might be."

"That's why I'm not stepping aside," Davis told him quietly.

Peatam laughed aloud. "Ah," he said, "but you are."

It really wasn't much of a fight, Bierce. Davis was a well-set-up fellow, but Peatam was nearly my size, and he was an experienced brawler. I heard two quick punches land and entered the room to find Davis stretched out on the floor, bleeding from the nose. Peatam glanced over at me as I filled the doorway.

"Well, Remington," he said, "would you like some, too?"

I merely bowed low.

The Pulitzer man was on me in an instant. He swung first, and the blow caught me high on the forehead. Peatam was a good-sized chap, but he, of course, had never been heavyweight champion of Yale. My first blow, a right, caught him squarely in the middle. I heard his breath leave him. He tried another halfhearted punch, but I brought around my left in a hammerlike fashion and struck him directly on top of the head. He dropped to his knees.

My instinct, of course, was to permit the fellow to regain his feet so I could knock him down again. But there was no referee in the room, and this was no time to observe the niceties suggested by the Marquis of Queensbury. I merely stepped back and, in my best imitation of McDonald's move, drove the point of my shoe into the chap's chin. Peatam fell over backward, quite unconscious. For a moment, I feared I might have killed him, but his breathing was regular, and his pulse was strong. I picked him up and threw him into the closet atop the guard. Then I gathered up Davis and his notebook and headed toward the waiting McDonald.

I congratulated the captain on his technique. I told him it didn't seem quite sporting, but this business of fighting with the feet seemed to work rather well.

TWENTY-TWO

As luck would have it, there was no moon that night.

We made our way along back streets, praying we wouldn't encounter a Spanish patrol and realizing too late how prudent it would have been to have tied and gagged both Peatam and the guard. As we huddled in the shadowy street outside Recojidas Prison, McDonald headed off to his vessel and returned not too much later with a stout length of rope, a tripronged grappling hook, two hacksaws, and a half-dozen of the most ferocious-looking cutthroats I've ever encountered.

"Me and my boys'll wait right here," the captain told us. "You just bring the girl, and we'll get you all to the ship. If we're not a good distance out to sea by daybreak, we might have to outrun Spanish patrol boats, and I'm not anxious to try that. Try not to get caught now, you fellows."

Davis was conspicuously nervous. He said, "You just stay right here. We'll have her down in half an hour."

The apartment house next to the prison was a disaster. It was a narrow, attached building with an apartment on each floor. It was simple to see why it had been so easy to rent. The place stank of wet, tropical decay. Windows were broken. At least an inch of filth covered the uneven floors. None of the apartments was occupied—unless you counted rats the size of cocker spaniels. You've never seen a rat, Bierce, until you've seen a Cuban rat. I swear you could saddle them and enter them in rodeos.

We fought our way without benefit of light up the stairs in a truly stygian darkness. After four flights, we emerged on the roof to a welcome rush of fresh air. The prison roof was a story above where we stood. I shed my suit coat and vest and tied the hook on the end of the rope. I motioned for Davis to step back. I swung the thing about my head a few times and tossed it to land with a disturbingly loud crash on the slanted red-tile prison roof. Then the hook slid with a stark, scraping racket until one of the prongs bit into the ledge. I gave it a

[178]

hard pull and then hung on it for a moment. It seemed secure enough to support my weight.

We were both in our shirtsleeves. Davis, being the lighter, went up the rope first. He scampered like a monkey and disappeared over the edge. In a moment, he poked his head over the side and whispered down to me.

"There's nobody here, Remington," he hissed. "Come on."

Well, Bierce, easier said than done. I wasn't then the Falstaffian figure I am today, but my body was built more for strength than agility. I made it up the rope with considerable effort. By the time Davis hauled me to the roof I was drenched in sweat and breathing heavily.

We perched high above Havana in the night air and pulled the rope behind us. It took us a moment to get our bearings, then we carefully made our way across the slippery tile to the Obispo Street side of the prison. I was amazed at how easy it had been to reach this point. There are some tasks, I suppose, that those of northern European stock perform better than Latins, and imprisoning people securely seems to be one of them.

When we reached the portion of the roof that we judged to be above Evangelina's cell, I dug the end of the hook firmly between two roof tiles. Davis tied the other end around his waist.

He whispered, "You hold tight to this end, Remington, while I go over the side. I just hope Evangelina has marked her cell properly."

I said in response, "Be careful, Davis. You're something of a fool, but I've grown attached to you."

He merely smiled and made his way to the edge. I sat on the roof, planted my feet, and grasped the line with both hands. I nodded silently to him, and Davis eased himself over the edge and down the side of the building.

From my own standpoint, what happened next was rather uneventful. I merely lowered him slowly, hand over hand. It took some muscle, but it was nowhere near as hazardous as the task Davis had carved out for himself. He'd bounced off the rough stucco walls several times as he cast about for some indication of which cell window belonged to Evangelina. If any of the other prisoners saw him come by, they refrained from raising the alarm. I imagine they realized immediately that this was some sort of rescue mission, and their sympathies could hardly have been expected to lie with their Spanish captors in such a matter.

Davis told me later that going down the side of the prison was considerably easier than climbing up it from the apartment house roof. He had the hacksaw blades in his trousers pockets. It was only a moment or two before he spotted what he took to be a bit of Evangelina's petticoat fluttering from the bars of one of the windows that looked down on Obispo Street. He swung his way over to it and finally managed to place his feet on the ledge.

It was a fairly large window, nearly four feet high and perhaps two feet in width. He had plenty of room to crouch on the window ledge as he clutched the bars with one hand and the rope with the other. He peered into the blackness of the cell and could see nothing. He shut his eyes, counted to thirty, and reopened them. Thus adjusted to the darkness, he was able to make out Evangelina's shadowy form stretched out on the bunk. He was surprised to hear her gentle snoring. Romantic that he was, it hadn't occurred to Davis that his angelic love might snore.

"Evangelina!" he whispered.

But the girl slept like the dead. Fearful of calling her name more loudly, he released his grip on the rope and dug into one pocket for some coins, which he tossed at her through the bars. He'd managed to strike her with coins twice before she finally came awake.

"Over here," he hissed.

The girl was astounded to see him, and who could blame her? He was forced to hang from the bars and the rope while she did the actual cutting with one of the hacksaw blades. The tool generated a certain unavoidable volume. To Davis it seemed as though the entire prison must have heard it. In his own mind, he'd always viewed this as the most perilous portion of his plan. He'd known it would take considerable time to cut through the bars, and he knew that if he were to be caught it would most likely be at this juncture in the adventure.

"You're going to fall," she whispered to him.

"Not if I hang on tight," he told her, "and that's what I'm doing. But you have to hurry."

Evangelina managed to saw through one bar and was at work on another when the hacksaw blade broke in her hands. Luckily, Davis had a spare, and this was a sounder implement than the first. She was slicing through the second bar with relative ease when Davis, from his perch on the ledge, spied disaster in the making.

From below him, he suddenly heard loud singing. He cast a glance downward and saw McDonald and his men emerge from the shadows in which they'd been hiding and begin to stagger drunkenly down the street toward the docks. For a moment, he was baffled. Why would they leave? And how had they managed to get so drunk in so little time?

Then he realized what really was transpiring.

McDonald and his colleagues were pretending to be drunken sailors to move out of harm's way. Davis observed their boisterous escape, and he saw the reason for the ploy. At the head of a troop of

Spanish soldiers rounding the corner were Weyler and—Davis could hardly believe it—a badly bruised Peatam, his eye swollen like a mango from where I'd walloped him. From his spot three stories above the street, Davis could hear their conversation.

Weyler was saying, "I hope you are not wrong, señor—for your sake."

Peatam was insisting, "I'm telling you, General, they've come up with a plan to bribe somebody and get her out of this prison. Davis and Remington would never have attacked that guard—or me, for that matter—unless they had something bigger than just a story in mind."

Davis turned his face back to the window and snapped to Evangelina to hurry. There was no need to worry about noise now. Evangelina went about her task in almost a frenzy after that. She'd already cut through the top of the second bar. When the blade bit through the bottom, the bar flew out into the air to land with a clanging bounce on the cobblestones of Obispo Street. It was, I'm certain, the loudest noise ever made anywhere by anything. From my position on the roof, it sounded like a bomb, but by then the entire troop of Spaniards was inside the prison.

Evangelina was a trim girl, and she managed to slip through the opening without difficulty. Davis grasped her tightly and pulled hard on the rope, which had been our signal. Then, Bierce, came time for my real contribution to the effort.

As Davis tried to scramble up the rope to the roof, I gained my feet, braced myself, and began lifting the two of them, hand over hand. Their combined weight, I imagine, would have been between 250 and 300 pounds. My footing on that slanted roof left a great deal to be desired, but I've always possessed two distinct skills. I have a certain small ability as a painter and sculptor—how distinctive an ability must be judged by others—and a physical force inherited from my mother's family, the Sackriders. My mother's father once lost his temper and tore completely in half a pair of leather riding boots. Try that sometime, Bierce. He was a powerful man, and I can say without false modesty that I inherited his genes.

I hauled the two of them up to the roof, a full story, without faltering. Davis was staggered by the feat, but we had no time to congratulate one another. When the pair of them scrambled up the tiles to the peak of the roof, Davis told me what he'd seen. We knew we had no time to waste.

I detached the grappling hook from its position in the roof tiles, and we made our way to where the prison joined the apartment house. We'd hoped we might make the street before the alarm went up.

Unfortunately, we weren't that lucky.

Ambrose Bierce
Mexico, 1914

Small Maria is visibly distraught.

"You must not stop here, Señor Bierce," she shouts at me. "You must continue."

My angelic nurse's lust for this tale has become all-consuming. I have explained to her that I know only what I have been told and can only guess at how much of this might be true. She cares not, of course. For the rabble, lies make life tolerable. A man who will not lie to a woman has no consideration for her feelings. My angel unquestionably desires submersion in that variety of ignorance that distinguishes the studious. Who am I to disappoint her?

But the fever has returned. My heart pounds, and extended conversation taxes me. I try to explain this, but her desire to hear this tale cannot be sated. Her charity is crucial to me, so I struggle to preserve it. I accomplish this by presenting her with this questionable account. My angel requires this good lie, I suppose, because she has spent her life hearing so many bad ones.

I say, "Peatam told me at a later date his version of the events that transpired that evening. He said he regained his senses in the hotel room closet and immediately roused the battered guard with whom he shared quarters. Peatam dispatched the poor bugger to the prison while he sought out Weyler at the governor-general's palace. Weyler was reluctant to accept Peatam's theory of why Davis and Remington had chanced an escape, but he was eager enough to recapture them that he would be led to the prison on Obispo Street.

"Once inside, Peatam scrambled to keep up with the general, who strode down the corridor snarling, 'This is ridiculous, señor. The entire Free Army, such as it is, could not free the Cosio girl from these walls.'

"Outside the third-floor cell-block, Weyler rapped on the barred door with the hilt of his saber. The mountainous Negro matron dozing in a nearby chair leaped to her feet.

" 'Open the door,' Weyler ordered.

"The woman did so—immediately. When they gathered before

[183]

Evangelina's cell, Weyler was startled to see that the window bars had been cut away. He ordered the cell opened, and rushed inside. He stuck his head through the now open window and glared down into the empty darkness of Obispo Street. He turned to Peatam.

" 'You were right,' the general conceded.

"Then Weyler ordered a search of the area around the prison, He ... he ..."

"Señor Bierce," Small Maria cries out sharply.

She fears that I shall perish, the tale unfinished. I gesture weakly with my hand, struggling to indicate my shortness of breath. My angel glares angrily at me, her eyes fierce in their intensity and her expression uncharacteristically harsh.

"You may rest for a moment," she says. "But then you must talk, Señor Bierce. You must finish."

I gasp for air. What a horrid sensation, to struggle for a commodity one has always taken for granted. Small Maria watches me. Clearly, she wonders if I can muster the strength to complete this story.

So, too, do I.

TWENTY-THREE

Frederic Remington
Cuba, 1898

The tiled prison roof seemed far slippier on our return trip. When we reached the edge beside the apartment house, I secured the hook and we three slid down the rope. I descended last to the apartment house roof and found that from that angle I was unable to dislodge the hook from the prison roof above.

From below, we could hear the sounds of soldiers in the streets. They were milling about, scattering street-tough Havana alley cats and generally making a terrible racket. We could hear the sharp voice of an officer calling out, "Search that building—and that one as well."

Moments later, we heard them milling about the lower floors of the apartment house. I felt a terrible knot form in my stomach, Bierce. We were on the lowest roof on the street. The only other roof to which we might escape was the prison roof, which we'd just left. We were trapped where we were, and we began a frantic search for a hiding place.

In only a moment, we concluded there was nowhere, and we were forced to engage in a frightfully risky maneuver. We simply moved to the rear of the apartment house roof and lowered ourselves over the slightly raised edge. There we hung by our fingertips over a fetid, shadow-soaked alley four stories below. I would never have gone along with such a harebrained idea, Bierce, but I was certain now that we'd be hanged or shot if we were caught. Or, perhaps worse, locked away in Recojidas prison ourselves, our fate kept secret.

We'd been hanging there, our feet in thin air, for only a few seconds when we heard the footsteps of soldiers pounding up the stairs to the roof.

Someone shouted, *"Una cuerda!"*

They'd found the rope, and they now knew how we'd gotten Evangelina out of her cell. This was the occasion for a good deal of incomprehensible chatter from the Spaniards while we terrified culprits dangled from our rapidly numbing fingers. Then they went storming down the stairs once again, apparently satisfied that we'd escaped by that path before they'd entered the building.

Davis was the first to pull himself back up. Once secure on the deserted roof, he reached down and quite appropriately brought Evangelina to safety next. Only then did they turn their attention to me. And I needed it.

My fingers had gone numb, and I was within seconds of losing my grip. Moreover, while I'd rather easily lifted their combined weight on the prison roof—pulling them in with the rope as though they'd been no more than a big fish—I found myself unable to hoist my own rather dense frame while hanging on with just my fingers. It took both of them, reaching down and clutching my wrists and pulling hard, until I was able to secure enough of a purchase on the roof to scramble inelegantly to its surface. I merely lay there, gasping unabashedly for breath and delighted to have been spared the fall into the alley, which surely would have injured me severely had it not killed me outright.

"Are you all right, Remington?" Davis whispered.

With a gesture, I indicated I'd survive.

Davis sneaked over to the Obispo Street side and peered down. He was startled to find himself gazing directly on Weyler and Peatam as the party of soldiers that had searched our building emerged into the street.

"Well?" Weyler demanded.

One of the soldiers said, "There is a rope, my general, leading from the roof of the prison to the roof of this building."

Weyler merely grunted. "Search this building thoroughly."

The solider told him, "It has been done, my general. All the buildings in the area are being searched."

"Then call for more men and saturate the area," Weyler ordered. "They cannot have gone far. That fat matron swears she saw the Cosio girl in her cell only a few moments before we arrived. We must blanket the streets."

As the soldier snapped off a salute and rushed off to carry out his orders, Weyler turned to Peatam. "Both of us had best hope that this girl can be recaptured, señor."

To Davis's delight, Peatam seemed deliciously disturbed. He said, "If they get away with that girl, General, you'll at least have your job. If the *Journal* rescues the Joan of Arc of Cuba, I'll be laughed right out of New York."

Weyler said, "There are worse fates, señor. If such a thing comes to pass, then the fire fanned by your fine New York newspapers will almost surely erupt into war between Spain and *los Estados Unidos*.

And if that happens, I do not know if my country could win such a war."

Davis crawled back from his lofty hiding place and recounted to us in a hurried whisper what he'd just heard. He said, "Let's wait another twenty minutes or so and get under cover inside."

I had my breath back and was deeply disturbed by the fix in which we found ourselves. Evangelina, however, was delighted to have gotten this far. Impulsively, she kissed Davis. Even in the darkness, I could see the man flush at her touch. It was most annoying, Bierce, to see the pair of them carrying on so when we were still in such unspeakable peril. I'm certain my expression revealed my distaste for such juvenile behavior because they broke off their embrace almost immediately.

We waited a respectable period, trying to stay low and listening to the commotion in the street. Then we moved downstairs to a large room in the front of the building and spied carefully out a window. Dozens of Spanish soldiers, a veritable flood of the damned fellows, were taking up positions all over the street.

Davis said grimly, "It doesn't seem as though they're going any-where for a while."

I said, "I don't see McDonald and his men."

Davis told me, "They cleared out when the troops arrived, so I'm not sure just where we might go from here."

"Oh?" I said. "Isn't that a bit inconvenient for us?"

"It would have been vastly more inconvenient," Davis said, "if they'd gotten themselves captured. We know where their boat is, at any rate. It's at a berth at the wharf down the street—that way."

Evangelina had crawled up beside us. She asked, "How will we get to this boat of which you speak?"

"He has no idea," I told her. "Neither do I."

"They can't stay out there forever," Davis said.

"Perhaps they can," I pointed out.

"You're a born pessimist," Davis chided. "I figure that if they fail to find anything of value in the next few hours, they'll widen the search at dawn and give us a chance to slip out."

"The streets are filled with people just after dawn," Evangelina said. "I have watched them daily. Perhaps we could mix with the crowd."

I shook my head wearily. I said, "Evangelina, yours is a rather well-known face, thanks to the marvelous sketches of you that have graced the front pages of The Chief's newspaper and others that have lifted them scandalously for their own use. Moreover, Davis and I wouldn't be exactly inconspicuous in the streets of Havana—two rather obvious

Americans in dress shirts and the trousers of what were formerly rather fine business suits."

Davis frowned at me. "Have you any other cheering observations you'd care to make, Remington?"

"Only one," I told him. "This has all become rather more complicated than I'd bargained for."

Davis slapped my shoulder with annoying playfulness. "You worry too much. We'll get out of this just fine."

He and Evangelina moved away from the window and settled along the rearmost wall of the filthy apartment. He gathered her into his arms, and she rested her head blissfully on his shoulder. In just a moment, each was asleep. I sat in the darkness, slapping occasionally at any rat that came too near. I found my mood growing ever more evil. I gazed at the unseemly spectacle of the lovebirds dozing in one another's arms as though they had not a care in the world.

I said to myself, "Considerably more complicated, now that I consider the matter."

TWENTY-FOUR

Dawn sneaked like a thief into Obispo Street. It arrived stealthily as pallid rays slowly suffused the tops of buildings before washing down the stucco and filtering through the grime-flecked glass of our window.

I'd slept only fitfully, and the arrival of sunlight put an end even to that pitiful period of rest. Lying in the accumulated dirt beneath the window, I stirred, then came awake with a start. Davis and Evangelina lay in one another's arms across the room. I crawled to my knees and slowly peeked over the windowsill into the street. What I saw there, Bierce, made me physically ill.

As Evangelina had predicted, pedestrian traffic was growing stronger with the sunlight, but Weyler's soldiers were still at their posts. They huddled in small groups at intersections or lounged in the doorways of shops and houses. People walking by eyed them with cautious curiosity, and several of the soldiers showed signs of fatigue. They were yawning or stretching. It had been a long night for them, I imagined, although without much sympathy.

I glanced to my right, straining to see what lay down the street toward the docks. If McDonald's vessel remained at the Obispo Street wharf, it was blocked from my view. Beyond the wharf, however, well out in Havana Harbor, I spied another boat flying the American flag. It was a gigantic vessel, bristling with big guns. I was astounded to realize it was an American warship riding at anchor. It must have arrived the previous day, after Weyler had ordered Davis and me taken into custody. Or it had come overnight, while we'd been in clandestine isolation in this rat-infested pesthole.

I immediately awakened Davis. He carefully extricated himself from Evangelina's sleeping embrace and came with me to the window. The light was not yet sufficient for either of us to read the white lettering on the bow of the distant American warship, but Davis was equally startled to see it.

"McKinley must have ordered it down here to confound his critics," he observed. "The pressure at home must have grown quite intense for him to have taken this step." Then he studied the street directly outside, where the very cobblestones seemed to be sprouting Spanish soldiers. "That's not good," Davis told me needlessly. "I was certain they'd be gone by daylight."

"It must be boring, Davis, being so right all the time."

He told me, "If they're still there, then Weyler must be confident that he managed to keep us bottled up in this area. If that's the case, he's bound to order another search of all the buildings around here in daylight."

"In which case . . ." I began.

"In which case," Davis said, "we'll be captured. We can't go back up to the roof and hang by our fingertips all day. There's only one course of action open to us, Remington."

"Which is?" I demanded.

He said, "One of us will have to try to get to the *Seneca* and obtain a disguise for Evangelina so she can sneak through the lines of Weyler's men."

I was aghast at the sheer brass of the idea. "A disguise? What sort of disguise, Davis?"

He said, "We could dress her as a cabin boy—put her hair up under a hat of some kind, put her in trousers. It might work."

"Highly unlikely," I judged. "And how do we get to the *Seneca* and obtain this disguise of yours—assuming, of course, that this McDonald fellow hasn't gotten cold feet and sailed away in the night?"

"I'll go for it," he said simply. "I'll wait a bit, until the street fills up with more people, then I'll slip out and make my way down to the wharf. They'll be looking for the three of us together, Remington, not one of us alone. And I'm filthy enough after a night in this foul place to pass as a wharf rat if those soldiers have grown weary enough to lose some of their attentiveness."

"You're unbalanced," I told him, "but let's suppose you somehow make it, just for the sake of argument. Let's even suppose you get back here with clothes for the girl and get her out. I have just one small question: How do I escape?"

Davis merely frowned at that question. Unquestionably, I would be a conspicuous figure on the street. Not only was I unmistakably a *norteamericano*, I was also unfortunately noteworthy for my sheer size.

"Perhaps you don't," he told me finally. "But what happens if they catch you? I'm little known outside New York journalistic circles, Remington. You, on the other hand, are an internationally known artist. They might slap a relatively anonymous sort like me in prison. That would be a newspaper story of a certain magnitude. But were they to mistreat you, it would be on the front page of every newspaper in America and Europe. It's much more likely that Weyler would merely speak harshly to you and then order you escorted to the next steamer out of Havana."

Then he motioned to the sleeping form of Evangelina. "If they catch her, though, they won't let her go—not now. Not for anything."

I said nothing, but I was less confident than Davis that Weyler would treat me so compassionately. I entertained visions of the squalid cells I'd glimpsed during our visits to the prison next door, and the thought caused me to shudder. Davis was surely right, however, about the fate that awaited Evangelina were she to be recaptured.

I said, "They'll give her twenty years now, if she's lucky. You realize, Davis, how foolish this entire enterprise has been. We should simply have let them pardon her."

He only shrugged. "You should have talked me out of this, Remington. You're a marvelous artist and a pretty hardy sort of fellow to boot, but you're too easily led."

I tell you, Bierce, I was all set at that moment to simply knock this outrageous chap right on his hindquarters, but he seemed blithely oblivious to that impending prospect. Instead, Davis moved to the window, gazed out into the street, and announced, "We can't afford to take any more time with this. I'm going to try right now to make it to the *Seneca*. Wish me luck, Remington."

My anger at his careless remark vanished immediately. I must say I found myself suddenly very much aware of how perilous a venture Davis was about to embark upon. We'd been through several frightening scrapes since we'd boarded the *Vamoose* back in Key West, but this one seemed rather more ominous than the others. I couldn't have said why, precisely. Perhaps it was because the incident with the patrol boat, the clash with the Spanish patrol in the cane field, and our capture by the Spanish in the mountains had occurred before we'd begun our real work in Cuba. Now it was nearly over, and we both understood that our likelihood of returning to New York unscathed had never been more remote.

Whatever the reason, I found myself suddenly filled with a feeling of union with Davis, who had so annoyed me so regularly. I felt an unmistakable concern for a *compañero*. I imagine that unexpected emotion showed on my face, because Davis reached out and took my hand. The next moment, we were embracing like long-lost brothers. Then we pulled apart, each feeling more than a bit foolish. He gestured toward the sleeping Evangelina.

"Take care of her for me, Remington," he said.

Before I could respond, he was gone—out the door and down the stairs. I moved immediately to the window, flattening myself along the wall to observe his escape attempt.

The building in which we'd found shelter fronted directly on the street. From the window, I could see that pedestrian traffic had picked up markedly. Several dozen people crowded Obispo Street in front of our refuge. Before our building, a group of dockworkers was passing by, engaged in cheerful early-morning discourse. Directly across the street, in a doorway, a weary Spanish soldier yawned widely, the distension of his jaw momentarily shutting his eyes.

When the fellow closed his mouth and opened his eyes once again, Davis was out the door and into the street, walking easily with the party of wharf laborers as they continued down Obispo Street toward the harbor. From my vantage point, I could see them move only a few yards before they passed from my sight.

I knew he could never make it.

AMBROSE BIERCE
MEXICO, 1914

I have always been a prohibitionist, striving most vociferously to prohibit the reckless use of water, but water is what I need now. The fever has grown unspeakably intense in its cruelty, robbing me of even the strength to speak. I need water, I crave it.

And I need my whore. I need my angel.

Small Maria deserted me last night. She stormed off in a rage when the power of speech failed me at what she regarded as a crucial juncture in this pointless tale that so captivates her. My angel obviously regards my companionship as worthless unless it serves to amuse. How disturbing to be dependent on someone with so little intelligence and so much sense.

This business of dying is untidy and demeaning. Death holds no terrors for me. My vision of heaven is a place where the wicked cease from troubling you with talk of their personal affairs, and the good listen with rapt attention while you expound on your own. But the process of transition from this world to the next is proving an irritation of considerable dimension. I cannot bear this fever. Truly, I burn.

As I lie on my cornhusked bier, I sense I am no longer alone. I turn my head toward the doorway, and I see outlined in it the oval shape of Big Maria, the neighborhood's other whore. She is a woman of indeterminate age and shape whose popularity with the patriots of the Insurrecto stems from her willingness to simultaneously entertain as many of them as can fit into her hovel across the dirt street. Small Maria, a creature of more delicate sensibilities, permits only one at a time.

I croak to Big Maria, "*Agua, por favor.*"

She replies, "So, you speak again. She will be pleased."

I beg once more for water. Big Maria merely smiles benignly and vanishes into the light. I despair. Without water, I will soon be a mummy. I fear I shall end up in a museum, dried and brittle, serving as a satisfaction of that vulgar curiosity that distinguishes man from the lower orders. Perhaps the moisture-free preservation of my sorry corpse shall prompt these simple people to designate me a saint—a dead sinner, revised and edited. It would be an ironic fate and not altogether without its humorous aspects.

As these thoughts dance in my fevered brain, I become aware that Small Maria has reappeared. She smells pungently of yellow lye soap, an improvement over her usual aroma of raw humanity. She lifts my head and places a cup to my lips. The water she pours down my parched throat stinks of something vile. The wetness is delightful.

She empties the contents of one cup and half of another into me. When I began to choke, Small Maria returns my head to its resting place. I manage to gasp, "You are an angel, child. I can never repay your kindness."

She says, "You can, Señor Bierce. You can continue to speak."

I groan. I grow weary of this story, which is a matter of monumental inconsequence compared to my current level of discomfort. Extended speech robs me of precious breath, a commodity whose limited supply is of growing concern to me. I begin to plead, "Small Maria, please . . ."

She shakes her head. I see in her dark eyes not even a glimmer of the kindness that radiated from them only a few short days ago.

"Speak, Señor Bierce," she instructs me coldly. "I would know more of this Cuban Insurrecto. And, if you do not speak"—she slowly pours the contents of the half cup into the dry dust of the hut's dirt floor—"then no more water."

Our eyes meet. My angel's eyes are hard and uncaring. The appearance of my own I can only guess at. From my own side, they appear large and frightened, which is probably a reliable guide to their general condition. We gaze at one another for a long moment, rickety storyteller and insistent audience. It is a test of wills. Pondering mummyhood, mine fails first.

I say, "Davis made it to the *Seneca*. It was only three blocks to the harbor, and Weyler's soldiers were less alert than Davis had any right to expect. Perhaps it was a miracle—an act out of the order of Nature and hence unaccountable, like beating a hand of four kings and an ace with four aces and a king. In any event, he enjoyed a fool's luck. He crowded close to the group of wharf workers, engaged them in carefree conversation, and walked with them through the knots of dull-witted Spanish soldiers in blissful delight over his good fortune.

"McDonald's sloop remained tied at the wharf. As the group of dockworkers passed it, Davis slipped away from them and crept furtively up the *Seneca*'s gangplank. He was met by McDonald, who was nothing less than amazed at seeing him.

[194]

" 'How the hell did you get out?' the smuggler demanded. 'The Spanish are all over the street.'

" 'I don't know," Davis replied truthfully, 'but now we have to get the other two out. I need to take back some clothing to disguise the girl and get her back to the boat.'

"McDonald shook his head emphatically. He said, 'Somebody has to go back, but you'd be pushing your luck if you tried it.'

"Davis asked, 'Who, then?'

"And McDonald told him, 'Somebody very stupid.'

"The crewman they picked was a fellow named Morgan. He was a big, bearded sort of about thirty-five who was in his bunk, sleeping off a drunk from the night before. McDonald awakened him, poured some coffee down his throat, issued him instructions, and sent him off up Obispo Street with a seabag over his shoulder. Morgan was nervous when he saw all the armed soldiers milling about Obispo Street, but he lacked intellect sufficient to support rational fear. He merely lurched up the slight hill, his head pounding from a night of debauchery, until he saw the building that had been described to him. Then he went inside, and . . . and . . ."

My chest heaves. There is no more breath to be had—I gasp for what air can be consumed in this foul little hut. Small Maria's pretty face darkens in menace.

"Señor Bierce . . ." she hisses. Her voice is a threat.

I feel her strong young hands on my face. She places a palm on each cheek and turns my face toward hers. She says, "I must know of this thing. I must!"

I am totally her creature, completely in her control. I gulp in air, suck at it greedily. My heart races. I know now that I am near my ultimate goal—a hole in the Mexican dirt. All that stands between me and this inglorious finale is this child-woman, so insistent on having her foolish way. I am prepared to die.

But not quite yet.

And so, I struggle for what little air I can find, and when I have mustered a sufficient amount in my burning lungs, I begin once more to speak, and once more recount Remington's tale. . . .

TWENTY-FIVE

FREÐERIC REMINGTON
CUbA, 1898

From our sanctuary in the filthy apartment on the third floor, I heard someone enter the building and begin climbing the stairs. Naturally, I assumed that the Spanish had intercepted Davis and were coming for us at last. I immediately awakened Evangelina, whispered to her of the precariousness of our circumstance, and took a position near the door with my fists cocked.

I was prepared at that moment, Bierce, to fight to the death with my bare hands. I'd given considerable thought to an extended stay in Recojidas Prison. It was a prospect with little appeal. I don't mind confessing that my nerves were frayed. Sitting here years later in Connecticut, it's obvious how foolish my decision to resist would have been. But when the big bearded man entered the room, I immediately pounced upon him and drove him to the floor with a spirited blow to the solar plexus. It was the sort of punch Ruby Robert Fitzsimmons used in dispatching Gentleman Jim Corbett. It wasn't until the poor chap fell that I realized he was only one man in seafarer's garb and clearly an American.

Holding his gut and gasping for air, he choked out, "You god-damned fool. You nearly killed me. I'm from the *Seneca*."

As I pulled him to his feet and hurriedly dusted him off, he treated me to a string of sailor's obscenities positively magnificent in their foul imagery. Evangelina stood by impassively. The girl was a cool customer, Bierce. All the women of the Cuban Insurrecto seemed to be like that.

"Are the soldiers still out there?" I asked the man, when he paused in his swearing.

He said, "They're thicker than fleas on a wharf rat, but this might help you get out."

He reached a brawny arm into his seabag and pulled out a wad of clothing. "The little lady better get into this," he said, tossing the bundle into Evangelina's arms. "And I've got some stuff for you, too."

He dug into the bag once more and emerged—God help me, Bierce;

this is what he had—with a swirling and gaily colored Cuban skirt. He said, "It's from one of the captain's lady friends. He likes 'em big. Strange trait in such a little fellow, but don't tell him I said that."

He handed me a white blouse from the bag and then turned to Evangelina. He said, "The stuff for you, ma'am, is from our cabin boy. He's only thirteen, and the things might be a bit snug. But you've only got to hold in your gut for a few squares."

Evangelina had laughed when she'd seen the skirt for me. Now, however, she reddened visibly. In a distinctly cold tone, she said, "Believe me, señor, I will not have to hold in my . . . stomach." She held up the dungarees in front of her, inspecting them. They were quite small. She said, "These will be more than large enough."

I was occupied with inspecting the skirt and blouse with more than a little distaste. I asked the fellow, "What about my mustache? What about my hair?"

"Ah!" he said, reaching back into the bag. He pulled out what I at first took to be a dead black cat, limp and bedraggled. I then recognized it was a wig. I appraised all this stuff, Bierce, and decided it was worth a try. I said to the seafarer, "Come on, let's go out into the hall and let the lady change."

His face fell. Even smudged with dirt, Evangelina was quite the vision, and he'd apparently looked forward to watching her undress. He said, "I'd feel safer in here."

I took his arm and said, "Outside."

Evangelina admitted to me later that the cabin boy's shirt was a tight fit and the dungarees had seemed impossible. She'd struggled mightily with the buttons, drawing in her breath and gritting her teeth to get them fastened about her trim waist. Finally, she was forced to lie down on the filthy floor and go through all sorts of contortions before she could button them. When she arose once again, her eyes bulged and she felt as though a steel band had been tightened around her middle. Her body had adjusted somewhat to the pressure before she opened the door to admit us. When she saw me, she burst out laughing.

I was nothing short of fetching, Bierce. The blouse was a puffy-sleeved peasant affair. The red, yellow, and green skirt was sufficient to accommodate a plow horse; McDonald did indeed like his women big. But the crowning touch was the wig. Perched atop my head and hanging down to my shoulders in ragged curls, it totally altered my appearance. Evangelina doubled up in laughter, popping the top button on her dungarees in her mirth.

"Dignity," I told her, "is no more than a state of mind."

McDonald's crewman, his chore complete, was anxious to be on his way. If we were to be caught, he wished to be nowhere near us, a sentiment for which I couldn't condemn him. He provided me with a black fan to hold over my face to obscure my mustache, then he was out the door and down the stairs. We heard him exit into the street.

We were to follow him in only a few moments, but we first needed to screw up our courage. I've never felt such tension in my life, Bierce, as I did in those last few moments in that shabby apartment in Havana. My knees were shaking, and I'm certain my voice was as well. Evangelina, however, appeared as cool as ever. I understood how aptly her prison nickname, the Ice Maiden, fit her. She fished a small cigar out of the cabin boy's pocket and said to me, "What should I do with this?"

"Smoke it," I advised her. "It'll help the disguise."

I found a match in the pocket of the trousers I'd discarded and lit the thing for her. She drew in, immediately coughing violently and letting loose a cloud of rich, blue smoke.

"Don't inhale it if you're not used to it," I advised her. "These things'll kill you on the spot. You won't even have to worry about the Spanish."

She coughed and waved away the smoke. "Must I smoke this?"

I ignored the question. I reached into the pile of clothing on the floor and pulled out a navy blue knit hat. I placed it on her head and carefully tucked her thick, black tresses up beneath its edges.

"Yes," I told her, inspecting her appearance, "you've got to smoke it. You're supposed to be a tough little sailor, and your face is far too clean."

I reached down to the floor, gathered up a liberal handful of dirt, and smeared it generously around the lower portion of her face, trying to make the stuff simulate several days' growth of beard. She looked almost pitiful in her men's clothing, with her cigar and the dirt on her face. Disguising her femininity completely was an impossibility.

I told her, "Unfortunately, you're still the prettiest cabin boy imaginable."

She laughed and told me, "No, you are far prettier, Señor Remington."

We moved down the stairs hand in hand. Near the bottom, I stumbled on the hem of that damned skirt, and the shaking of my knees was no particular help. She said to me, "Are you all right?"

"For now," I told her.

At the doorway, we halted. My heart thumped madly, Bierce, but Evangelina appeared almost unconcerned with the formidable task confronting us. She seemed to sense my reservations about our chances.

She said, "Richard got through."

It was the first time she'd referred to either of us by our first names. For a finely bred woman in a Latin country, this passed for a gesture of considerable intimacy. I was touched by it. I unfurled the broad fan. Evangelina placed the smouldering cigar between her white, even teeth. I inspected her one last time.

I said, "Just keep that thing in your mouth and keep your eyes fastened on the cobblestones all the way to the wharf. Those gorgeous eyes of yours could give you away. Walk at a normal pace. And remember, keep your face down. Now, go out ahead of me."

For the first time she appeared to falter. From the moment Davis had appeared at the window of her cell, at least one of us had been with her constantly.

"I am going alone?" she asked, and her voice was a soft wail.

I told her, "I'll be only a dozen or so paces behind. Of the two of us, I'm the more conspicuous in this silly getup. If we're out there traveling together and I'm stopped, then both of us will get caught. This way, if they spot me for what I am, you'll have a better chance to make the boat."

Evangelina paled visibly. She said, "I am afraid, Frederic. I cannot go alone."

We couldn't argue forever. I opened the door suddenly and thrust her into the entranceway as I flattened against the inside wall. She clutched my hand and simply froze. I could feel the fear flow like a river from her hand into mine. The long night of her ordeal had robbed her of her bravery. I tried to pull my hand free, but her fingers dug into my flesh.

I whispered, "I'll be right behind you."

Anyone passing by in Obispo Street would never have guessed I was there. I was obscured from view, and Evangelina, at a casual glance, appeared to be nothing more than a young sailor in a stocking cap and work clothes leaning against an open doorframe with one arm out of sight. Only her eyes might have betrayed us. Those luxuriant brown eyes were enormous. I patted her hand gently.

"You must go," I whispered pleadingly. "Go now, Evangelina."

Then, with the fluid slowness of flowing maple syrup, our fingers parted. She stepped off the doorstep and into the street. Pressed against the inside wall, I heard her footsteps merge with those of the passing crowd. I counted twelve seconds. Then I, too, stepped out the door into the street with the black fan across the lower portion of my face.

After the musty dimness of the hallway, the light in the street was unbearably bright. For a desperate moment, I could only squint helplessly against the morning sun. I was immediately caught up in the press of moving bodies. As my eyes adjusted, I searched for and finally spied a knit navy blue cap bobbing in the crowd a dozen paces ahead. I smiled to myself behind the fan. I cast an anxious glance over the heads of the crowd to the sides of the street. Instantly, my heart began to pump with renewed vigor.

Soldiers were everywhere, Bierce. It seemed there were many more than I'd spied only moments earlier from the third-floor window. Had Weyler reinforced the area, fearful that time might be running out? They lined the edges of the street, standing almost shoulder to shoulder. Some of them were yawning or chattering in weary bonhomie after the long night's vigil. Still others, however, seemed sharply alert and intent on inspecting every face in the bobbing mass of heads and shoulders and hats.

For a moment, I was certain my heart would burst. It was racing wildly, pumping my blood with a horrendous rushing sound that filled my ears. Surely the soldiers could hear it, too. I fought a seemingly irresistible urge to break and run, to put an end to this agonizing ordeal. I held myself back only with a ferocious effort. I forced myself to take one step at a time, one after another, eyes fixed over the fan on that bobbing blue knit cap, one at a time, one, two, three, four . . .

It seemed to take a lifetime, but we were finally at a cross street— first Evangelina, then, a few steps later, me. And we were still walking unmolested and unrecognized. I couldn't believe it. Good God, Bierce, we were actually getting away with it.

After the first block, as the crowd began to thin out at the intersection, the throng in the street started to disperse. My heart was pounding even more wildly now. It threatened to burst from its moorings and through my rib cage. I shut my eyes as I walked. I had to think of something else—anything else. I forced myself to think of Cuba as I'd seen it that first day from the *Vamoose*. I recalled that silvery beach bathed in sunlight. I thought of the tropical wind herding a flock of fluffy clouds above waving palm trees.

After what seemed like forever, I opened my eyes again. We were now halfway through the second block—midway to the boat, clearly visible at the wharf at the foot of the street. I saw, too, the armed, stony-faced men in their tan uniforms as I passed only a few feet away. I concentrated on the path of cobblestones gently sloping toward the sun-splashed blueness of the harbor. The *thump, thump, thump* of my heart was maddening. I had to keep my mind off this. I had to *think!*

So I thought of the cane waving like thin fingers in the breeze. I thought of the stench of sweat and fear and the coppery smell of blood as Gonzales wiped off his machete. I recalled the crisp clarity of the mountain air and the softness of gray, volcanic dirt on the slopes. I thought, too, of Delores—of her elegantly slanted eyes, her smooth olive skin. I felt her softness and warmth. I recalled the intoxicating smell of her in the night.

And then I became aware of the disturbing fact that I'd lost sight of Evangelina.

Over the fan held so closely to my face, my eyes sorted frantically through the pedestrians ahead of me. Finally, I spotted her moving along as carelessly and as unhurriedly as before. I also realized that my self-imposed reverie had slowed my pace. I'd fallen behind by a good two dozen paces. And that turned out to be a good thing because it permitted me to see something I otherwise might have missed.

It was clear that if I maintained my hunched-over posture and kept the fan across my face, the chances were reasonably good that I would be taken as nothing more than an unusually tall, fat woman worthy of no more than a glance from these woman-ogling Spaniards. But, as Evangelina stepped around a blind, legless beggar in a wheeled cart, I realized that our inept efforts to disguise her gender had been doomed from the start.

As the crowd thinned out, and as I was afforded a more distant view of her as she walked, I realized that the cabin boy's dungarees clung tightly and alluringly around the gently swelling curves of Evangelina's hips and buttocks. Even the blind beggar should have been able to see it. God help our society, Bierce, if women are ever permitted to wear pants in public. There'll be no controlling the animal lusts that are our unfortunate legacy from our shaggy ancestors.

Now, as the crowd grew thinner in the last block before the wharf, I realized it would be unlikely for even the dullest Spanish soldier to fail to note that this little sailor, this cabin boy with his cigar, was the possessor of a startlingly lush female body. I breathed a fervent and silent prayer that this wouldn't be noticed.

A futile prayer, I'm afraid.

As Evangelina strolled by a knot of five soldiers leaning against the wall of Saint Teresa's convent, one fellow was loudly regaling his comrades with a bawdy story. I could hear him. His story featured himself, the lascivious wife of an Andalusian judge, and a third woman who'd viewed romantic relationships with a decidedly commercial slant. The storyteller was quite obviously a chap with a practiced eye in such matters, and he seemed to react almost instinctively as Evangelina came by. His eyes riveted on what were surely the most artfully formed hindquarters the chap had appraised since Andalusia.

He shouted suddenly in Evangelina's direction. She pretended not to hear, so he shouted more loudly. Immediately, she froze in her tracks, although she had the good sense not to turn around. The soldier with the roving eye stepped away from his companions into the middle of the street. His rifle hung casually on his shoulder as he approached her. I, in turn, stepped up my pace until I was walking almost beside the fellow, my fan over my face and my eyes seemingly glued on the harbor ahead.

He glanced casually in my direction, seeing only a large, dark-haired woman behind a fan. Then he turned back to the suspect sailor and placed a hand hard on Evangelina's shoulder. He spun her about rather roughly and leaned back on his heels to examine his quarry. Her eyes were the size of silver dollars, but with the cigar and all the rest I'm not sure this fellow immediately understood what he had here. He might even have thought he'd accosted only a rather feminine man.

I had no choice, Bierce. I knew it would be only a heartbeat before he realized he was looking not at a cabin boy but at a woman in disguise. And before he could raise the alarm to his chattering comrades several yards away, he was on the ground, his rifle clattering harmlessly across the cobblestones. My fist had caught him high on the head, just above the left ear. It hadn't been one of my better punches, but it had been sufficient.

He began instantly to scramble to his feet. As he did, his compatriots began to move toward us. I tried to run, but the Spaniard had already gotten to his knees. He reached out and grabbed my legs as I went by. I was caught by surprise and went down. The fellow then climbed atop me and began pummeling me. I could tell from the level of force in his punches that I could make short work of him if I could get my hands free. Peatam, for example, had been much more powerful than this considerably tinier chap.

But there was no time for me to work free because the Spanish soldiers were almost upon us. Evangelina, God bless her, sized up the situation instantly. What she should have done, of course, was to desert me and run directly to the *Seneca,* which was only a half-block away. Instead, she picked up my antagonist's rifle, worked the bolt as her father had taught her, spat out the cigar, and snapped off a shot over where the soldier and I lay struggling in the street.

Her first bullet whistled by the head of one of the charging Spaniards by little more than inches. All four of them turned and bounded like deer back to the safety of the low wall that surrounded Saint Teresa's. Evangelina's second shot took the hat off another soldier, who executed a magnificent leaping dive to safety behind the wall.

While all this unfolded, I was freeing my arms and pushing the struggling Spaniard off me. We both clambered to our feet. He accomplished this more quickly than did I, and he was on me before I'd fully regained my balance. He caught me with two or three harmless blows before I managed to reach out with my left hand and grasp his head. I then lifted him by the hair completely upright, almost to his toes, and struck him once in the middle and once squarely on the nose with my right. The coach at Yale, Bierce, had always complimented me on my right. When I let the Spaniard go, his face was a bloody mess, and he toppled over as though boneless.

I had no time to admire my handiwork, however. Evangelina's two shots had raised the alarm all along Obispo Street. At the first sound of gunfire, civilians had cleared the open areas. They'd dived into doorways and beneath merchants' shopping stalls. Several dozen Spanish soldiers were moving down Obispo Street at a dead run. I simply turned, grabbed Evangelina, and pulled her roughly along with me as I began running toward the wharf. As I pulled her with me, she lost her grip on her rifle. It jerked free and hit the street with a dull clatter just as the four soldiers behind the convent wall rose up to their knees and began to bring their rifles up to their shoulders.

We had only a few dozen yards to go to the boat, which we could see had already started her engines and was casting off. Any moment, I expected bullets to rip into our backs. I put down my head and simply ran for all I had in me. In football, I'd always been rather quick over short distances, if a bit disappointing over the longer ones. I was literally dragging the girl as I raced toward the *Seneca*, my head down and my legs pumping wildly beneath my billowing skirt.

Which was why, when the first volley of shots sounded, I failed to recognize that they weren't coming from Spanish rifles but from McDonald's motley crew of cutthroats. Davis told me later that the first shots struck the wall of Saint Teresa's just as the four soldiers were preparing to fire. The Spaniards ducked low. The second volley, directed up the street at the two dozen soldiers running to catch us, sent the Spaniards scurrying for cover.

Evangelina and I knew none of this. All we knew was that bullets were flying and the same was required of us. We reached the gangplank of the *Seneca* just as the boat was pulling away from the wharf. I pushed Evangelina ahead of me, and she made it to the deck just as the boat pulled away from the dock and the gangplank dropped into the harbor.

I was less fortunate. I was no more than a pace away from the deck when the gangplank dropped from beneath me, like the earth opening up in a temblor. The gangplank splashed into the harbor; I dropped like a stone. It was only luck that I managed on my way down to grab the edge of the deck. By one hand, I hung there for a moment that seemed to last forever, my feet dragging in the water. Then a strong hand reached over the gunwale and grasped my wrist, and a multitude of hands were on my arm as I was dragged inelegantly onto the deck of the *Seneca* and to blessed safety.

I lay with my eyes closed and chest heaving as the vessel pulled away from the wharf. Gradually, I was aware of a crowd gathering on deck above me. I had no breath left, so I was unable to frame a suitable response when I heard the voice of Davis in the milling crowd of deckhands.

"Nicely done, Remington. Remind me to recommend to The Chief that you get a bonus."

"What is the rest?" Small Maria demands.

My response is delivered in a feeble whisper. I am, I fear, ill almost unto death. I gasp, "It is finished. There is no more."

"There must be," she insists harshly. "There must be more."

I manage to get out, "There was a war, of course. Weyler knew it could not be avoided. When he and Peatam arrived at the wharf, the *Seneca* was well out into the harbor, beyond rifle shot and heading for the open sea. Weyler said, 'I can send word to the harbor batteries, but it will not reach them in time.' Peatam could only moan when he heard that. He said, 'This can't happen. I'll lose my . . . lose . . .' "

My breath has deserted me. I cannot find air.

"And what did Weyler say?" demands Small Maria. "What did he say?"

I struggle to please my angelic prostitute. I choke out, "He said, 'You'll lose your job, señor? It could be worse. I strongly suspect I have lost a country.' "

I lie gasping.

"And now you have finished?" Small Maria asks quietly.

I care not for the sound of this question. It is almost ominous in its demand for finality. I can only gaze at her, my nurse and captor. I gaze into eyes transformed by growing awareness of a world beyond this mean little village into orbs devoid of remorse or charity. I fear this woman, my savior and tormentor, whore and angel. To placate my childishly angelic nurse, I say this:

"Only a minor addendum. That day in Connecticut, Remington told me what he saw as the *Seneca* moved out of the harbor into the sea. He said he looked back at Havana. He looked back and saw . . ."

TWENTY-SIX

Frederic Remington
Cuba, 1898

The city huddled in a semicircle around the shining water of the harbor. The sun glinted off it, Bierce. It was almost blinding. I found myself struggling mightily to capture the image in my mind. I'm not a landscape painter as such. Mere real estate has never captivated me. But there was something about Havana as I left it that begged for interpretation on canvas. I stood at the stern of the *Seneca* and studied Havana's colors. I studied the sweep of the scene over the open water.

The picture was almost perfect—the city encircling the harbor like a bracelet of gleaming gems. It was spoiled only by the presence, in the middle of it all, of this great, hulking American warship riding at anchor.

We'd read the name as we'd gone by in our flight. It was the *Maine*, the unprepossessing possessor of the name of a lovely state. Sailing vessels have their own special beauty, Bierce, as do trim, elegant yachts like The Chief's *Vamoose*. But it's difficult to picture anything uglier than the huge, squat presence of an oil-fired warship in an otherwise pristine setting. The vessel was like a giant troll floating atop the water—squat and fat and repelling. As is always the case when I'm confronted with something so incongruous with the rest of any image, I couldn't keep my eyes off it.

I imagine, therefore, that I might have been the first to have seen it. It happened with startling suddenness. A long, thin tongue of red-yellow flame licked out of the bowels of the *Maine*. The flame rolled slowly and majestically across the surging whitecaps of Havana Harbor. It was only a moment or so later that the thunderous roar of the explosion reached the deck of the *Seneca*. It assailed my ears, and I felt the force of the wind the blast generated.

Flames surged out of the stricken troll and billowed hundreds of feet into the clean Cuban air. The flames hung momentarily, like an obscene flower. As the sound died away—and as the explosion's plume lost color to be transformed into a roll of thick, oily, black smoke—hundreds of bits of metal and wood and what had to be human flesh and bone came bursting out of it. They, too, hung in the sky for the briefest of moments, then fluttered downward into the harbor and into the shattered, smoking hull of what had been, only a heartbeat before, an American warship.

I never did paint that scene of Havana Harbor. I always meant to, but every time I tried to recreate it in my mind I always found myself focusing instead on the horror of what I'd seen when the *Maine* exploded—on the sheer ghastliness of it all. That explosion cost me a painting, Bierce.

I shouldn't really complain, of course. The fiery death of the *Maine* cost me a painting; but it cost Spain so very much more. . . .

Ambrose Bierce
Mexico, 1914

"And then?" she asks.

I am profoundly weary, but I muster strength enough for righteous outrage.

I gasp out, "And then? Life goes on, Small Maria. Human events repeat themselves indefinitely. Would you hear of all that has transpired on this earth since those events of so many years ago? Tell me what would you know, child, that I may quench this insatiable curiosity with which my tale seems to have afflicted you."

"Tell me," she orders calmly, "what happened next."

Struggling, I say, "What happened next was war. Two hundred and fifty crewmen of the *Maine* met their ends in that explosion. No one ever learned what caused it, although The Chief was convinced it was Spanish treachery, and his angry headlines proclaimed that loudly. Weyler wept when he learned of the blast, but his grief could save neither him nor his country. The United States declared war against Spain. The Spanish were defeated in four months."

She says, "And what happened as a result of this war?"

I tell her, "T.R. led his Rough Riders in an insane charge up San Juan Hill. His foolhardiness made him so immense a national hero that McKinley was impelled to take on T.R. as his vice-president. And when McKinley was murdered by a lunatic in Buffalo, T.R. ascended to the throne. One lunatic unwittingly befriended another."

"The fortunes of but a single man," she says. "Tell me more."

I shake my head wearily. Will this child never cease to plague me?

I tell her, "The war did all the things Curry had predicted. It gave the United States possession of Puerto Rico, of Guam, and of the Philippine Islands. It gave the United States control of Hawaii. It made possible the construction of the canal through the Isthmus of Panama. It helped The Chief defeat Pulitzer. It accomplished, child, precisely what all wars accomplish; some men become richer and more powerful and others, less fortunate, become crippled or dead."

[209]

"And what of Davis and Evangelina?" she demands. "Did they marry?"

"Of course not," I respond, astounded at her naïveté. "Evangelina was married to her Insurrecto. Davis was married to his scribbling."

"How did they part?" she asks.

"When the war broke out, Davis and Remington went back to Cuba in the service of The Chief. Davis later wrote a book, which sold poorly. I have no idea what happened to Evangelina. Whatever it was, my friends played no role in it."

"And Remington?" she presses.

"My friend? He grew richer and immensely fat and bought a gracious home in Connecticut, where he invited me one day not long before Christmas five years ago. It was there that he told me of his adventures in covering the Insurrecto. After I left, he complained of stomach pains. His ailment was discovered to be a burst appendix. He passed on the day after Christmas, at only forty-eight years of age. Unlike me, Remington had the good fortune to die before his health gave out."

Small Maria is silent for a long moment. Then she says, "So there is no more to tell? How went the Insurrecto, Señor Bierce?"

I tell her truthfully, "The war resulted only in an abrupt change in the form of misgovernment, child. Every government merely protects by force the property of the indolent and the unthrifty, staving off the outrage of the envious and the luckless."

She is again silent. I suspect she is thinking, and I once again curse myself for sparking in her this distressing habit. After a while, she rises and leaves the hut. I am grateful for the respite. I have no more stories to tell, and my weariness is immense.

I doze.

It is night when I awaken. The hut is dark and forbidding. My fever has returned. I can feel it consume me in its fires. My heart beats with effort and far less vigor than before. I know that merely by living I am pressing it beyond its capabilities. Also, I thirst mightily. I struggle to cry out, but my voice is as thin as paper.

I manage to rasp softly, "Maria, I thirst."

A shadowy form appears in the doorway. I crane my head to achieve recognition. It is Big Maria, not the Maria I seek.

I move my mouth. No sound emerges, but my lips form words. Silently, they ask, "Where is she?"

Almost in tears, Big Maria tells me, "My daughter is not here, Señor Bierce. She has gone to join the Insurrecto."

I am distraught beyond all imagining. I struggle vainly to say, "She is gone? She will not return to me?"

Big Maria cannot hear my words, but she can read my mind. She says, "Who knows of these things? Who can say what will become of her?"

Then I notice that Big Maria is not alone. With her is Padre Pio, the shabby priest who serves this village. He is an old man, perhaps as old as me. His visage is worn and lined and solemn. He looks down upon me. Then he kisses his rosary, and he places about his neck a scrap of purple cloth. He is preparing to perform the last rites. Padre Pio deludes himself that this soiled, sorry thing that is my soul can be saved from the fires of the hell in which he believes so fervently. And in which, I fear now, I also believe.

He tells me, "I am here to listen to your confession, my son."

I struggle to find voice, but there is none. Small Maria has robbed me of it. The priest understands. He makes the sign of the cross over the bed that contains my fevered body. He mumbles words in bad Latin. I am alert as shadows consume me—alert and angry to the very last.

I do not want this black-clad mumbler of dead languages, this prattler of pointless prayers. I do not want the empty comfort of a man who has never known the joy of human flesh in all its sad, degrading glory. I want no priest at my deathbed. I want only Small Maria—purveyor of lust, newborn revolutionary, and the last woman who will ever love me.

I want my angel. . . .